21/10   £2.50

GW00726063

TOURNAMENT

Jennifer Goebel & Dagmar Jacisinova

Menotomy Press
© 2013 Jennifer Goebel & Dagmar Jacisinova

All rights reserved. No part of this book may be used or reproduced by any means, graphic, electronic, or mechanical, including photocopying and recording, except for brief quotations in critical articles or review, without the written consent of the publisher.

Please visit tournament2044.com for permissions.

ISBN: 978-0615817651

This is a work of fiction. Names, characters, places and incidents are either the products of the author's imagination or used fictitiously. Any resemblance to actual persons living or dead is purely coincidental.

Printed in the USA.

June 19, 2014

Central Security Service, National Security Agency,
Washington, D.C.

Recorded conversation between Brig. Gen. Steve H. Peterson, USAF,
Deputy Chief/CSS and Lt. Gen. Hayden Keith,
DIRNSA/CHCSS/CDRUSCYBERCOM

Keith: The North Koreans declared a state of war with South Korea. And we have reason to believe it's not just saber-rattling this time.

Peterson: If they are as paranoid as I fear they are, it's not just a possibility that they'll strike first, it's a matter of when.

Keith: Their long-range weapons are operational. How good they are, we don't know. The Atlantic Ocean may not be enough protection anymore.

Peterson: We would have to retaliate, even if they confine their strikes to the Korean peninsula.

Keith: China would have to respond. And then we're committed, and it's a full-out nuclear catastrophe.

Peterson: The human casualties would just be the beginning. Whoever survives would have to struggle through the worst depression of all time.

Keith: Depression! There are times I wonder if we're not sleepwalking into Armageddon.

Peterson: So what is your recommendation to the President?

Keith: I'll tell him what we know. And what we suspect. He has to make the decision. He's not going to like it.

Some people believe football is a matter of life and death.
I'm very disappointed with that attitude.
I can assure you it is much, much more important than that.

- Bill Shankly, Scottish Footballer and Manager

RICK

July 22, 2014

"Pass! Pass!" Rick was yelling at Henry as he broke for the goal. A beautiful pass came his way, and he tipped it with his left foot right past the goalie. In the midst of the high-fives and whoops and hollers with his Colorado Rapids teammates, there was an enormous flash in the sky.

When Rick came to, he sat up. He must have only been out for a few minutes. All around him, both teams and the fans in the stands were either unconscious, or beginning to move.

Rick looked over at Henry, who was rubbing his eyes.

"What just happened?"

"I don't know. Why's it dark?" Henry was still rubbing his eyes.

"It's not dark," said Rick. "What's going on?"

"What do you mean, it's not dark? I can't see a freaking thing!" Rick held out his hand to Henry to help him up, but Henry just sat there. Rick spotted the team's goalie coach.

"Coach! Coach! What's going on?"

"I have no bloody idea! Maybe an earthquake? Coach Cox went into the clubhouse. Look, I'm going to try to find out, just don't panic." The sounds of people yelling and crying filled his ears. Chaos. People were stumbling around the field, looking for a way out.

"I think Henry's gone blind." Rick yelled, to the coach's departing back.

"What?" barked Henry.

"Well, you can't see and it's broad daylight," said Rick.

"You're kidding me." Henry rubbed his eyes, but nothing happened.

"What's the last thing you remember?" asked Rick.

"I was just high-fiving you and over your head I saw this enormous flash, and then next thing I know you're telling me I'm blind."

Rick let out a swear that would have gotten him kicked off the field if a ref had been around. He grabbed Henry's arm, pulled him up, and tried to keep calm as he tracked what looked like an enormous ball of fire heading in their direction. It was about the size of a bus, and was whirling like a tornado, picking up papers and trash in its path.

Rick pulled Henry along with him, following the stampede off the field. The noise made it impossible to talk, though he could tell Henry was trying to say something. He pulled Henry's shirt up over his nose and did the same with his own, trying to breathe the hot, smoky air. Like an 18-wheeler hurtling down a highway, the fire charged by, heading out toward the parking lot. Rick dragged Henry over to a sheltered corner, where they sat huddled with a few of their teammates from the Rapids, some LA Galaxy players, and a few fans. Time seemed to stand still as the winds blew at hurricane speeds, pelting them with all kinds of debris, picking up anything that wasn't bolted down plus several things that were. A set of four bright blue stadium seats came at them, shattering into splinters when it hit the cement wall. Even though it hurt, he didn't cry out. It felt like it was happening to someone else, and he was just watching. They were going to die. Rick closed his eyes and prayed: please God, please God, please God. He wasn't sure what he was praying for exactly. The noise was deafening.

Finally, the winds died down. It could have been minutes or hours, Rick had no idea. They stayed huddled in the corner. When he finally looked out, he couldn't believe his eyes. There was debris all over the stadium, and the bodies... there were mangled people on the ground, looking like dolls carelessly tossed around by children.

He had to get home. He had to. He pulled a stupefied Henry up with him, and they headed toward the parking lot. Around him, he heard people saying it was a bomb. A nuclear bomb. Things had been increasingly tense on the Korean Peninsula lately, they were saying, but Rick hadn't been paying attention to the news. He had games to win.

"I can see again–things are a little fuzzy, but I can see," said Henry.

A guy in an official stadium windbreaker walked by, looking oddly normal after all that had gone on. He was holding a walkie-talkie to his ear.

"They hit NORAD," he said.

"Hit NORAD? What the heck is that?" yelled one guy wearing an LA Galaxy shirt.

"North American Aerospace Defense Command. At Peterson Air Force Base, in Colorado Springs. It's the place that's supposed to *warn* the country if there's a nuclear attack…" said another player, his eyes glued to the enormous, ballooning cloud off in the distance.

"Who hit NORAD, then? And with what?" screamed the LA Galaxy player, who seemed on the verge of hysteria.

"A nuclear bomb!" yelled the stadium guy, back at him, running off toward the stands.

"That's 60 miles away," said one of Rick's teammates, quietly. "Oh my God."

They stared at each other, dumbfounded. Most of the stadium was still standing, but with some chunks missing, like a kid missing a few teeth. Cell phones weren't working and none of the televisions were on.

Rick and Henry walked over piles of debris, searching for Rick's car. They found it. Hemmed in by a mountain of blue stadium chairs on one side and a pile of turned over buses on the other, was his beloved 1972 faded orange Volkswagen Beetle. Untouched. Like a faithful pet. He put the key in the ignition and prayed. The car engine coughed and then rumbled to life. By pushing against the end of a line of crumpled chairs, the Beetle had just enough juice to shove its way out. Rick stopped when one of his teammates waved him over.

"My car won't start," he said. "It was fine this morning." It was a late-model black Audi with all the bells and whistles. Rick had eyed that car jealously in the parking lot. But now he was grateful for his trusty Bug.

"EMP," said Henry. They looked at him. "Electro-magnetic pulse. Supposed to happen when a nuclear bomb explodes–kills all electronics."

"Excellent," said the guy sarcastically, staring at his useless lump of metal. "You guys go on, I'll figure something out."

Rick puttered onto the main road. All the traffic lights were out. Cars were stopped everywhere, blocking the roads and the intersections. He navigated carefully around them, while Henry fiddled with the old-fashioned radio knobs. There was nothing but static. Not a single station coming through. Henry slammed his hand against the dash.

The highway looked like a scene from an apocalyptic movie. Henry tried his cell phone again, but there was still no signal. Their phones were useless. They realized a lot of the towers were probably destroyed in the bombings, and who knows what else was gone or what was going to happen to them. As they drove south towards Centennial, where Rick and Henry both lived, they were getting closer to the bomb. The roads were sometimes blocked by piles of unidentifiable debris, and Rick tried to avoid looking at what he was passing. Sometimes he had to zigzag from one side of the highway to the other. But there weren't many other cars on the road. His heart was beating too fast. He didn't let himself think about what he might find or not find at home, he only knew he had to get there. Had to. The smoke made it impossible to see in some parts, and hard to breathe. Far off in the distance, they could see gray hazy clouds and the glow of fire.

He stopped at a gas station where several cars were already lined up. The pumps were out of service–no electricity. Someone had already hooked up a hand pump to get the gas out of the underground tanks, and he and Henry filled the Beetle's tank, stopping when it started to overflow. A guy in front of him handed him two large empty plastic containers to fill.

"Take them while they last," he said.

As they approached Centennial, it looked like enormous tornados had hit the town. Some streets looked completely normal, but there were wide swaths of complete devastation.

Rick hoped this was just a dream and that he would wake up soon. He could go back to worrying about things like his credit card bills and whether the grass needed to be cut.

After he dropped Henry off, Rick pulled into his driveway, where his small rental house looked exactly the same as it had when he left in the morning. Except there were flakes of white, gray, and black all over his tiny front lawn. Flakes of what, Rick didn't want to think about. He opened the door, and there was Dana, who looked beautiful to him, even in her sloppy sweatpants and tear-stained face.

"It's okay, I'm here. I'm okay. You're okay," he murmured into her hair, as he rocked her back and forth. He had loved her from the moment he set eyes on her, back in the 7th grade.

"I was so worried," she sobbed. "I couldn't get you. Just before the TV went out, there was an emergency alert about bombs in New York. The phones are completely jammed. The cable is out. The internet is out. I didn't know what to do."

"We have to get out of here, Dana. It's not safe. It sounds like most of the country has been bombed. We'll probably get sick from the radiation. We have to get out of here. I think our best shot for survival is to get far, far away from here. Where the survivalists go."

"Idaho?" she asked.

"Alaska," said Rick.

Chapter One

JASON

February 1, 2044

Thud. Thud. Thud. Jason sat on his bed, bouncing the soccer ball off the gray cement wall across from him in his dorm room. All the rooms were the same. No posters, no pictures, just endless dull gray wall in the old military barracks. Not much to look at, but what they lacked in charm, they made up for in smooth bounce-ability. The ball came back to him with perfect regularity. He tried to focus on catching the ball with his left hand, which was his weaker side.

Thud. Thud. Thud. The clock by his bed taunted him. 3:12. It was like each minute was lasting an hour.

On the bed by the window, his brother was reading a book. They almost never had time to read. When they did, Jason usually went for comic books and sports magazines, which were thrown haphazardly on the bottom shelf of their bookcase. Nate's small collection of pre-War paperback books sat next to them, lined up, alphabetically arranged by

1

author. The rest of the shelves were filled with rows of gold and silver trophies, plaques, medals, and team pictures. Jason bounced the ball closer and closer to Nate, to see if he would respond. Nate's head leaned back on a pillow propped against the wall by the room's only window, and he held the book over him to catch the sunlight. Lights were usually off in the dorms during the day to save energy. Everyone was at practice from 8am to 6pm anyway. But today, being a special day, they had electricity. Jason thought about reminding his brother of that fact, but decided not to. Let him try to read in the waning February afternoon sunlight. Nate turned a page. Jason went back to bouncing. 3:13.

"How can you read?" Jason asked, exasperated. Some-times his brother, twin though he was, completely mystified him. Jason had tried reading his comic books earlier today, but he had read them all before. The words swam in front of his eyes, making no sense, while his brain raced around in circles. He needed motion. But there was nowhere in the soccer training camp that he wanted to go. Some kids were probably at the gym or the video room. He had been in the video room earlier, blowing things up with weapons that no longer existed. Even though they were gone, he knew their names: AK-47s, M-16s, M-249 SAWs, ACRs, M203 grenade launchers, Kalashnikovs. Battling virtual enemy forces was fun for a while, but he had beaten all the levels on the games they had. He had hung out with his friends, talking about the teams, speculating about who would make it, and pretending he wasn't worried. Just another day in the country's most elite soccer training facility.

He could go back to the cafeteria. But nothing seemed appetizing. His stomach felt queasy, like he had felt the time his family had driven the 350 miles to Anchorage and gone on a whale watch. They hadn't seen any whales or dolphins, and his stomach churned the whole trip. He ended up leaning over a rail and heaving his breakfast. Pretty much ruined sunny-side-up eggs for him for life. Toast was the only thing that had looked possible this morning, and even that had stuck in his throat at breakfast. Nate, on the other hand, had managed to consume his usual cafeteria breakfast of protein shake, fruit, and yogurt. He could be so annoyingly calm.

"Have they found Earth yet?" Jason asked, more to get some kind of answer from Nate than because he cared at all about a stupid book.

"Nope," said Nate, moving across the bed and tilting the book to catch the waning light.

Thud. Thud. Thud. Thud. Thud. 3:14. Bang.

"Oops, sorry," Jason said as the ball careened off the wall and onto Nate.

"Yeah, right," Nate said, sighing. He put down his book. "Stop stressing out. You'll make it. You're the best goalie here." Nate paused. "But I won't make it. If it weren't for this stupid knee..."

Jason stared at the floor, running his eyes along the lines dividing the worn linoleum squares. Knees gave out in even the best athletes. Sometimes it just happened from overuse in training. For Nate, though, it had been a foul by another player that resulted in a badly torn ACL. Surgery, then rehab, had taken most of the last three months. If he had another six months, Jason was sure Nate would have made the team. But the Tournament started in July.

"If I don't make it, I wonder where they'll send me. Do you think I could end up going home?"

"Home?" Jason repeated.

Jason stared into a corner, holding the ball, while images of home—a small apartment in west Fairbanks about an hour from here in a butt-ugly boring high-rise building—flashed through his mind. It was in "the projects," groups of post-War buildings constructed too quickly for anyone to care how they looked. They were lucky to have gotten one at all. The two-bedroom apartment was too small for the six of them, so it was a good thing he and Nate had been recruited for training when they were in the third grade. He was sure their neighbors were thrilled, too. The walls were thin, and the sounds of two boys jumping on the bed, throwing things against the wall, and wrestling on the floor were probably not missed. It had been more than eight years since they had lived there, and Jason had stopped calling it home ages ago. He went back to bouncing the ball against the wall. Nate went back to his book. Jason glanced at the clock: 3:16. Forty-four more minutes to go… maybe. If they posted the results on time. Forty-four more minutes when he and Nate were on the same team. Nate obviously didn't want to talk.

Jason bounced the ball against the wall about a foot above Nate's head. Nate jumped.

"Hey! Chill out." Nate sat up.

"You might make the squad, even if you don't make the starting line-up," said Jason. "Your knee is getting better. You still have a chance. Aren't coaches always saying soccer is a mind game? Well, you've got that."

"Yeah, I've got that," Nate said, "but this knee isn't ready. Probably not even to sit on the bench."

"This sucks," Jason knew Nate was probably right. They had carefully avoided talking about it, but both knew that Nate's knee wasn't ready yet. He still had another month of rehab to go. Of the 22 players who would make the squad, only 15 would be on the roster to play each game. Eleven starters and four subs. The other seven players would be warming the bench. With more than 100 kids trying about for 22 spots, competition was fierce. And even if you made the team, there was no guarantee you'd be one of the starters.

"Maybe they'll let me be the water boy. I'll pass out all your personalized water bottles at half-time. That'll be fulfilling." Nate joked. If things were reversed, Jason would be pissed. He'd really want to take it out on the kid who injured him. But Nate wasn't like that.

Maybe it was because he was older. Four minutes shouldn't make any difference, but for some reason, it did. Sometimes those four minutes seemed like four years. Jason looked at his brother. Like him, but also not. They both had long, muscled legs from all the soccer training, blue eyes, and dark, straight hair that was cut short, in accordance with Alaska training camp rules. Nate's eyes were a slightly deeper blue and a little wider apart, and his face was a little narrower. People who knew them well could tell them apart by how they walked and how they stood, but that was a small group. The last time they had been home, their little sister Sarah, who was just ten, had kept mixing them up. That had been awkward, but not surprising, since they hadn't lived at home since Sarah was a baby.

Jason went back to bouncing. Nate went back to his book. 3:17. The ball bounced off the wall and off one of the desks by the door. Their computer monitors were both asleep, just the little blue light in the corner indicating power was on. Jason thought about going to check his email inbox or the weather page. See what parts of Alaska were under radiation alerts. But that seemed like too much effort. He thought about taking his ADD pill, which he only used occasionally for school work, to see if that would calm him down. But he had a feeling that the only thing that would put an end to his misery would be the arrival of 4pm.

Jason kept bouncing the ball, slowly. 3:18. He tried to focus on the ball and how it met his left hand. His mind kept wandering, though. He remembered the look on Coach Chip's face during tryouts as he watched Nate. In the high stakes game of The Tournament, they weren't willing to bet on a player with an injury. But he hoped they would put him on the team as an alternate or something. They had to find a place for him. Nate had worked so hard, and he was one of the best defenders on the team. He was "the wall." Together, Nate and Jason were the cornerstone of their team's defense, and worked together seamlessly to shut down scoring. It worked, and their team had the lowest goals-against in the league. What if, without Nate, he wasn't nearly as good a goalie? That little thought gnawed at his insides.

Thud. Thud. Thud.

Nate closed his book.

"Look, tomorrow, when the media come, no matter what happens to me, you better act like it's the best day of your life," Nate said seriously.

Jason faked throwing the ball at him, and Nate ducked.

"Got ya," said Jason. "Okay, yeah, I know. I will."

"Let's practice your interview skills," Nate said, putting his book down, and sitting up.

"I'll be the reporter, and you'll be the star 17-year-old athlete who just realized his life's ambitions, who has been training for this day since he was eight years old. Ready?"

"No." Jason kept bouncing the ball off the wall. Thud. Catch. Thud. Catch.

Nate looked at him.

Jason sighed.

"Fine."

Nate picked up a sweaty shin guard from a pile of cleats, socks, shorts, and t-shirts under his bed, and held it in his hand like a microphone. He sat down next to Jason on his bed, held the shin guard in front of his face, and said in a deep, serious voice:

"So how does it feel to be 17 years old and have the weight of the country riding on your shoulders?" Nate poked the shin guard-as-microphone into Jason's chin.

Jason shoved it away, and pushed Nate off the bed. His landing was cushioned by his own pile of workout clothes and cleats.

"Oh, that's really mature," said Nate, sarcastically, as he scrambled up from the floor. "You'll end up in the detention center instead of on the team if you pull something like that, you moron."

"Well, keep that disgusting shin guard out of my face," grumbled Jason. "It stinks. The microphones probably won't smell like they came out of the sewer."

"Whose turn was it to do the laundry? Oh, look at that handy color-coded chart by the door. What does it say? Wow, I can even read it from here. Oh yeah, I think it says *you*," countered Nate.

Jason looked at the list, and sure enough, there was the big blue J on the chore calendar.

"You didn't sweep or mop the floors, either." Jason crossed his arms in front of his chest.

"Yeah, but we never do that," said Nate. They had agreed that the dirty clothes did a fine job of wiping up the floors, and so generally skipped that part of the required chore list. So far, the dorm monitor hadn't challenged their methods.

"Just humor me. I don't know where I'll be tomorrow, and I want to make sure you have this down," said Nate.

"Fine," said Jason, annoyed. He grabbed another shin guard from under the bed, and stood in front of the mirror that hung on the back of the door. He took a deep breath. Then he smiled winningly at his reflection and said, "I'm just happy to be chosen. I will work my hardest to show the world that Alaska is the greatest country in the world!"

"Pretty good," agreed Nate. "Now try a harder one: How do you feel about all the sacrifices you've made to get here?"

"It's been hard, not seeing our parents or my sisters, but it's been worth it," said Jason, to the mirror, flashing another broad smile. He could almost see his molars.

"Okay, glamour boy, stop admiring yourself, and think," said Nate. "That's a trick question, you know."

"It is?"

"Jason, come on. We haven't made sacrifices. We've been chosen. We're the lucky ones. We've had good food, clothes, school, and plus Mom and Dad got those good jobs at the university, and they have that apartment—okay, it's tiny and ugly, but it's in a good part of town and it has electricity most of the time. And it's all because of us." Nate looked at Jason.

"They won't ask that, you know. Because it only seems like sacrifice to us." Jason could tell he'd surprised Nate.

"Okay, what would I really say? I'd say it was a great honor to be chosen, and I'm so happy to be on the team. I love soccer, and I love Alaska. This year, we'll win the Tournament, and everyone will see Alaska's glory! Go Alaska!" Jason raised his arms in the air, as if he was on the podium receiving a medal. He bowed to an invisible audience, waved, and smiled so hard his face muscles hurt.

"Okay, okay. No need to overdo it," Nate said. "You really think I could make the team?"

This was the first time Jason had heard some hope from Nate.

"I bet you will," said Jason. "Coach Chip knows how good you are, and he knows you're almost done with rehab. Evan, Jack, and I were talking about it earlier, and they both think you'll make it. They have 22 spots. You have one more month of rehab, and the Tournament doesn't start until July. Even if they don't put you on as a starter, they'll probably put you on the bench. I mean, look at all that stuff." Jason gestured to the top shelf of the bookcase, where Nate's lineup of statues and plaques for league championships stood. "You have more 'man of the match' awards than anyone else. They know you're awesome."

"Who am I kidding?" Nate shook his head. "We all just train, train, train, hoping we'll make it, but most of us won't. And I never really thought about what I would do after soccer, you know? Never thought beyond today, and being on the national team." Nate slumped back on his bed.

"It's crazy. I mean, whoever came up with the idea that a bunch of 16- and 17-year-olds should decide the fate of the world?" Jason went back to bouncing the ball off the wall. The clock read 3:25.

"Don't be such a drama queen. It's not the fate of the world, it's just who gets to run the Global Government for two years. But, yeah, it does seem like a strange way to run things. Before the War, they just had soccer tournaments for fun. People cared who won and who lost just because of national pride."

"You sound like one of those government videos about World War III, and the downfall of the world's major cities, blah blah blah," said Jason. "But, I don't get it. Remember when Coach told us about how there used to be riots when soccer teams won or lost. Why did they care so much?"

Although he'd seen the history videos in class that explained what the world was like before the War, it was hard to imagine people going about their daily lives knowing that nuclear-armed countries were able to start a war at any time. It must have been awful, knowing that you could see missiles coming at you while you were sleeping or at your birthday party. Even though most of the world was still struggling to rebuild 30 years later, Jason thought it was probably less stressful living now. The fear of another nuclear holocaust was completely gone thanks to the Global Government. Sure, people were poor, hungry, and sick, but from what he could tell, things hadn't been perfect before the War, either.

"Well, maybe that's why most of Europe was completely flattened," said Nate. "And maybe that's why Alaska is all that's left of the United States. Maybe they all just cared too much about stupid stuff like sports championships, when they should have been actually paying attention to where the nukes were and whose finger was on the button." Jason and Nate were both quiet. 3:31.

"I think we can win this year," said Jason.

"Alaska has never won. What makes you think we can win this time?" Nate asked.

"Us, stupid. We can win it. We're unstoppable. Duh." Jason swung his legs over his bed, and leaned down to look for his blue flip-flops.

Suddenly they heard, "The lists are up!" and feet stampeding toward the main gym.

"But it's too early! They said they wouldn't be up until 4," yelped Jason, as he frantically felt around for the second flip-flop.

Nate reached under his bed, and tossed one of his green flip-flops to Jason.

"Use that. Let's go!" They ran out the door, letting it shut behind them.

Chapter Two

CASSIE

Cassie was lying on her back on the floor of her room, with her legs bent above her, juggling a soccer ball with the soles of her feet. It was pretty tricky, and required a lot of concentration. She had been doing it for the last hour, and her body was starting to feel the strain. Her feet started to shake just a tiny bit and sweat was running down her back and tightly focused face. Practicing her freestyle soccer tricks helped pass the time while she was waiting. Her roommate and best friend Karen was on her third chocolate chip muffin.

"I feel sick, but I can't seem to stop," said Karen, with her mouth still full. She was looking at the plate with the solitary muffin on it.

"Pass me that one. Because I'm such a good friend, I'll save you from yourself," said Cassie grinning. Karen sighed and tossed it to Cassie. She caught it in her right hand, her feet still working the ball.

"Geez, you're unbelievable," Karen sighed again. Cassie brought her knees into her chest, legs together, and gently rolled the ball up and down along her lower legs by raising and lowering her feet a few inches. She pinched off pieces of muffin and chewed slowly while keeping the ball in motion. It was hard to swallow lying down.

"I wish I could do what you're doing instead of what I'm doing," Karen said, as she started pacing around the room. Again.

Cassie gave up, and let the ball fall to the ground. She took another bite of muffin standing up.

For the last two hours, Karen alternated between pacing and running to the cafeteria, scavenging for food.

"Do you think we'll make the team?" asked Karen for at least the forty-seventh time.

"Yes. No. I don't know," said Cassie, taking a big bite.

"No girl has made the team for the last four years. We must be crazy," said Karen dispiritedly. Now that the sugar rush was gone, reality was coming back.

"We might be crazy, but we kick butt, Karen. No one works as hard as we do." Cassie was trying to be optimistic, but the thoughts nagged at her. Had she done enough? Should she have added an extra mile in her training routine? Should she have pushed herself more? She took the towel from her bed, wiping the sweat off her face. Too late to change anything now.

"Cassie, it's really you who kicks butt. I bet you'll make the team. I hope you'll come to see me when I'm tying shoelaces for the next group of budding soccer stars," said Karen.

The chances of two girls making the national team were slim. One was a long shot, as it was. Cassie felt bad for thinking it, but she knew she was a stronger player than Karen.

She and Karen had been together for the last eight years, and Karen was like a sister and a best friend all rolled into one. Cassie still remembered the first day they met. They were sharing a room with 18 girls and Karen was on the bunk next to her. She had come to the training camp with her old beat up soccer ball and she held on to it for the next month, even taking it to the bed. Some girls had a stuffed animal, Karen had her soccer ball. She and Cassie had bonded immediately over their adoration for Lauren Osborne, the girl soccer star who had been on the national team the year they started training. Lauren had played first string in the Tournament. All the girls admired Lauren, but Karen and Cassie had taken it to a new level, sneaking off to watch her practice whenever they could, copying her hairstyle, and taping their shin guards in place with colored tape, like she did.

They'd been through a lot together. When Cassie broke her ankle and had to hobble around on crutches for six weeks, Karen got her food from the cafeteria, found her some new books to read, and made sure she didn't miss any gossip. When Jonah kissed Karen, and then ignored her for the next two weeks, Cassie was there with tissues and sympathy. Cassie didn't let too many people into her life, but Karen knew everything about her. They were no secrets between them. The thought of going on without her was terrifying, almost as bad as the thought that she might not make the team herself.

"If I make it, I promise I'll come rescue you after we win the Tournament. We can get an apartment together or something," said Cassie.

"Apartment? Are you kidding? If you win the Tournament, I want a mansion! And a cook! And a driver. And maybe a cute gardener."

Karen was laughing.

Cassie smiled. "You and your cute gardener fantasies and cute coach fantasies."

Karen blushed deep red.

"I can't help it." She looked at Cassie with a dreamy look on her face that told her she was thinking about their new assistant coach Jack. Then she refocused on Cassie.

"You know, you're the strange one. Walking around all these gorgeous hot guys and not seeing them at all," Karen teased.

"I see them. It's just that I know what they are—our competition," said Cassie. "There will be plenty of time for *that* after the Tournament."

"Yeah, I know," Karen sighed. She started picking the crumbs off the muffin wrapper, and staring at the ground.

"Ok, mansion it is. With a swimming pool," said Cassie. But her thoughts kept coming back to that list. All that running, conditioning, and endless drills, even in her two daily hours of unscheduled time. While other girls were doing homework or hanging out, she just ran more steps in the arena. And, of course, spent every waking moment with a soccer ball. Cassie drove herself so hard that, when she was 12, she almost stopped growing. Coach had to step in and force her to rest, eat, and "take it easier." He gave her some books to read about soccer stars from before the War. Pele, Maradona, Kaka, Messi, Ronaldo, Rooney, Beckham. It was interesting reading, and at least it kept her sitting still and gave her body a chance to convert her food to muscle, said Coach.

Cassie had obsessively watched all the archived soccer matches, studying their moves, learning their tricks. Coach always said you win games not just with your speed and skill, but also with your head. She was his best player, fast, clever, always able to see "the big picture" on the field. Up until now, she had played only on the girls' teams. But the national team drew from the best, regardless of gender.

"Just imagine, if you make the team, it'll be you and 21 hot guys," teased Karen.

"Great. Me and 21 sweaty, smelly, Neanderthals that I have to convince I can play as well as they can, if not better," Cassie made a face. But Cassie knew she could show any bunch of adolescent jerks quickly enough what she could do, and the smart ones would respect her for it. And the dumb ones, those she could handle, too.

"Oh come on, some of them are good guys," said Karen. "I've seen those twins around—they'll probably make the team. And you have to admit, they're just flat-out hotties."

"If I make the team, boys—nice guys or creeps—are going to be the *last* thing on my mind!" said Cassie. "Well, I mean, in that way. God, I hope I make it."

"You will," said Karen, absolutely confident. "I know you will."

In her heart, Cassie knew she was good enough for the national team. She had watched the boys. Some of them were amazing, but she was just as good. If the evaluations were fair, she would make it.

Karen sat on her bed, leaning against the gray cement wall. She was looking lost all of a sudden. "What's going to happen if we don't make it? Do you think they'll send us home?"

"They better not," Cassie muttered. "That would be the worst. I'd rather be the team's laundry girl than go back there." Her family lived in Alaska's Matanuska Valley, a farming area that was being swallowed up by the sprawling suburbs of Homer to the south and Anchorage to the north, both of which had ballooned with post-War refugees. It was a seven-hour car ride from Fairbanks, and making the trip once a year in December was about all her parents had time for since the farm and the greenhouses kept them busy. The Palmer family had been farming in Alaska since the 1800s, through good times and bad.

"I can just see you out there in one of those radiation suits on your hands and knees, weeding onions or turnips or whatever," said Karen. "Or driving one of those big tractor-things." Karen giggled at the thought.

"Ugh! That would totally suck," said Cassie, flopping back on her bed. She stared at the ceiling. "I can just see their happy faces when they find me on their doorstep, and realize that all their extra food vouchers are going to vanish, and that Eric and Peter will have to fight for spots at the university. Oh yeah, the whole family is just going to love having me back."

"They're probably out boarding up the greenhouse windows just in case," joked Karen. When Cassie was seven, she had broken so many of the glass panels playing soccer with her brothers that it was legend. In fact, the scout had found her in rural farmland only because he happened to be in the Matanuska Valley Agway when Cassie's dad had come in to buy 10 more replacement glass panels–for the second time that week. The scout decided he had to see who was causing all this damage with a soccer ball, and that's how she ended at the Fairbanks soccer training facility.

"You're so hysterically funny," said Cassie, sarcastically. She got back up and started juggling the ball, keeping it low and in perfect control. "Maybe I could live with Adam in Anchorage instead of on the farm."

"Didn't he just have another baby? What is he, 20, now? They're popping them out pretty quick, just like our dear leaders tell us to. I'm sure your brother and sister-in-law would love someone around to help with the kids," said Karen, mesmerized by Cassie's feet keeping the ball in constant motion.

"Yuck," said Cassie. "Bottles and spit-up, wouldn't that be fun?"

"Oh, come on. I've seen pictures of your nephew. He's a cutie, with that baby blond hair and big, brown Palmer eyes. And your niece must be adorable, too," said Karen.

"Um, yeah, I suppose so. I just don't see the appeal," said Cassie. She didn't get how people liked hanging out with little kids. They were messy and boring. And they cried a lot. At least, that's what she remembered from her brothers when they were babies and her mom left her in charge. If she got assigned to coach little kids, she didn't know how she could stomach it.

"Maybe the farm wouldn't be so bad after all," said Cassie, wrinkling her nose at the thought of screaming babies and smelly diapers.

"Cassie, don't worry, you aren't going back to the farm. They would be crazy not to put you on the team. Certifiably insane. Believe me," said Karen.

A knock interrupted their conversation.

"The lists are up!" Their friend Samantha was running along the corridor, knocking on everyone's doors and letting them know.

Karen and Cassie looked at each other.

"Oh God," Cassie moaned.

"May as well go see," said Karen, getting up off the bed and brushing the muffin crumbs from her shirt.

"Wait. You better wipe the chocolate off your face," said Cassie. They both looked in the mirror.

One tall girl, lean and long-legged, with big brown eyes, looking serious, and one shorter, with long black hair, olive skin, and lively dark eyes that matched the chocolate smeared on her face. As Karen wiped off the brown smudge, Cassie eyed her messy light brown ponytail critically, and wished it hung as neatly as Karen's. Oh well.

"Here we go," she said to Karen, and they walked out the door.

Chapter Three

REED

David Beckham ran down the field, where he received a perfect pass and executed an amazing bicycle kick into the goal.

"Score!" Reed screamed and punched his fist into the air. It was 4-2, with his virtual team of long-gone super soccer stars winning. Slide tackle. Red card. Oh well, didn't matter in this game. Another slide tackle, and boom. Another red card. Wish I could do that in real life, he thought. Coach Chip was always on him about keeping his arms down and controlling his body, but Reed liked to use his body in the game. And if someone else fell down or got injured, that was just part of the game. Winning is what matters, not how many fouls or yellow cards or red cards you get. And he had the awards to prove it: 16 years of trophies, medals, and plaques stacked neatly in rows on the shelves across from his bed. Well, 12 really. There were pictures of Reed dribbling a soccer ball with a baby bottle in one hand, but he didn't think he could count anything before the age of four as part of his "career." He remembered blowing out the four candles on his birthday cake vividly. He had known what four candles meant: he was old enough to play on a real team, like his dad. He remembered his mother's big smile as she handed him a big square box wrapped in red foil, with a blue ribbon on top. He had torn open the paper, and there was his first soccer kit–miniature professional blue jersey, black shorts, blue socks, shin guards and the best of all–cleats! Real cleats!

Reed checked the clock on the game console. 3:55. He wasn't worried. For the last five years, he had been the country's top scorer for his age group. And now his age group, U-18, was ready to go to the Tournament.

Rosa walked into the den.

"I brought you some cookies and milk," she said, and put a plate of huge chocolate-chip cookies and a tall glass on the table next to Reed.

"Don't put them there!" snapped Reed.

"Don't snap at me, mister," she replied. But she placed them on a smaller table next to the sofa.

"Sorry," said Reed, sheepishly.

"You sound tense. I guess you didn't find out yet." Rosa asked, as she came to sit down next to Reed on the sofa.

"Nah, I'm not tense about that, I'm just concentrating on beating the hell out of FC Dead Guys," said Reed. "Watch this." Rosa watched as he maneuvered his players to shoot on the goal, and then, once the ball went in, he had two of his players do cartwheels.

"Nice. But I've never seen you do that on the field. Why not?" she said, teasing him. Rosa had come to take care of Reed's mom before she died, and then she stayed. To Reed, she was a combination of grandmother and hired help. Though she was an ample woman in her 60s who favored long skirts and cardigan sweaters, she was a whiz at card games, knew the names and stats of every player on all the world's national teams, and was an amazing cook besides.

Reed put down his controls and reached for the cookies.

"I thought you would have found out by now," said Rosa, reaching for a cookie herself. Reed slapped her hand.

"Hey, I thought you were on a diet!" Reed grabbed the plate away from Rosa.

"Right, I forgot," said Rosa, sighing. She was always on a diet, and yet she never seemed to lose any weight. This mystified Reed. Hard-core exercise took up most of his days, so keeping weight on was more of a concern for him. "So did you decide if you're going to live in the dorms or at home once you're on the team?"

"I talked to Dad the other night. He said I should go live in the dorms because it would be better for team cohesion, but he also said he'd really miss me. So I thought maybe I'd just go during the week and come home on weekends," said Reed.

"Seems like a good compromise," said Rosa. "He's been really busy since he got promoted at the Ministry, but he would really miss you."

"Plus, I don't think I could stand being in those stupid dorms all the time, and the food." Reed shuddered.

"Okay kiddo, let me know when you find out. I'm going to go out to get some stuff for dinner," Rosa said, as she heaved herself to her feet.

Reed grabbed another cookie, and picked up a game controller, but didn't start playing. He would really miss the den if he moved out—it was the perfect room, with comfortable dark leather sofas, a 64-inch screen for games and TV, an awesome music system, and his favorite family pictures—his mom and dad in Colorado before the war, his dad holding up a soccer trophy with the rest of his team, his mom holding him as a baby in the hospital. He didn't really want to trade all this comfort for the dorm. Add to that the horror of cafeteria food and sharing bathrooms with 21 other guys and it really seemed unappealing. But if his father said he should live in the dorm, he should go. He sighed.

Reed heard the house door open and his father's voice talking to someone on the phone. I bet that's the call, he thought as he lined up his next team of players. A minute later, he heard his father's steps as he came down the hall. The door opened.

"Reed," his dad said.

"Yeah, Dad?" Reed said, not looking up.

"You made the team, kid. Well done," said his father.

"Cool." Reed continued playing. He was surprised that he felt a little relieved. Of course he made the team. He was, after all, the best.

"I'm the Captain, right?"

"No. Some kid named Jason Carey. Do you know him?"

"Yeah, I know him. He has a twin brother. They're both pretty good. But why'd they pick him to be Captain?"

"I don't know, but I'll make a call. See if anything can be done about it." Reed's father started scrolling through his contacts list on his phone.

"Don't bother. I don't really care. Let him do all the talking, I'll be scoring the goals." Reed was disappointed, but didn't want his father to know.

"Are you sure? Henry could probably do something about it. I'll just give him a quick call." Henry Knox was in charge of the elite sports program. His father and Henry Knox had been soccer teammates in Colorado back before the War. Henry was a frequent guest in their house, and, unlike his father who never seemed to want to talk about his past, was happy to tell Reed stories of their pre-War glory days on the soccer field.

"Nah." Reed turned back to the game. "Come here, Dad. You just have to see this move." As Reed's fingers flew around the controller his player slide-tackled two opponents at the same time. "Wasn't that sick? I've got to learn how to do that!" Reed's dad shook his head.

"Just don't let the ref see you." Reed knew his dad didn't always approve of his physical way of playing. But he didn't object to all the wins.

"Hey Dad, when do we have our first practice with the whole team?" Reed asked.

"Not until the day after tomorrow. Tomorrow is the media day. You'll have to be up early and look your best, so you better get some sleep tonight. The whole country is anxious to get to know our new star soccer players."

"Okay, Dad, I'll get ready after dinner." Reed wasn't looking forward to the media attention. He knew his story was good. His father was a former soccer star whose dreams were interrupted by the war, and he was carrying on the legacy. He was happy to have the attention, as long as they didn't bring up his mom. But he had a feeling they would.

"I wish your mother was alive to see this. She'd be so proud of you." Reed closed his eyes for a second. He wished that, too. Reed's mother had died when he was eight years old, after a long battle with cancer that the doctors said was caused by radiation exposure. Sick as she had been, she always found the energy to read to him at night, and he still missed her. His father was crushed, and buried himself in his work. He never remarried, luckily. Reed liked it this way, with just the two of them. And Rosa, of course. They couldn't make it without Rosa.

"I'm sorry I can't celebrate with you. I have to go into the office for another emergency meeting right after dinner. And I have a conference call at 5. Rosa said dinner should be ready at 6. Maybe we can do something this weekend. Do you want to invite some friends over tonight?"

"Not really. I want to enjoy my last night of living at home. Will you take me tomorrow morning, instead of the driver?"

"I'll do my best." Reed saw his dad heading toward the door.

"Okay, thanks, Dad." His dad closed the door behind him.

A message popped up on the game screen.

SamStrikesFirst: Did you hear?

Reed stopped playing. Sam was one of his best friends. He replied.

Im#1: Yeah. You made it, right?
SamStrikesFirst: Yup. Max too. We're unstoppable
Im#1: Cool. Can't wait to kick some butt
SamStrikesFirst: Some cute butt. A girl made the team
Im#1: What???
SamStrikesFirst: Some girl called Cassie Palmer
Im#1: Never heard of her
SamStrikesFirst: Me neither
Im#1: That sucks
SamStrikesFirst: What were they thinking?
Im#1: Nutcases. Probably an alt
SamStrikesFirst: She'll probably break a nail don't worry
Im#1: Not worried

SamStrikesFirst: Bet $100 she won't last
Im#1: Not taking that bet. U r right
SamStrikesFirst: Gotta go almost chow time
Im#1: C U tom
SamStrikesFirst: K bye

Reed stared at the blank screen. A girl on the team? It was rare, but it did happen. Could a girl really handle the pressure, take the hits, and, most importantly, score goals? Not likely. On the other hand, the news of a girl might distract the press. He really hoped the reporters wouldn't ask about his mom, but he was pretty sure they would. Unless they had something more interesting to go after, like this girl. She wouldn't last, but maybe a good temporary diversion.

Reed went to his desk and pulled out a photo hidden under some notebooks in the top drawer. It was his favorite picture of his mom, sitting on a picnic blanket, laughing, her long hair flying around in the breeze. He touched his fingers to her face, pausing for a second. Then he put the photo back into the mess of his drawer and went back to his game.

Chapter Four

JASON

The gym smelled of fresh paint and glue. The newly installed wood floors were shiny, not a scratch on them yet. Twenty-two kids in plain white t-shirts and black soccer shorts were standing around or sitting on the gym bleachers, some in groups, some alone. Jason looked at all the faces around him. He knew most of them from training camp, but only a few of the other kids from his green training team had made it. He saw Carlo and Jack. Everyone was nervous and waiting. A few kids said hi to him as he walked in. His attention was drawn by three guys who were horsing around and talking too loud, telling stupid jokes, in the corner. Jason exhaled. He recognized the three yellow team "stars"–Max, Sam, and Reed. Jason suspected that if there was any trouble– and with 22 super-competitive kids on a highly pressurized team, there would be trouble–he could pretty much count on it starting with those three.

"They're clearly compensating for something," said a voice behind him.

Jason turned around and smiled at a tall, pretty girl in the corner juggling a soccer ball, passing it easily back from one foot to the other with perfect control.

"No kidding," he said closing the distance between them. "I'm Jason. What you do with that ball is pretty sick." He watched her pop the ball up to her arm and roll it along her back.

"Thanks. I'm Cassie."

"Yeah, first girl to make the team in four years. You're kind of hard to miss."

"Look who's talking. You're kind of hard to miss yourself, Captain." Cassie returned the smile, never breaking her juggling routine. If her playing was anything like her juggling, she had to be pretty good. It was hard to say who had been the bigger hit of the press day–Cassie Palmer or Reed Martinez, the son of the nation's Security Minister, who everyone knew had once been a soccer star himself. Of course they had brought out videos of Reed's father's glory days, before the War. The father's hopes dashed by a devastating war, his wife dead due to radiation cancer, and left with a son who would fulfill his father's dreams by winning the Tournament. Had all the makings of a TV miniseries.

Cassie caught the ball in her hand and stood next to Jason.

"Hey, I'm sorry about your brother not making it."

Jason looked around the gym.

"Yeah, it kinda sucks," he said, trying to sound nonchalant, but not really succeeding. "I was hoping he'd make the squad, even if he didn't make the starting line-up."

"My best friend didn't make it either," Cassie said. "We knew two girls on the team was a long shot, but it's really weird being without her." She looked at Jason. Jason nodded his head to show that he understood.

"Where'd your friend go?" asked Jason.

"She got put into the junior coaching program. She was really bummed about not making it, but she likes little kids, so it wasn't the end of the world. If they had done that to me, I would have jumped off a bridge," said Cassie grimly.

"Yeah, I know what you mean. But after this is all over, you know, we'll have to do something with our lives, and I guess I'd rather be a coach than sit at a desk all day." Jason grimaced at the thought of spending his days at a computer terminal.

"Or work on a farm." Cassie said, making a face.

"Right," said Jason, as he picked up a soccer ball and started juggling, too.

"What about your brother?" asked Cassie, balancing the ball low on her foot.

"They assigned him to some kind of training facility in the north somewhere. I don't know much about it, and he had to pack up pretty quick to get on the bus. It's really weird not knowing where he is or what he's doing." Jason frowned. "But, he was relieved he wasn't going into the coaching program, I think. He's like you, he would have thrown himself off a bridge."

"You don't know where he is?" she asked.

Just then a tall, athletic man in a navy blue track suit walked in.

"Gather around everybody," the man called out. "I'm Coach Andrews, I'll be whipping you all into shape and turning you into the international champions I know you can be."

People were staring and whispering. Where was Coach Chip? Coach Chip had coached the national team for the last 10 years, and Jason had always been impressed that he had taken time out to watch the training games. He'd even talk to Jason and Nate sometimes afterwards about their plays, and gave them suggestions and tips on what they needed to focus on. Jason had really looked forward to finally being on his team. Sounded like he wasn't the only one.

"Where's Coach Chip?" Reed shouted out. Reed, Max, and Sam made their way to the front of the circle.

"Coach Chip retired. He's no longer with the program. I'm your new head coach," said Coach Andrews.

Everybody was quiet. Jason remembered seeing Coach Chip a few days ago, and he had seemed friendly and joked with him and Nate as usual. He hadn't mentioned anything about retiring or leaving the program. It was strange that there had been no official announcement of his leaving.

Jason felt unsettled, but there was nothing he could do about it. This was the new coach. This was the guy he had to impress.

"There'll be more changes, too. We're going to do things differently. Coach Chip was never able to produce a winning team, but I'll do it. And you'll do it. No matter what it takes, we're in this to win this," said the coach.

"We're in this to win this? Hope he doesn't expect us to talk in rhyme," Jason said under his breath to Cassie.

Jason looked around at his new teammates. Everybody was staring at the new coach.

"The President has promised us anything we need," Coach Andrews continued in a stern voice. "There is no room for failure."

"Gee, intense much?" Cassie muttered under her breath.

"We'll start with a scrimmage. I want to observe you, and see your weaknesses and strengths. We'll do a 4-4-2 formation. Carlo, you take the far goal, and Jason the near one. Anton, I'll put you in after 20 minutes. The rest of you, I'm dividing you into A and B offenses and defenses. We'll have the A offense against the A defense for this first scrimmage, and we'll see how you do. I'll be watching you and making adjustments as we go." As he spoke, Coach handed out blue and yellow pinnies.

Jason grabbed his goalie gloves and put on a green long-sleeved goalie jersey. Anton and Carlo were both great goalies. The keepers at all levels attended intense monthly training sessions, so they knew each other. Competition for the first-string position was going to be tough.

As he looked down the field to see who Coach had put on the "A" offense, he felt his heart sink a little. Reed and Sam in forward positions, Max and Josh in the center. Great, Reed would be in his face.

Jason took his place in the goal. This was where his body took over and his brain was along for the ride. The whistle blew, and the game started.

Observing from the goal, it was pretty obvious that Reed, Max, and Sam were used to playing together. They were great at anticipating each other's moves. They might be jerks off the field, but they would be great assets for the team.

Jason watched as Cassie, who was playing left midfield on the B offense, intercepted a pass between Reed and Sam. As she bolted down the field, she faked out several players, dribbling easily around them, until Reed charged her from behind and knocked her down. In a game, that would have been at least a yellow card offense, maybe red since it was so obviously intentional. Cassie was on the ground, holding her ankle. Max and Sam snickered. Coach didn't stop play, and kept walking along the sidelines following the action as it moved up the field. Jason couldn't tell if he really didn't see or had decided to ignore it. Reed had offered his hand to help her up with a big smirk on his face. Cassie brushed his hand away and limped off the field.

So that's how they were going to play it, thought Jason. They were going to give the girl a hard time and see if she could take it. Jason looked over to Cassie on the sidelines. She was rubbing her ankle.

The play moved toward Jason now. A pass from the left mid up to the left wing, and then a nice cross right in front of the goal, where Sam ran it to kick it in the top left corner of the goal. Jason anticipated the kick, leaped up into the air, caught the ball and fell with a dramatic flourish. If Nate had been there, he would have laughed at Jason for the dramatics—but hey, new coach, gotta make an impression, thought Jason. He had to show he was worthy of being the first-string goalie. And he knew it looked better to dive and fall to the ground with the ball firmly in his hands than to simply jump and catch.

A few steps out to the edge of the box, and a big boot sent the ball sailing past the midline, where Cassie, who had come back in, trapped it and set off towards the opposite goal to Carlo.

Cassie passed it to Oscar, who looked ready to take it up the field. Max intercepted it, booted it to Reed, who charged past Evan and was about to take a powerful, close-range shot at Jason, when Jack ran in to block it, taking the brunt of the shot with his body. Reed headed the rebound right over Evan and toward the goal. It was an impossible shot to predict, but Jason managed to grab it, and hurled it out.

Jack grinned at Reed and made a rude hand gesture. Jason's confidence surged.

Cassie dribbled the ball up the field, around two other midfielders, Josh and Mateo, and nutmegged Max.

Boo-yeah! Jason thought to himself. After that dirty trick, he was rooting for Cassie. Max seemed to wonder where the ball went before realizing he'd been gotten. He turned around, and chased after Cassie. She had legs like a gazelle, thought Jason. Speedy and graceful. She ran up the field, keeping up with the play. Coach had to be impressed. He'd probably move her to the A offense. He had to. She was amazing, and was proving she could keep up with the boys. Reed was right behind her, breathing hard, aiming to take her out again, but Cassie outmaneuvered him and kicked the ball to Oscar, who took a beautiful shot into the upper right corner.

"Way to go!" shouted Jason.

After the kick-off, Max and Sam executed a series of one-touch passes, and sped down the field toward him, where Reed was perfectly positioned to take a shot. It was a tough one, but Jason was able to punch it over the top of the goal. Not pretty, and a corner kick, but at least it wasn't a goal. It was a tough scrimmage, with everyone out to prove they deserved to be there. After that first knock-down, Cassie stayed just far away enough from Reed that he was never able to get her again.

At about 20 minutes, Coach pulled Carlo out and put in Anton, moved Cassie to the "A" offense with Reed, Sam, and Max, and moved Luke into center back. From midfield, Max lobbed a ball to Cassie, who executed a beautiful high pass to Reed. Reed headed the ball toward the goal, where it bounced off the bar. Sam was there, and pounded it into the goal.

There was nothing Jason could do. Reed and Sam high-fived each other, and Max came in for some back-slapping, but Jason noticed Cassie stayed outside the circle, even though it was her pass that had made it possible. Cassie's addition to the offense made a big difference. Jason pulled out everything he had. Luke and Jack blocked about half the shots, leaving Jason to deal with the rest. He let in half a dozen more goals, and felt pretty good about keeping them to that. It was a real workout. In the other goal, Anton was really struggling. The "B" offense was having a field day with him.

Half an hour later, Coach called them off the field for a water break. Sweat dripped off Jason's hair into his eyes as he jogged off the field. If Luke and Jack were getting beat, this had the potential to be a high-scoring offensive line-up.

"Line up, everybody," Coach yelled. "I hope this wasn't your best, because if it was, we're in big trouble. You are nowhere near ready for the level of play we'll see in the Tournament."

"Hey coach, that was our first game together," said Reed. "You can't expect us to be perfect." Jason guessed if your dad was the Security Minister, you could say whatever you wanted to whomever you wanted.

"Yeah," said some of the other kids, happy to back Reed up, though none of them probably would have said it themselves. They were used to being the best, not being told they weren't.

"Defense wins the games. What I saw out there wasn't much defense. A bunch of kindergarteners could have run through those lines. We've got some serious work to do. Your placement was terrible, your communication was sloppy, and you did a lousy job of setting up plays at free kicks and corner kicks. If you're going to be a team, you're going to have to learn to work together, to know where your teammates are going to go, not just where they are, and to be there to back them up. And don't think you guys on offense were much better. You have some strong midfielders. Use them. Strikers, you need to work on your precision. I don't want to see so many balls going over the net. Midfielders, you need to work on awareness about when to switch fields. Quick switches will be key in this Tournament. I know you are all used to being the best—that's how you got here. But none of you are stars on my team yet. Everyone starts from zero with me."

That was good to hear. And it was satisfying to see that Reed wasn't getting any special treatment. If they were going to be a team, they had to work together and value each other.

Coach sent them back out to the field. He spent the rest of the three-hour practice moving players around and trying different combinations. He brought some players off the field to work with the assistant coaches, three former Tournament stars. His coaching style was to scream at them as a group, but he was patient and helpful one-on-one. Jason noticed he was coming back to Cassie-Reed combinations, even though Reed seemed to take every opportunity when Coach wasn't looking to push her off balance or trip her. That would have to stop.

* * *

At the end of the practice, Jason's legs felt like jello. He had seen some great moves on the field today. Luke was an amazing sprinter. Cassie was smart and had excellent placement. Reed could be a problem. He was really talented, but a ball hog. Jason would have to talk to him. He groaned inside. He wished Nate were here to help him with this one.

Heck, if Nate were here, he'd probably be Captain, and Jason would just be offering advice in the background.

"Hey Reed," Jason called as they were leaving the locker rooms after another few hours of grueling practice.

"What?" Reed turned around and faced Jason.

"Good job, today," started Jason.

"Gee, thanks, *Captain*," Reed replied sarcastically.

"But it was not cool what you did to Cassie."

"What do you care? Are you into her or something?" Reed snickered.

"No. Idiot. I'm talking about the game. She's really good. Those passes she gave you were the only reason your sorry butt even scored on me. So stop beating on her." Jason had about an inch on Reed, and used it to glare down at him.

"If she's that good, she can take it. She doesn't need you to protect her," Reed said, as he turned his back on Jason and left.

Maybe that was a mistake, thought Jason. Nate would have known how to handle Reed. Jason felt like had just pissed him off. Great. He packed his gear and headed to the cafeteria for dinner. At least since they were in hard training again, there should be a lot of it.

Chapter Five

CASSIE

Jerk. Arrogant moron!

Cassie was taking a shower, still fuming after the incident with Reed in practice. It was no accident the way he barreled into her and knocked her down. She wanted to smack that smirk off his face. Idiot!

Cassie let herself imagine just for a second how it would feel to punch him in the face. Nice.

And those two "buddies" of his were not much better. Cassie could still see how they patted Reed on the shoulder and high-fived him after he knocked her down. At least now she knew what to expect. Cassie turned the faucet to brutally cold for couple of seconds before she turned the water off. It was supposed to be good for your muscles after an intense workout. It better work, because it was an awful way to end a shower.

She forced her mind away from Reed and his buddies, and replayed the rest of the scrimmage in her mind. A couple of guys looked really good. She had to admit that even though Reed was a colossal jerk, he was the best striker she'd ever seen. If he wasn't a soccer player, he could probably be a model. He had those typical blonde, blue-eyed boy-next-door good looks. Luke's stockier build, round face, and messy dark blond curls were as far removed from Reed as could be, but he and the other tall, skinny blond kid, whose name she couldn't remember, were great in defense. She had never seen anyone sprint like Luke. Coach flattened the defense at the practice today, harping on every little mistake they made, but she thought they were really solid.

And then there was Jason, the Captain. Even though she just met him, she really liked him. He was observing the game and directing all his players, yelling encouragements and keeping any frustrations to himself. Not too bossy, but bossy enough to keep them focused. And what a goalie. Some of those saves she would have said were impossible.

Too bad his twin brother didn't make the team. It might have been fun to have identical twins on the team. Confuse their opponents. And cute, she thought. She shook the thought away. She had seen the two of them together around the Training Center sometimes, but the first time she had talked to Jason was at the practice.

It was partly because their practice schedules were different, so even though they shared a cafeteria and classrooms, logistically it worked out that the girls' and boys' teams weren't often in the same space at the same time. That didn't stop them from having relationships, of course. But she had, so far, steered clear of any complications. Karen, on the other hand, was like a rubber ball, bouncing from one crush to the next. Cassie and Karen spent hours dissecting what a look or a comment meant in the roller coaster that was Karen's love life. She missed Karen, and the excitement of her ups and downs.

Cassie looked around her private shower and locker room. The maintenance guys must have been really annoyed to have to build this so quickly. She knew they worked overnight to divide the boys locker room into two sections. Because of one girl.

As Cassie walked out of her locker room, she thought about what Coach had told them after practice. Tomorrow they would each visit the nurse's office for physical exams. Their optimal diets would be calculated, and from this point on their food intake would be monitored. Ugh, thought Cassie. The last thing she wanted was someone watching over her every mouthful. What if they wanted her to eat when she was full? Or didn't give her enough?

The cafeteria served pretty good food. Heavy on the fruits and vegetables, lots of lean protein, and whole grains. Plus, occasional cupcakes, cookies, and muffins. They better not take those away! Sometimes, when she caught a glimpse of a crate of tomatoes in the kitchen, she wondered if it came from her family's special radiation-free greenhouses. Sometimes she felt guilty that she had escaped the farm, while her family was still there, working long days and doing hard work, while she basically played all day. She also knew that her "play" was worth more than all their work combined to the government, and she felt guilty about that. But knowing she was contributing to her family's success, with the extra food coupons and scholarships for her brothers, helped. They all appreciated what she was doing, and her mom and dad even talked to her about the sacrifice she was making, but it never felt that way to her. She felt like she had won the jackpot. She not only got food and a roof over her head, but she also got to spend her days doing something she loved and something she was really, really good at.

Before the War, Alaska had not had a lot of food production. Most of the land had been frozen, and the state had a very short growing season. Their income was mostly from oil and fish. Fallout had polluted much of the world's farmland and radiation was everywhere. Levels were much lower than they had been, but radiated food was still a problem. For many people, radiated food was just part of everyday life–they had to eat, and if the soil was contaminated, that was too bad. They hoped the potassium iodide pills distributed by the government would keep them from succumbing to radiation poisoning.

It was easy to forget sometimes how lucky the kids in the training camps were. And if they actually won the Tournament, there would be nothing she couldn't have. Being on the national soccer team guaranteed you national celebrity. Even though people were sick and hungry, they loved watching the Tournament and they loved their soccer stars.

Every two years, the Tournament brought the whole world together. Everyone was given holidays from work and school to watch the games, and the host country would go all out with parties and celebrations. The Tournament was a reminder that, despite the devastating failures of the past, humans could rise above their baser instincts and live in a peaceful world.

* * *

The next day in the cafeteria after practice, while Cassie was waiting in line, Jason came in behind her.

"What's the hold up?" he asked.

"I think it's our new customized food they were talking about yesterday."

Jason looked over at some of the other kids' trays.

"Oh, great. If it tastes anything like it looks, we're in for a treat. And what's this?" He looked at the supplements in paper cup.

Cassie laughed. "Yeah, it looks like the cook doesn't believe in the power of presentation." Cassie's tray had some sort of meat, a scoop of mushy pasta, a pile of something green that didn't look that appetizing, but was probably very good for her, a pile of mixed berries, and a little paper cup of pills.

"Ugh. I hate pills. But they were pretty convincing telling us about all the great things these vitamins will do for our 'adolescent' bodies," Cassie said, imitating the way the nurse said adolescent, as if it was some kind of disease.

Jason laughed.

"If this soccer thing doesn't work out for you, you could do vitamin commercials," he said.

A nurse in white scrubs was walking around the tables with a clipboard, checking names off. Reed opened up his mouth and dumped the entire cup in at once, swallowing them without water and giving a big grin. Show off.

"Let's go sit with Luke," Jason said.

They walked to where Luke was sitting alone, eating his meal. He looked like he was actually enjoying it. He smiled at both of them.

"What's up with the long faces?" He was just finishing the pile of the green stuff on his plate.

"Wow, you look like you actually like that stuff," Cassie said.

"Sure I do. This is totally like my childhood. My grandma was Russian. She cooked all the food for so long it practically dissolved into molecules. This tastes exactly like her cooking," Luke said. "Are you gonna finish that, Cassie?"

"Not if I can help it. Do you want it?" Cassie looked around to see if lunch monitor was watching.

"Sure, pile it up, baby," Luke said and moved his empty plate next to hers.

"Luke, you're gross, seriously," Jason was slowly chewing his meat, trying to keep himself from barfing. "This food is disgusting."

"Not to me. But you can take my pills anytime. Those I can live without," Luke said as the nurse approached their table, and then checked them off on her clipboard. After she seemed satisfied that the right pills had been swallowed by the right kids, Cassie and Jason watched Luke clean his plate.

"The culinary experience of lifetime is over. Let's get out of here." Jason said, when Luke was finally done.

"It wasn't so bad," Luke mumbled as he walked out of the cafeteria over to a potted plant in the corner and quickly spit out the pills.

"How'd you do that?" asked Cassie.

"Just one of my many talents," said Luke, grinning his crazy grin. He was pretty cute when he smiled like that, Cassie realized.

"On what planet is a talent like that useful?" Jason asked.

"Well, when you're a hyper little kid in an orphanage with hundreds of other little kids, sometimes they use chemical means to keep control," Luke said. "But, like I said, that's just one of many."

"Yeah? So what are your others?" Cassie asked.

"Do you really need to ask? Haven't you seen my bicycle kick?" Luke asked, pretending to be devastated that she hadn't noticed his prowess on the soccer field.

"I've seen you on a bicycle and I've seen you kick," said Jason, "But can't really say I've seen them together." They all burst into laughter.

"I'm wounded!" said Luke, pretending to hold his heart and fall to the ground.

"That is sooo mature," Cassie laughed, offering him a hand up.

"Maturity is grossly overrated," Luke grinned at Cassie, not letting go of her hand.

"Are you guys going to the game room?" she asked.

"Yeah, I built my dream team and I'm ready to kick some butt!" said Jason. They were all heading to the game room for two hours of required strategic computer soccer games. The games were in 3D with holographic players filling a field, everything scaled to size. They looked almost real, except when they occasionally flickered due to low power. Sometimes opposing team players were designed according to actual famous players, like Zhang, the 7-foot-tall Chinese player from the 2042 Tournament. Usually, you had to play as the holographic version of yourself, with all your physical limitations. The rumor was that the coaches were monitoring the games, and kids who showed mastery of strategy were awarded more time on the field. Cassie had never really cared about computers or playing the games. Jason, on the other hand, was a natural. Maybe that's why they chose him to be the Captain, she thought.

After two hours in front of their holo fields, Cassie was wiped out. As they were leaving the game room for the dorms, Luke jumped on Jason's back like a monkey.

"Jason, you beast! How are you doing it?" Luke asked. "You won every single game!"

Jason just grinned.

"That's one of *my* many talents," he said.

"You guys are crazy. I'm going to bed," Cassie said, going out the door.

"Can't wait to do it again tomorrow," said Luke, and he and Jason headed off to their room.

* * *

As she was showering after another brutal practice, Cassie admitted to herself that it was hard being the only girl on the team. She could handle the training. But could she handle some of these guys? It turned out the shoves on the field was just the beginning of the fun for Reed and his buddies.

In the past few weeks, she had been knocked down four more times and been kicked and tripped more times that she could count. She had the bruises to prove it. The physical stuff was not so hard to take. What they said about her bothered her more. She had heard them, as she was obviously meant to, saying that she looked more like a giraffe than a girl, with her long legs and her long neck. She was some kind of athlete freak. They were all class, those guys.

Not all of them, of course. Jason always chose her for his scrimmage team and he and Luke had started to run with her in the mornings. They were becoming good friends, in fact. As they ran, they talked about the soccer, the team, their families. Jason was not what she expected, seeing him on the field as a goalie and Captain. On the field he seemed to work hard to be all business, focused and committed. Off the field he was funny, cracking jokes, imitating Reed and his buddies, bouncing off the walls, and making fun of himself.

And Luke. Luke was really nice, sweet, and relaxed. You would never guess from looking at him. He was solid as a rock, and when she faced him on the field as a defender, he actually scared her. Until he smiled. When Jason started to get wound up about practices and his responsibilities as captain, Luke kidded the seriousness out of him. She knew Luke didn't have any living family. His parents died in car accident when he was two and his grandma took care of him until she died. That's how he ended up in the orphanage at the age of six. Luke didn't talk about the orphanage. Cassie wasn't sure if he didn't remember anything or chose to forget. Whatever his story was, there was something about his warmth and openness that made her want to get to know him better.

Cassie never complained to them about the bullying. She wanted to fight her own battles. She didn't have any time for self-pity. Coach was running all of them ragged. They were doing more wind sprints, running more stadiums, doing more sit-ups and push-ups than they ever had. One of the assistant coaches had come up with the brilliant idea that they should race each other to be dismissed for dinner. The winner of the first lap got to leave first, and then the winner of the next lap, and so on, until 11 of the 22 were dismissed. The first 11 were rumored to be the ones who'd make the starting line-up. If you were last three days in a row, Coach said, there were plenty of kids just hoping for someone to drop out.

She came back to room each night and collapsed on her bed. She missed Karen, but didn't have the time or energy to try to connect with her.

Chapter Six

REED

"Shoot, for God's sake, just shoot!" Reed screamed at Max. They were at Reed's house on a Friday night. It had been the toughest week of training Reed could recall, but the more Coach pushed him, the more he could feel himself improve.

Max swore loudly, fiddling with his control.

"Bang, you're dead again, Max," said Sam, laughing.

"You loser! You always get shot at the beginning of the game," said Reed.

"Shut up. I'm starving," said Max, his stomach growling. "Do you have anything to eat?"

"Sometimes I think you only come here for the food. Go ask Rosa for something," said Reed, not taking his eyes from the screen and hitting his targets.

"Get some for me, too," said Sam. "Just nothing that looks like anything they serve at the cafeteria."

"Man, I wish I didn't have to eat that crap all the time. At least you get weekends off," said Max, as he went out the door.

"Stop complaining. I think you guys eat more at my house than I do. After you guys leave, it's like the locusts have been through the kitchen." Reed was repeating what Rosa had said last time, as she vacuumed the crumbs the trio had left strewn around the room.

"Sorry, but you have all the good stuff. Hey, I know. If you let me eat here, I'll give you all my food back at the Training Center," Sam offered.

"Yeah, right. I'd rather eat my shoes than eat all my meals in that cafeteria," said Reed, making a gagging noise.

Max came back with his hands full of potato chips, granola bars, and cookies, and dumped them on the table. Sam dove in, grabbing handfuls of cookies.

"The nurse would really approve of your nutritious choices," Reed remarked, looking at the cookie crumbs flying everywhere and thinking how Rosa would complain. Oh well. "Hand me a cookie or two. Tomorrow's weigh-in day and I can't let you clowns beat me again."

Max moved in front of the mirror, as he stuffed his mouth with a cookie. He pulled up his shirt sleeve, mouth still full of cookie, and started flexing his muscles.

"I think I've gained 10 pounds this month. My arms are totally buff. Check it out."

"That's nothing, you loser," said Sam, nudging Max aside and flexing his own arms. "Check out these guns."

"It looks like the whole team is going through a major growth spurt together. Have you noticed Luke? He's like majorly buffed now. I wonder if he's lifting weights at night or something," said Max.

"He's probably trying to impress the giraffe. Haven't you noticed how they're always hanging out together?" said Reed.

"No, I haven't noticed. I've never really liked giraffes," said Sam. "How come you noticed? Do you like giraffes?" Sam leered at Reed, "They have really nice big brown eyes, and loooonggg legs..."

Reed rolled his eyes.

"They belong in the zoo, not on my team," said Reed.

"So you say, but it doesn't seem like your heart is in making her life miserable anymore," said Max.

"Yeah, well, the Tournament is around the corner and we're stuck with her. And she's not that bad of a player. She's been first in the lap-running competition three times in a row, which is more than I can say for either of you." He paused. "And yesterday Coach told me to lay off her. So we all lay off her, okay? She's not as bad as I thought she would be," Reed looked at Max and Sam. They were back on the sofa, stuffing their faces again. "And watch out for the chocolate on the sofa. Rosa almost killed me last time."

"Okay, okay, *mom*," Max said. Sam nodded to indicate he had heard, still chewing.

Later, after the guys went back to the dorms, Reed started picking up crumbs and wrappers that were scattered all over the den from the feeding frenzy. He wanted to make sure his dad didn't see this stuff. Reed knew how his dad felt about athletes and junk food, but kids who were working as hard as they were deserved some time off, right? A few cookies couldn't hurt anyone who trained as hard as they did. Besides, Rosa kept making them and someone had to eat them.

The team looked strong. Everyone, including Cassie, was playing really well. They might actually win it this year. Reed imagined the uproar in the country. They'd be heroes. Coach was really hard on them, but very determined. He was tough, but fair, and was always available after practices for kids who needed help or wanted advice. With his father so busy lately, Reed had started staying after practice and talking to Coach, which was how the whole Cassie thing had come up. Coach had actually thanked him for pushing her hard, because he had his doubts about whether a girl could handle the pressure. But then he told Reed it was time to lay off, and Reed had agreed.

Lately, his dad was always tied up at the Ministry. When Reed asked what was keeping him so late, he never wanted to talk about it. "Just boring stuff," he would say, "Nothing for you to worry about." And then he'd ask Reed about training. That's all they talked about anymore.

They used to talk about everything. But now, his father had shut down. Reed knew something was going on. Rosa told him that his father wasn't sleeping well, and Reed had seen her taking the empty liquor bottles out to the recycling bin.

Reed had just finished cleaning up when his father came in.

"So, how was your day?" his dad asked.

"Pretty good. Coach worked us really hard today." Reed paused.

"And?" Reed's dad sat down on the sofa, and watched Reed sweeping crumbs off the coffee table.

"Well, coach said my shooting has gotten a lot stronger," said Reed, focusing intently on the crumbs.

"That's good," said Reed's dad. "And why is this room such a disaster area?"

"Max and Sam were here tonight," said Reed, sighing. "They pretty much ate the entire kitchen. Hope you ate already."

"They're the two messiest boys I've ever met." His father smiled in sympathy. "And yes, I ate at the Ministry. So what else did Coach say?"

"Coach told me to lay off Cassie. Which I guess I was ready to do anyway. He also thanked me for pushing her, so it wasn't like it was criticism."

"I agree with your coach. Having a girl on the team is a gamble. You have to be able to rely on her, so it's important to make sure she's up to the job. You performed a valuable function." Reed breathed a sigh of relief.

"But Reed, I need to warn you against developing any feelings toward this girl. I know from experience, girls can get in your head and mess with your game," he continued.

"Are you kidding?" Reed protested. "I have no interest in that girl. None. Zero. I'm just glad she's proved herself and as long as she helps me score goals, I'm happy to have her on the team." He came up from the table, and looked his dad in the eyes.

"Good," said his dad. "I also wanted to let you know that we'll be hosting a big dinner party next weekend for the President and the other Ministers. I want you to be here, of course, but I think Sam and Max should probably stay at the dorms, okay?"

"Yeah, okay. What's the party for?" Reed asked.

"We're getting together to do some pre-Tournament planning and talk about some of the events. This stuff can get pretty dry, so we thought we'd liven it up by having a party," said Reed's dad.

"Do I have to dress up? I don't think any of my good clothes fit me anymore," said Reed.

His dad looked up at him.

"You really have grown these past few months. I'll tell Rosa to take you shopping this week. You don't have to stay for the whole evening, just make an appearance and say hello to everyone. Everybody is excited to meet one of our soccer stars in person, and I'm sure they'll all want to talk to you. Since this is our first time hosting the Tournament, everyone at the Ministry is very excited. I've never seen the President take such an interest in our teams before."

"Okay Dad. I'll do my best to be charming. Hope the food will be worth my sacrifice," Reed grinned. "Hey, Dad, how's work?"

"Things are crazy. Security around the Tournament is always a big deal, especially since we're hosting, so there's a million things we have to think about and plan for. We really want it to be the most amazing Tournament ever. It's a chance for our country to make a name for ourselves and I think we can beat China this year." His dad paused. "Sorry if I've been a little distracted and busy. I'll make it up to you after the Tournament."

After his dad left, Reed went to his room. He got into bed, and picked up a soccer magazine to read for a few minutes. But he couldn't concentrate.

The Tournament was everything right now. Being part of the team and training hard consumed his every waking moment. Usually. But every once in a while he wondered what would happen next. In a few months, the Tournament would be over. He really thought they could win this one. He looked up at his top shelf, which held his only world competition trophy. There were an assortment of silvers and bronzes from his age-group regional championships on the lower shelf, but the top shelf was just for Worlds. The silver trophy from last year's Junior World Cup, the informal competition that happened in off years between the Tournaments, stood alone, slightly off-center. Reed knew exactly where his new gold medal would go.

At the Junior World Cup, China had taken gold, as they almost always did. But for the first time, Alaska had given them a real run for their money, only losing the game in overtime 2-1. He remembered feeling that they were going to win. When they went into overtime, he really thought they could pull it off. Reed remembered the horrible feeling of watching as the goalie—not Jason—just missed a hard shot that went into the corner. If their defense hadn't been so tired out, if the goalie had just been anticipating a little better, they could have won. Reed had been watching Jason carefully during practices, and was happy with what he saw. Jason blocked shots that easily defeated Carlo and Anton. He never seemed to tire, either. Just kept going. He couldn't put his finger on it, but there was something different about the way Jason approached the games.

Chapter Seven

NATE

Nate woke up to loud speakers blasting in the building.

"Line up in five minutes in the yard," announced a loud computerized female voice in the quiet of the room. Nate got out of his bed along with 19 other exhausted and slightly disoriented boys, who all started scrambling around the room getting dressed.

Nate looked at the bed next to his and pulled the sheets off his friend Nikko, who was still sound asleep.

"Leave me alone!" Nikko growled and put the pillow over his head. Nate was trying to put his pants on with one hand while tugging the pillow off Nikko's head with the other. No luck. Nikko was holding the stupid thing like a drowning man clutching a lifejacket. Nate tripped on his pant leg and swore. He just about had it with his friend.

"Get up or you'll have bathroom duty for the rest of the week, idiot!" He tried pulling the pillow of Nikko's head one more time.

"What the heck?" Nikko mumbled sleepily, turning over.

"Another insane line-up," Nate said. He could see the first streaks of sunrise out the windows. "Wake up, Nikko, or

I'm leaving you here and don't expect any help with cleaning the toilets." This wouldn't be the first time Nikko couldn't get his butt up for the lineup. His offenses were piling up nicely.

"What time is it?" Nikko asked, sitting up drowsily and rubbing his eyes

"Four a.m.," Nate was all dressed and ready. "That's sleeping in, compared to last month. You have exactly one minute, Nikko."

"God, I hate this, hate this," Nikko grumbled as he thrust his feet into his pants, then boots, his eyes barely open. "This is the second time this week."

Nikko's shirt was inside out, but Nate was just happy Nikko was finally moving.

Nate was sick and tired of it, too. He had been in the new "training facility" for more than four months now, but it wasn't the sports training he had expected. He still wasn't sure exactly what they were training for, but he was starting to get an idea. The transfer to the new training camp had happened so quickly that he barely had time to say goodbye to Jason. Nate and the others in his program were given an hour to pack up and get ready to leave. They boarded a large tractor-trailer, fitted with benches on the inside. The only window was in front, a Plexiglas partition between the back of the truck and the driver's seat. It had been impossible to see where they were going. When they arrived late at night, they were given a room assignment, issued gray nondescript sweatpants and t-shirts, and send to dorms to sleep. The training had started the next morning. Running, endurance, weight lifting. Lights out at 2200, wake-up call at 0600.

The training compound was in a remote area, several hours from Fairbanks, where he had spent most of his soccer-training life. Judging by the amount of daylight at the beginning of June, they were pretty far north. The nights weren't completely dark at all anymore, just a few hours of deep blue to purplish sky. The compound looked brand new. It seemed like somebody hastily cleared a couple of acres of wilderness and put together ugly gray buildings made from prefabricated panels. Two long, rectangular one-story buildings housed the kids and staff. In between them stood a large two-story building housing a cafeteria that doubled as TV/game room in the evenings. There was also a kitchen, a gym, and some offices. A mile-long outdoor track circled the compound and a couple of athletic fields. Nate had not even been inside most of the buildings. Just the room they all slept in, the gym that they used when the weather got exceptionally foul, and the cafeteria where they ate and spent evenings watching TV or goofing around.

Nate's room held 20 boys ranging in age from 16 to 18. He knew some of them from soccer training, but there were many others who he'd never seen before. They came from Junior Leaders camps all over Alaska.

Nate had never heard about those camps, but no wonder. His life up to now had been all about soccer. Nikko came from a JL camp in Fairbanks, where he had spent the last four years. Nate learned from some of the other JLs that Nikko was a genius, with IQ scores off the charts. By 14, most college professors couldn't keep up with him. Everybody wanted to see Nikko play the strategy games, and the game room had been flooded with kids whenever word got around that Nikko was playing. That didn't help him here, in the land of endurance, strength, and running. Short and thin, he looked younger than anybody else out here. When some of the bigger guys started to give him a hard time, Nate stepped in. Nikko was grateful and latched on to him. That's how they started hanging out together.

"I wonder what fun they have planned for us today," Nikko muttered under his breath as he lined up next to Nate in the yard.

"Maybe a few hundred push-ups and then a nice jog through the cold river like two days ago?" Nate ventured a guess. "Or maybe they'll let us loose in the woods again and will have to find our way back."

Nikko had hated that assignment. Last week they had gotten separated in the woods, and Nikko had ended up lost, or as he preferred to say, "disoriented." They all teased Nikko about it afterwards, but there were some tense moments while the search party was trying to locate him. The woods in these parts were thick and wild, and grizzly bears and mountain lions were not uncommon. Even the search party got a little disoriented while looking for Nikko.

"I don't think they'll pull that one on us again, at least not without some supplies and compass," Nikko said. "Not after all that trouble last week. It was fun riding the rescue helicopter, though."

Nate looked around the yard. Four months of training had paid off, at least in terms of line-ups. Their trainers stood to the side, rather than starting their warm-up. A tall middle-aged man with short severe haircut, dressed in Army fatigues, walked toward them. Nate nudged Nikko, and Nikko shrugged, as if to say, "don't ask me."

"My name is Colonel Gladov. You will address me as Colonel. From now on, I'm in charge of this unit. You've been with us for four months now and you're all ready to begin your new training in earnest." The Colonel had their full attention now.

"You're part of very special elite security force that our President created to meet new challenges our country might face in the future. In the near future. You're some of the best and strongest athletes and strategists our country has, and should count yourself very privileged to be chosen for this training. You all know about World War III and the Peace Treaties that were signed in its aftermath. Every two years, the country that wins the Tournament faces the responsibility of keeping the nuclear sites around the world safe from unscrupulous hands. It worked for last 30 years, but now we have intelligence telling us that one country is prepared to use force to get hold of the weapons and use them to control the Global Government."

Nate shifted uncomfortably and looked around at the other boys. They all stared at Colonel.

"People have short memories. Some have forgotten the events that led to the War, and how quickly destruction followed. We haven't. Our President is determined to keep Alaskans safe, and you'll be part of that effort," said the Colonel.

Nate didn't buy this. He looked at Nikko, whose face was grim.

Nikko swore under his breath.

Nate totally agreed. Every four-year-old knew that no country was allowed an army. Military training was illegal. After the Peace Treaties, there had been only one country that was discovered training a secret army. It was about 10 years ago. The country—Nate couldn't recall the name—had been caught with weapons. Nate remembered because he and Jason had been obsessed with weapons since they were little, and loved going through old books and videos about armies and battles. And when they showed machine guns on the news, he and Jason had been able to tell their parents the names of every weapon that came on screen TV. After that, Nate remembered their books and videos disappeared, and they started going to play soccer every day after school with their dad. He learned later that the consequences for the country were harsh: No food from global distribution centers, no agricultural supplies, no medicine, no technology. The country had become an international pariah, cut off from the rest of global community, which would mean slow death by starvation and illness.

Nate looked around cautiously as he whispered to Nikko, "You'd think they'd tell the Global Government."

Nikko whispered back, "No kidding."

Colonel Gladov continued, "We've contacted the Global Government, and it's their recommendation that we prepare for all possibilities. I don't want to sugarcoat it for you gentlemen, but one of those possibilities is war. From your previous training programs, we know that you have the skills and intelligence to be our future leaders in the case of armed conflict."

Future leaders? Was he insane? Did anybody notice they were teenagers? Nate wished he could talk to Jason. Maybe he knew something. He hadn't had any way of getting in touch with him or anyone else for the last four months. They had no access to the computers or phones. They were kept dumb and deaf here. Their only source of outside information was a TV in the game room. The news channels were blocked, but nobody really cared. After 10 grueling hours of training, all they wanted was something to take their minds off their sore muscles. They watched mostly sports, especially now, so close to the Tournament.

"Starting now, you will begin a new training regimen. In addition to the strength and endurance training, you'll also train with conventional weapons. And for strategy, you'll be doing computer simulations. We just received a shipment of top-of-the-line computers and are setting up new computer training rooms as we speak. We have high hopes for you. Your country needs you, so I expect you to do your best," continued Colonel Gladov in his thick Russian accent. Where did they find this guy? He was as cheerful as death. The yard was quiet. You could hear a pin drop.

"It goes without saying that this is all classified information, and you may not share it with anybody outside your units. Your country's future depends on it." Gladov finished.

Nate and Nikko looked at each other. Nikko's eyes were lit up like Christmas tree. "I want to see these weapons. What do you think we have? Rocket propelled grenades? AK-47s?"

"Don't be stupid. All those weapons were destroyed years ago. We are probably talking about swords or something," Nate replied, and they both chuckled. The image of 400 boys charging with ancient-looking rusted swords quickly flashed in Nate's mind. Jason would really enjoy that, Nate thought, remembering some of their favorite ninja warrior games.

"This is going to be so cool. I never even had a toy gun! I had to make them out of sticks and paper," said Nikko. Nate rolled his eyes. Trust it to Nikko to find a silver lining in any situation.

"It looks like your dreams are about to come true," said Nate. He wondered what kind of weapons survived the last war, and were they really going to use them? He never thought there would be another war. Not in his lifetime. For as long as Nate could remember, he had been taught that another war would probably mean the end of civilization.

Nate felt like throwing up, but that would probably not make a good impression on the 400 kids assembled in the yard who had all just found out they were future leaders. He really wanted to talk to Jason. Shooting off ideas with his hyper brother somehow brought clarity to stupid situations. Boy, he missed him. He missed their ugly dorm room, his teammates, even the cafeteria. He wished he could pack up and leave. He hadn't signed up for this, had he? Could he just talk to Gladov and ask to go home? Fat chance of that, now that he was in 'possession' of highly classified info.

At least now they would have an access to the computers and the Web. Maybe he'd do some careful digging around. And maybe he'd get in touch with Jason. Email was probably out since it was sure to be monitored, but there was always online gaming. He was sure his beast of a brother couldn't stay away from blood and gore if he had access to a computer. Jason sometimes got a little intense, and Nate couldn't help but rile him up. Nate almost laughed out loud when he remembered the time he beat Jason by squirting at his eyes with a tiny water gun so he couldn't see at the very end of the game, and then Jason taking his revenge across Nate's nose–some real blood and gore. Nate's nose hadn't been broken, luckily, but he had two black eyes for a week. It was so worth it.

Chapter Eight

JASON

It was 8 p.m., and Jason, Luke, and Cassie were in the game room. They'd spent the first hour working through a series of exercises on ball angles and bounces, and now were on the second hour of soccer strategy games against the computer teams. Jason was winning every game.

"How'd you get past the 11th level?" Luke asked, leaning over to look at Jason's screen.

"The 11th level? I beat that three days ago," Jason said, pretending to yawn.

"Overachiever," said Cassie. She was still struggling with level 12.

"Okay, let me show you. You have to switch fields here instead of trying to run it up the side, and then the field just opens up," Jason said, working the controls.

"Wow, I can't believe I was stuck on that the last 45 minutes. Switch fields. Ugh!" Luke slapped his hand on the table.

"You overthink things. Soccer is a simple game. One-touch pass to the open man and put the ball in the net," said Jason.

"Yeah, simple for you," said Luke.

Jason looked over at what Cassie was trying to do.

"Okay, it's not *that* simple. You can't use the same move on every level." Jason said, exasperated. "Here, let me do it for you or you'll never get out of here." She gladly handed him her controller.

"I don't know what this has to do with real soccer anyway," Cassie mumbled grumpily, as she rubbed her eyes and stretched her back. Jason made a few moves, and sent a hard kick sailing toward the upper corner of the goal.

"Here you go. You're a level 13 now, baby. And don't tell me I never did anything for you," smiled Jason, handing back the controls.

"Thanks. Yeah, I think I'm done for the day now. How about you guys?" Cassie looked tired.

"Me too," said Luke. "I'm ready to go if you are. Coming, Jason?" Luke looked at Jason, and gave a short "no" shake of his head while Cassie was putting back the controllers and shutting off her monitor. Jason looked back at his screen and smiled.

"Nah, I think I'll stay for a little bit longer." Jason got the hint. As the Captain, he really wasn't sure what he should be doing, but as their friend, well, they seemed good for each other. Luke seemed to give Cassie back the confidence that had wavered while Reed, Sam, and Max were pulling their stunts. And Luke seemed happier with Cassie around. Plus, they were just friends, he reasoned. Dating was against the rules for the Tournament team. Truthfully, it was a relief to have that off limits. He could focus on his play. No distractions. If Luke wanted a distraction, well, that was up to him.

"See you guys," said Jason, pretending that his attention was totally on the controls. As soon as they left, he signed out of the soccer game. Boring stupid game. He was ready for some blood and gore. He signed into Outlander, his long-time favorite video game. He and Nate used to play it all the time in the training center. He logged on using his old user name, Castor51. He searched the net to see who was online playing the game. A few gamer tags he recognized, but no one he knew well. In a few minutes, he was completely immersed in hand-to-hand combat, and blood spatters filled the screen. Whoever this gamer was, he was good, and Jason couldn't keep up. Time to run. As he made his character run down an alley, throwing obstacles behind him, out of the corner of his eye he saw a message pop up that Pollux51 was online and wanted to join his game. Pollux51? In the half-second it took for that to penetrate his consciousness, his character was pummeled by the enemy and died in a humiliating pile, but he didn't care. Nate!

When Jason had returned to his room after the team list was posted, Nate's bed had already been stripped and he was finishing packing. Nate told him he had been assigned to a new training center up north, and figured it was better than coaching small kids. He promised to be in touch as soon as he was settled, but Jason hadn't heard from him at all. He had gone to the Administrative offices to see how he could reach Nate, but the Administrator, a pudgy older man who seemed friendly, had explained that Nate was chosen for a special assignment. It was top secret and classified, so Nate would not be able to communicate with him.

The Administrator smiled at him. Jason wanted to bash his smug little face in. After he nagged him some more, the guy allowed him to send his brother an email, but warned him that Nate was probably too busy to respond. Jason doubted that. This was Nate.

Every day after practice, Jason went by the office to see if he had gotten an answer. The Administrator had started closing his door when Jason approached, so Jason talked to Margaret, his assistant. Margaret smiled a lot, too, but had nothing for Jason. After two weeks, Margaret had whispered to him that he had better stop coming by. The Administrator was starting to worry about his mental state.

Reverting back to a normal voice, she said, "Jason, I'll let you know as soon as I hear anything from Nate." She shooed him toward the door.

Jason had left, and hadn't been back since. He hadn't stopped worrying, but it was clear that he wasn't going to get anything through official channels. He tried his parents next. Although they only lived on the other side of Fairbanks, he rarely spoke to them. They emailed weekly, but it was mostly perfunctory. How are you? I'm fine. Practice is hard. I hope we win. Say hi to my sisters. That kind of thing.

When he called, his Mom sounded surprised to hear from him. She didn't have any more information about where Nate was or what he was doing, but she said the government had told her he was on a special assignment, and was fine. And apparently that was enough for her. But not for Jason.

Whenever he had a spare minute at the end of a game session, he had looked for Pollux51. After four months of not hearing anything from his twin, Jason had given up. He tried not to think about it, since there was nothing he could do. If Nate hadn't contacted him, it must be because he was somewhere where he couldn't. Or they were lying to him. But if something bad had happened to Nate, he would know. They were twins.

He went back to the invitations list, found Pollux51 and joined his game. He turned his headset on.

"Nate?"

"It's me," said Pollux51.

Jason jumped up off his seat and walked toward the screen. Not that he could see anything other than the game right now, but he couldn't sit still.

"Where the heck have you been? Why didn't you answer my emails or anything?" Jason hammered the questions at his brother.

"Slow down, Jase. I'm okay. Everything's okay." Nate said, reassuringly. "Sit down."

Jason grinned. Nate couldn't see him of course, but he knew Jason well.

"Okay, I'm sitting. Spill. What's the deal?"

"We only just got computer access a week ago. I've been checking every day for you whenever I could. But we don't have email or phones. You wouldn't believe this place," said Nate.

"So, where are you?" Jason asked.

"In the middle of nowhere," answered Nate.

"What do you mean?" said Jason.

"They brought us here in the middle of the night. There doesn't seem to be any civilization around us, just mountains and woods. And believe me, we've seen a lot of the surrounding area in our training."

"What are you training for?" asked Jason. "All they told me is that you're on a special assignment. That's what they told Mom, too."

"You talked to Mom? Is everything okay?"

"Everything is fine. Well, at least I think it is. I called her to see if she knew anything about you. She didn't have any more info."

"Jason, if I tell you, you have to promise not to breathe a word to anyone. I mean it."

"So if you tell me, you have to kill me or something?" Jason joked.

"I'm serious," said Nate.

"Just tell me what's going on."

"Look, I don't know if anyone monitors these games. They probably do. So I can't say much.

"Well, talk fast then." Jason said.

"We're training for war," Nate said quietly. So quietly, Jason could barely make it out.

"What?"

"We're actually training with weapons, you know, guns and artillery and grenades and all the stuff we learned about in the old video games," explained Nate.

"I thought all that stuff was destroyed," said Jason.

"That's what I thought, too, but here I am, part of a 'special elite security force'," Nate said, using his best approximation of Colonel Gladov's thick accent. Nate kept his voice very low as he told Jason about Colonel Gladov and their training.

"It's probably just a precaution," whispered Jason. "It can't be a real army. That would be illegal. We could get in serious trouble with the Global Government for that. Maybe it's just some kind of new mental exercise. Remember when that other country started an army? Way back. Remember how that went?" Jason asked.

"I thought about that," Nate paused. "But we're using real weapons."

"That is seriously cool!"

"Yeah, you wouldn't believe the armory. When I walked in, it was like walking into one of those weapons caches in Battlefield 57. I never thought I'd see any of this stuff live and in person."

"So it's a real army?" Jason kept his voice hushed.

"I guess so," said Nate. "But I don't really get it. They just gave us an official story, but I don't have any way of knowing if it's true. Have you heard anything?"

"Nothing," Jason said. "But you know how it is here. Soccer 24/7. I'll see what I can find out."

"So, what's new in Fairbanks?" Nate asked, his voice returning to normal decibels. Jason took his cue. Their conversation couldn't have lasted more than two minutes, so he hoped that whoever was supposed to monitor these things had gone to bathroom or something.

"Training's mega intense. The Tournament starts next week," said Jason.

"How's the new coach?" asked Nate.

"How'd you know about the new coach?" Jason asked.

"About the only thing we get up here is the sports channel. Some cartoons. Most of the time after training I'm too wiped to even think about TV. I haven't even touched a soccer ball since I've been here. Can you believe that?"

"No soccer? Isn't that against the Peace Treaties or something? Doesn't everyone have a constitutional right to a soccer ball?"

"Yeah, well, they keep us pretty entertained without one. So how's the team shaping up?" Nate asked.

"This team is amazing. And Coach is working us really hard, harder than anyone ever has before. Could you imagine if we actually won? We'll never have to work for the rest of our lives!" said Jason.

"That would be great. Except I don't know if it would make any difference for me."

Jason looked at the clock. It was almost curfew.

"I have to go."

"Yeah, me too. I'll try to find you here again in a few days," said Nate, and then the screen went blank.

Jason signed out of the game, and jogged back to his room, making it with just minutes to spare before lights out.

Chapter Nine

CASSIE

"I still don't get how this is supposed to make me play better," Cassie sighed as they left Jason behind in the computer room. "Ugh. You can't even control the character's skill levels. None of those guys would be able to take the ball from me in real life." Cassie's rant was getting into full swing. She despised computer games, and especially soccer holo games. She looked at Luke.

"If they really decide our field time on computer results, I'm toast," she sighed.

"Cassie, Coach would have to be brain dead not to play you because of some soccer simulation. Your ball skills are out of this world and you always come in the top three in our races," Luke said, giving her shoulder a little friendly shove.

"Always on your heels, Petrov," said Cassie, shoving him back.

"Come on, let's do something to take your mind off all this stuff," said Luke. He smiled at her with those sparkly eyes. Cassie was in so much trouble. She checked her watch. An hour till lights-out. She had planned to go back to her room, relax, and try to erase the memory of today's practice and how much of a moron Reed was. Good luck with that.

"We should get some sleep. I'm wiped," she said.

"Oh, come on. You need a little fun. Let's do something crazy. Break into the cafeteria and steal some ice cream or something." Luke had a point. Cassie was hungry. But she was also mad. A thought stole into her mind.

"I have an idea," Cassie lowered her voice to almost whisper, even though the corridor was totally deserted. "Is Reed staying at his house tonight?"

"Yeah, he was bragging all day about not eating in the cafeteria," Luke confirmed.

"Do you think we can get inside his room, somehow?" Cassie whispered.

Luke looked at her with a stony face.

"Palmer, you're scaring me. Are you suggesting we break into our teammate's room? The son of the Security Minister, not to mention super-mega-star of the team? That sounds morally questionable and extremely dangerous." He broke into a grin. "So what's the plan?"

"Well, it might require breaking a few rules," Cassie started.

"What, you?" Luke said in mock horror.

"Hey, what do you mean by that?"

"I just mean that you seem like the kind of person who always, always plays by the rules." Luke said, "I bet you haven't ever broken a rule in your life."

"Maybe I haven't broken many rules, but I did break someone's nose once," she said, trying to sound cool. "And yours might be next."

"Okay, okay," said Luke, putting his hands up and taking a step back. "You're a badass. Sorry. My apologies. So what's the plan, Ms. Badass? You want to get into the golden boy's room?"

"After what he pulled in today's practice, I wouldn't mind making him pay a little. Or a lot." Cassie's face flushed as she remembered how she had fallen flat on her face. While Coach was talking to them, Reed had taken advantage of her untied shoelace and tied it to the bench. And to make matters worse, Coach had seen it all and scolded her for untied shoelaces. And he had said nothing to Reed! She was still furious. As the team headed out to the field, Reed had looked back at her and had given her a wink. A wink! Her blood had been boiling. She told Jason and Luke about it at dinner, and they had both been ready to go beat the crap out of Reed.

"God, that guy is a complete jerk," Luke muttered. "Cassie, I know you said you like to fight your own battles, but if you ever want somebody to redecorate his face, I'd be more than happy to oblige."

"I'll keep it in mind, thanks. But tonight, I have an idea about a little redecorating myself," she said. She leaned closer and whispered in Luke's ear. His face split in huge grin.

"Brilliant! Remind me to never piss you off. If you have everything you need, I can get you in," he said.

"I just need to stop by my room. Karen left some stuff behind when she moved out, so we'll put it to good use. Come on."

A couple of minutes later, they were both standing in front of the door to Reed's room. His beat up door had a huge "#1" sign hanging on the outside.

"I'm surprised he and his ego can both fit into the room," she muttered.

Luke squatted down and took a good look at the lock on Reed's door. "At least he didn't change his lock to something fancy. It's the same cheap stuff we have on our doors."

"Great, so what do we do? It's a cheap lock, but it's still locked." Cassie looked at Luke.

"Now you get to see another one of my many talents," Luke said. "Give me your hair thing." Cassie unclasped her ponytail clip. Luke took his ID badge and slid it along the edge of the door above the lock while he simultaneously jiggled the pin in the lock. The lock clicked.

"Cool. Do I even want to know where you learned how to do this?" Cassie asked.

"Nah, probably not," Luke looked down the hallway, and Cassie looked too. It was empty. Luke gave the door a quick shove, and it opened.

"Ladies first," he gave Cassie a little bow. They both stepped into Reed's room and quietly closed the door behind them. Reed's room was surprisingly clean and orderly. His walls were covered with posters of international soccer players, and, no surprise, one of the posters was of him wearing the national team uniform and standing with one foot on a soccer ball. He looked pretty good, thought Cassie, if you didn't know what a complete jerk he was. His bed was made, his soccer uniform hanging on the chair. A few soccer trophies were lined up on a shelf, along with a couple of game cases stacked neatly and arranged alphabetically. A small TV and game console stood on his dresser.

Luke whistled.

"First, how is he allowed posters? And his own TV? And his own game console? Wish I was the son of a Minister."

Cassie walked around Reed's room. His bed was made perfectly, not a wrinkle to be seen anywhere. How is this idiot more of a neat freak than she was?

"I bet he has his housekeeper come in here every day to straighten his stuff," she said to Luke.

"That, or we just found his one redeeming quality," Luke said. "The boy wonder knows how to clean his room."

"Let's do this before I change my mind," Cassie said, heading for the bathroom. She carefully emptied Reed's shampoo bottle down the drain and refilled it with blue dye Karen had left from Halloween. This was no subtle blue or blue highlights, this was a neon blue. And it really worked, too. Just one application and Karen's nearly black hair, along with her scalp and the tops of her ears, were a bright, screaming blue. It took a couple of weeks for it to wash away.

"I really think blue is his color," said Cassie. She closed the bottle tightly, and put it back in the shower basket where she had found it. She stood back, trying to see if anything looked out of place. She nodded in satisfaction. "I'll have to send a little thank you note to Karen, maybe with the photo of Reed after he washes his hair," she said, relishing the thought.

Luke laughed.

"I can't wait to see it."

"Well, that was entertaining," Luke said, when they were out in the hallway. "You know, I'm really glad we're friends. You have a serious mean streak, Palmer."

"I don't have a mean streak," said Cassie. "It's more like I have a strong revenge streak. Comes from living with four brothers," said Cassie smiling.

"When do you think we'll see the results of our efforts here tonight?" asked Luke.

"I'm sure we won't have to wait too long. Our international soccer star probably has another photo shoot or something coming up and I'm sure he'll want to look his best."

As they rounded the corner, Luke grabbed her hand and broke into a run. The exhilaration of having fought back against her bully got to her, and she surged along beside him. They slowed down as they reached the point where the girls' dorms split off from the boys. Cassie didn't want to leave Luke.

"I don't know about you, but I'm starving," Luke said. "Want to check and see if maybe there are any brownies?"

Cassie looked at him.

"You know there aren't any brownies, right?"

"Yeah, but there might be something," said Luke.

"Okay, why not? I'm already a fugitive from justice," she laughed and they took off towards the kitchen.

Luke was trying to pick the lock on the kitchen door when they heard the five-minute warning announcement for lights out.

"Just in time," he said and swung the door open. "In we go, before dorm monitor starts checking the hallways."

This whole evening was so unlike her, Cassie felt like she was in some parallel universe where she was a reckless girl who broke rules and held hands with a boy.

"I think it's you," she said to Luke.

"You think what's me?" Luke looked confused.

"You're a bad influence on me," Cassie said. "That, or I ate something very strange for dinner."

"There's no telling what that mystery meat really was," said Luke. "But, it's about time you loosen up a little. Being too responsible and mature isn't natural for a 16-year-old," he reached out and touched her hair, which was hanging softly around her face. "I love your hair loose," he said softly.

"Thanks," she said shyly.

The lights-out buzzer sounded, and the lights all over the dorms went out. It was pitch black.

"We'd better get back to our rooms," said Cassie.

"There you go, being all responsible again," kidded Luke. He looked around.

"Guess there weren't any brownies here after all. But wait just a minute." Luke let go of her hand and disappeared. Cassie stood there, waiting. She heard his footsteps recede, then saw a light at the end of the kitchen, and then heard him jogging back to her. She felt a small cup thrust into her hand.

"Pudding," said Luke. "Hope you like chocolate." He grabbed her other hand.

"Of course I like chocolate! How'd you know where it was?"

"Oh, I can't tell you all my trade secrets…at least not right now. Let's go." And they headed back toward the dorms, moving carefully in the dark, hand in hand.

Chapter Ten

REED

Blue! Why was the shower stall blue?

He should have showered at home, but Sam and Max had convinced him to hang out with them in the game room, so he had decided to use his dorm room shower.

He had noticed that the shampoo smelled a little different than his shampoo at home, but hadn't thought anything of it until he looked down and saw streaks of bright blue circling the shower drain. But then it was too late. He pulled the white shower curtain back, splattering it with blue, and looked across the bathroom to the small mirror over the sink. Even through the fog on the mirror, he could see that his hair was neon blue, and that there were streaks of blue down his face and body.

He got out, rubbed the steam off the mirror, and started to laugh. It was definitely bright, he'd give her that. It had to be Cassie. Who else would do this to him? He remembered vividly how she had jumped up off the bench and fallen flat on her face. It was one of the best ones he had pulled off. Okay, Palmer, you got me. He grinned at his reflection. Good one.

He returned to the shower with a fresh bottle of shampoo from the medicine cabinet, and scrubbed for 15 minutes, expecting the blue to be gone. Blue dye again circled around the drain. But when he looked in the mirror again, it was just as blue. This wasn't funny anymore. He rooted through his pile of towels, leaving drips of blue all over them, until he found a rough washcloth. He jumped back into the shower and scrubbed and scrubbed, pulling the washcloth through his hair and across his skin to peel the color off. When he checked again, he had managed to remove most of the blue on his face and body, along with a good part of his skin. There was one spot on above his left eyebrow that was stubbornly light blue. He grabbed his toothbrush, piled it thick with soap, and scraped it across the spot until it started to bleed a little. Well, at least it wasn't blue anymore. Maybe he should shave his head.

He heard a knock on the door.

"Hey Martinez!" It was Sam and Max.

"Just a minute!" he yelled to the door, and toweled off his hair and body before grabbing a pair of shorts and opening the door.

Reed decided he wouldn't give Cassie the satisfaction of knowing how well she had gotten him. The gears in his mind turned quickly. When he saw Sam and Max's jaws drop, he just smiled a huge smile, and said,

"What do you think? Awesome, right?"

"Dude, what did you do? Why is your hair blue?" Sam looked doubtful, but Max came to the rescue.

"That's brilliant! Matches the uniforms. Do you have any more?" Max stepped into Reed's room, to the bathroom and looked for the shampoo bottle. "Is it this one?" Max picked up a bottle with blue smudges down its side. Sam looked skeptical.

"Are you sure that's okay? What will Coach say?"

"Don't be such a baby. It's just a little hair color. Just to show our team spirit," said Max. "Right, Reed?"

"Absolutely. You know how crazy the fans go, right? They even paint their faces and bodies, so I figured it would be cool to dye my hair." Reed pushed Sam into the bathroom with Max. "It'll be even more awesome if we all do it together."

Max pulled back the shower curtain, but Reed stopped him.

"It can really get all over your skin, so let's just do it in the sink. Your hair's already wet from the shower, so all you need to do is just massage it in." He gave them both towels for their shoulders, and then dropped a few dollops of dye on their heads. They rubbed it in. The effects were instant.

"Wow, that's good stuff!" Max admired his new do in the mirror. His light brown hair had completely vanished. "I look pretty snazzy, huh?"

Sam's eyes were wide as he looked in the mirror. His short curly black hair was now brilliant blue. Then he grinned too. He pointed at Max's ears.

"Your ears are all blue." Max turned his head, and sure enough, he had dripped dye on his ears, and one side was really blue. Reed handed him the toothbrush.

"Try scrubbing." Max looked at it skeptically.

"No thanks, my ears can be blue, I don't care," he said.

Sam was looking at his reflection, grinning widely.

"Hey, now I'm black and blue, get it?"

"Wouldn't be the first time," said Max. "How's that bruise Palmer gave you?" Sam leaned over to inspect the side of his calf.

"Palmer gave you a bruise?" asked Reed. "What did you do, trip over her? That's the only way she could get you. She doesn't have enough power to hurt anyone," said Reed.

"I thought you were laying off her," said Sam, raising an eyebrow at Reed's tone. "Anyway, it's no big deal."

"Right," said Reed, busying himself with picking up the avalanche of blue-spattered towels that were now all over the floors.

"Yeah, I saw the way you laid off her with those shoelaces," said Max, holding up his palm. "High five, dude. That was perfection. Smack! Her face was in the mud. I could barely keep myself from exploding. Coach has been on her about those shoelaces, so he couldn't even get mad." Max laughed. They left the bathroom, and stood in front of the full-length mirror on the back of the door, admiring their blueness.

"Okay, blue team, off to the game room!" said Reed, as they all headed toward the door. He really hoped they wouldn't pass Cassie in the hallway.

* * *

The house was full of guests. From his room, Reed could hear the hum of conversation and the tinkle of glasses and laughter. Reed was in his new suit, getting ready to make a short appearance, like his father had asked. He looked in the mirror, trying to focus on the suit and the body, and ignore the bright blue hair. He had shampooed his hair another fifteen times in the last 24 hours using shampoo, vinegar, and nail polish remover on Rosa's advice, but it was still very, very blue. Maybe not quite as neon as it had been, but still there was no getting around that it was a long way from blond and not anywhere in the realm of a normal hair color. This was going to be bad. He was not nearly as worried about what the President would think as what his dad would say. There was a knock on his bedroom door.

"Ready to go?" His dad asked.

"As ready as I can be," said Reed, opening the door.

"Oh my God! What happened to you? Reed, what did you do?" Reed's dad's voice was stern. "Go wash that out right now! You can't meet the President like that."

"Dad, it won't come out," said Reed. "Rosa tried everything and we couldn't get it off."

"What possessed you to do something so dumb?" asked his dad.

"It was just for team spirit, Dad. I didn't know it wouldn't wash out," said Reed. He was sticking to the story, no matter what.

"Team spirit, you say?" Reed's dad looked skeptical. "Nothing else you can do to get back to your normal hair?"

"Could shave my head?" Reed said. Reed's dad smiled.

"No, then you'll look like a radiation victim. Can't have that. Okay, then, if that's what we've got, let's go sell it." Reed's dad put his arm around Reed's suit-covered shoulder, and started walking him down the hall.

"When did you get taller than me?"

"Last week," grinned Reed.

"Let's go. I guess I've got to go introduce you to the President, blue hair or not. You'll just have to explain it to him. It's a big honor, you know, he doesn't usually come to these parties." Reed's dad led him toward the living room. Big honor or not, Reed wished he didn't have to do it especially with weird hair.

"Okay, let's get it over with. How long do I have to stay?" asked Reed.

"Not long, I just want to show everyone our future Tournament champion, even if he is a little blue," his dad replied.

"Just shows how committed I am to the team," Reed said.

They walked down the hall towards the dining room, where members of government and their spouses were eating hors d'oeuvres and chatting. A string quartet was playing in the corner, and waiters in black tuxedos were carrying trays of champagne. Reed felt like all eyes were on him. He heard whispering as we walked through the room, and more than one smothered laugh. Oh well.

Reed's dad approached the President, who was standing surrounded by a cluster of men. He looked up as Reed approached, and broke off the conversation.

"Ah, this must be our star," said the President, offering his hand to Reed. He was smiling. "I understand you colored your hair to show your commitment to the team. The blue hair suits you."

Reed breathed a sigh of relief.

"Good to meet you, Mr. President." Reed recovered his confidence, as his hand was engulfed by the President's powerful grasp.

"I hear you have quite a powerful boot, and are not afraid to be physical," said the President, his attention fully on Reed.

"Yes, sir," Reed flashed a deprecating smile, "I do have that reputation."

"And how is the team shaping up? Is Jason Carey doing well as Captain? Is Cassandra Palmer pulling her weight? What about Carlo Rossini, the back-up goalie?" The President seemed to know all their names. Reed wasn't expecting that.

"Yes, sir," he answered. "Jason's a good Captain, and Cassie is much better than I thought she would be, I have to admit it. And Carlo isn't Jason, but I supposed if Jason's injured, he'll fill in okay."

"You must be very proud," the President turned to Reed's father. "I guess athletic prowess on the soccer field runs in the family."

"Yes, sir, Mr. President," Reed's dad was smiling.

"Our nation's hopes are riding on your team. I've been kept informed about your team's progress, and I'm sure you won't let us down. I won't keep you now. I know you're in training. Best of luck."

"Thank you, sir," Reed nodded his head toward the President, not sure if he was supposed to bow or what.

The President rejoined his group, and Reed's dad steered him over to a table with a carving station for several kinds of meat, accompanied by mounds of fluffy mashed potatoes, spicy rice casseroles, mountainous salads, and piles of fresh vegetables. It was more food than even Reed was used to seeing in one place.

"Well, that was very nice of the President." Reed's dad said as he filled a plate.

"Yeah, I didn't know he knew everyone on the team," Reed said.

"The President is taking a strong interest in all of you. It would be a great accomplishment for him if the team won this year," his dad replied.

"Uh, Dad? I don't think I can eat all that." Reed's plate was now piled high with mashed potatoes. "I really think that's too much, even with my appetite."

"Oh, sorry." Reed's dad looked down at the mammoth mountain he had created. "Well, just eat what you want. Why don't you take your plate to the kitchen? That way no one will bother you."

Reed moved aside some trays and piles of dishes and found a place to eat. As he plowed his way through the mountain of food, he watched the hired kitchen staff whirling in and out with trays of food and wine glasses, and returning with piles of dirty dishes. Rosa kept them moving with orderly precision, almost like one of Coach's drills, thought Reed. As he finished, Rosa offered him a cupcake with bright blue frosting and winked. He rolled his eyes, and headed for his room.

As he passed his father's study, he heard voices inside. He stopped to say goodnight, but before he opened the door he listened to see if he could interrupt.

"We have more than enough supplies. When we start depends on how the Tournament goes. What do you think, Rick?"

"They'll win. I've never seen my son training so hard. And the whole team has grown." That was his dad.

"Yes, they have, haven't they? They won't suffer due to their size, this year. We made sure of that. We may not have the food resources of some of our competitors, but we do have other resources." The voice chuckled. Was that Henry Knox, the Minister of Elite Sports?

"And getting rid of that old coach didn't hurt either. Hope he's enjoying his state-sponsored retirement in the Big House," said another voice. "Coach Andrews knows what's at stake for the team, and for him personally, if they don't win."

"I talked to Coach Andrews and he is confident. No team in history has ever worked this hard." Reed's dad again. "I'm sure they'll win."

"Your belief in your son's team is heartwarming, Rick. But, remember China. They always push the boundaries, and even if we should win, we'll still need the security team to play their part. I don't expect China to give up control easily. We may need to use force," said the President. "How is the security force training coming along, General?"

"The soldiers are improving every day and are learning to manage the new materials. I expect them to be ready for conventional warfare in a matter of weeks, Mr. President. They won't let you down."

"Excellent. Now, gentlemen, I suggest we return to the party before we are missed."

Reed sped down the hallway to his room. What the hell was going on? Using force against China? Soldiers? What new materials were they talking about? The last couple of months started to make sense. His father spending so much time at work, stressed out, not sleeping. Everyone on the team growing like crazy. Those pills. Whatever they were, they were bulking them up for the Tournament. And Coach Chip's sudden "retirement." The only thing he clearly understood was that they had to win this Tournament. He wished he could talk to his father, but somehow, he had the feeling that wasn't a good idea. He had a hard time falling asleep.

Chapter Eleven

THE OPENING CEREMONY

CASSIE

Cassie and the rest of the team were sitting together on the sidelines of the enormous soccer stadium. Cassie had watched many of these ceremonies over the years on TV, but this was the very first time she was sitting in the actual stadium, watching it live. The field below was filled with hundreds of people in Native Alaskan costumes. Some were also dressed like moose, salmon, or raven, reenacting native Alaskan legends, moving gracefully to the sounds of old songs. On the stage in the middle of the field, an enormous raven with a huge black beak brought the first light to the world. He released the light from his beak and the entire stadium became flooded with colorful sparkling lights. The stands exploded into thunderous applause. The performers disappeared into the sudden darkness. Then, in the quiet, enormous red fireworks burst over the stadium. The red sparks slowly faded away into the night. This time the darkness lasted longer. Then a yellow light slowly rose, like the sun, and one by one, performers emerged from piles of ash and ice, and began an elaborate dance, with more people adding in as they emerged from spots all around the stadium. The beautiful and intricate dance told the story of the new Alaska, the only one of the 50 states where the human spirit had triumphed, overcoming the obstacles of a ruined environment, a rapidly shifting climate, and a devastated population. The dance then expanded to include the other 31 countries that had survived the nuclear holocaust. At the end, a short video recounted the history of Global Government's formation, its role in bringing together the remaining human civilization, and the agreement that brought about the Tournament.

Cassie felt proud to be Alaskan. It was her parents, of course, who had survived the disastrous War, but she felt like it was a part of her, too. Her parents had told her stories about the years of hunger and how "rat surprise" had been a big part of their diets, about losing Cassie's grandparents to radiation sickness, and about fighting to protect what little food they were able to grow on their farm from looters. The giant dark blue flag that rose over the field, with the North Star and the solitary red stripe that represented Alaska's survival, was spectacular.

She glanced at her teammates. Sam and Max were fooling around, as usual, flipping their program books at each other. Those two would probably pay attention only if the story was reenacted by naked women. She had almost fainted when she saw them with blue hair. The story they were spinning about "team spirit" was pretty good. So good that there were some other kids on the team who were actually considering dying their hair blue for the first game.

After she had left Reed's room with Luke, she had been elated, felt invincible. But later, when she was alone in her room, she had started to worry about Reed's reaction and the fact that he was the Security Minister's son started to freak her out. But the little jerk had somehow gotten the better of her again. She hadn't seen Reed until the next day, when he strode to the soccer field with his two blue-haired buddies looking like he owned the place. As he was passing her, he gave her his full-blown, all-perfect-white-teeth-smile, and then he winked at her. Ever since, Cassie had been jumpy, expecting some kind of retaliation.

Cassie looked at her partner in crime. He had never seemed worried at all. As Luke caught her watching him, he took her hand and gave her fingers a little squeeze. He was smiling at her, but his face was pale.

"Are you OK?" Cassie mouthed, looking at him closely.

"Yeah, just a little tired," his smile turned a little wicked, "I didn't get too much sleep last night, you know."

Cassie flushed bright red. She was mortified. What if Jason heard him? She knew all right. They had spent most of last night in her room, sitting on the worn rug, leaning against the wall, talking. Talking and holding hands.

Yep, she was definitely going off the deep end. It was the day before the start of the Tournament and instead of staying focused and getting some sleep, she had been up all night, snuggly with a boy. Karen would laugh her butt off if she only knew. Cassie undid her ponytail and massaged her scalp. Even her hair was tired.

Luke was so easy to talk to, and Cassie told him things about herself that only Karen knew. He amazed her. He had lost his whole family. Living with his grandmother, whom he adored, was the only nice part of his life that he remembered.

Everyone he had loved and who had loved him back was dead. To Cassie, it seemed like a sad life, but Luke somehow didn't see it that way. He was perpetually cheerful and optimistic. She didn't understand it, but she loved it.

Cassie looked around. All 32 national teams participating in the Tournament were sitting in the same section of the stands, a friendly, colorful jumble. She heard languages she didn't recognize around her. The other players said friendly hellos, and she had even found a few girls in the Tournament. Despite the language barriers, they had managed to make a connection at the players' lunch. The bond of sisterhood—in the face of all these sweaty boys—was easy. But tomorrow, that would all change. Once the competition began, there would be no mixing with the other teams for next four weeks.

Winning mattered more than anything else and all the athletes knew it. Alaska was opening the Tournament with a game against New Zealand, which they were widely favored to win. Cassie was looking forward to getting on the field, and testing her skills against another team. Her teammates were all in great mental and physical shape, except maybe Reed. She had noticed that Reed's mind was somewhere else these last few days, even though his moves were as strong as ever. He wasn't joking and goofing around with Sam and Max. Maybe the blue hair dye affected his brain and Reed grew up a little? Sure, and maybe pigs could fly, Cassie looked at Reed again. That stupid blue hair actually suited him.

* * *

REED

Reed couldn't enjoy the ceremony. He barely noticed the kids from other teams sitting near him. He knew as the host, he should have been friendly–even though he planned to completely squash them during the games. That was Good Sportsmanship, according to his dad. Reed tried to focus on the ceremony, but the dancers blurred in front of his eyes as his mind jumped from weapons and war to soccer and the Tournament. He had deliberately taken a seat at the end of the row so that he could avoid talking to anyone. Sam and Max were next to him, and they were hyper enough for all three of them. No one would notice that he was a little out of it.

Reed kept trying to work it out. Their first game would be against New Zealand, and he knew that would be an easy win. He jumped over the next couple of games to the final game and then what? What would happen when they won the Tournament? Other Alaska teams had gotten close in recent years, and Reed thought the training and the pills would give them an unbeatable advantage. Even over China.

When Reed had confronted his father about what he had overheard at the party, his dad at first refused to talk to him, but after Reed kept asking questions, he gave in and told Reed what he knew. The President had persuaded a majority of the government that Alaska deserved to have a greater share of the world's resources and power, as the sole remaining state of the former world leader. If they won the Tournament, the President would be in charge of the Global Government, and would be able take over peacefully. However, he had a back-up plan. If they didn't win the

Tournament, Alaska would seize control of the Global Government by military force. A military force no one would expect Alaska to have.

Dad told him about the weapons that were discovered just as the new President came to power. It had been a fluke thing–a group of geology students out on a field trip at the site of the old Matanuska Glacier had stumbled across some secret bunkers. They had gotten inside and found enormous stockpiles of weapons that dated back to the Cold War, and had probably been safely hidden under ice and ash for the last 60 years. Ironically, it was probably the huge Russian peat field fires that melted the glacier and exposed the weapons. The geology students had reported their finding back to the University, who reported it to the government. Reed's dad said he and some of the other ministers had tried to persuade the President to report these weapons and turn them over the Global Government, as was required by international treaty, but the President had refused. With this kind of firepower, along with a well-trained army to back it up, Alaska's days of poverty and obscurity were about to end, the President said.

He looked around at his teammates. They were so lucky. He wished he could take back that walk down the hallway and be as ignorant as his friends of the possible consequences. He thought about telling Jason. That's what a Captain is for, right? To handle morale issues on the team? Well, he was having a crazy morale issue. Reed turned his attention back to the field. He wanted to be out there playing soccer. He wanted to outrun other players, out-maneuver them, and slam balls into a goal. He wanted to win. Whatever stupid politics his father was dealing with weren't his problem. Suddenly he felt like a burden was lifted. It really wasn't his problem. He leaned over and cuffed Sam across the head. Sam turned, grinned at Reed, and pounded him back. Reed couldn't wait till tomorrow.

* * *

JASON

Jason was watching the ceremony and thinking about the first game. New Zealand should be a piece of cake. In preparation for the Tournament, they had watched all the friendly matches the team had played. New Zealand had a couple of good players, but coming from a country where there were more sheep than people, they would probably be out of the Tournament pretty soon. The next team would be much harder. Brazil used to be the soccer powerhouse before the war, and they were still strong. That game would be the first real contest. Jason wondered if Nate would be able to see them play.

Thinking about Nate brought back their conversations. They had talked one more time while playing online. Nate had told Jason more about the combat weapons and explosives they were learning to use and the training they were doing. Jason glanced around at the other 31 teams, wondering which one of their governments was the cause of the trouble. What if Nate got killed in a war? He felt sick. There was nothing that Jason could do except hope that the intelligence the army received about the country going rogue was wrong. The only thing that he could influence was his game, and he needed to focus on winning. The whole team needed to focus on the game. That was what they had trained for all these years.

The President himself had come to meet the whole team before the Tournament started. He had told them how proud he was of the team, and how all of Alaska's hopes were riding on them. No pressure, Jason thought. It was an honor to meet the President, and a surprise to find out the he seemed to know each of their strengths personally—well enough to comment on them, anyway. He didn't even seem surprised by all the blue hair. While the others were psyched by the President's personal interest in the team, Jason found it kind of unsettling.

He looked around and saw Luke taking hold of Cassie's hand. Cassie looked up at Luke, with a faint pink glow about her. Hmm. Jason had gone to sleep early and had no idea when Luke finally showed up in their room. Jeez, on top of all this craziness, these two could not have chosen a worse time to do this. Whatever this was. Jason looked at Luke, trying to catch his attention to cut it out. He noticed that Luke didn't exactly look his best. Pale as plaster, with dark circles under his eyes. There would be no fooling around tonight. He would tie Luke to the bed if necessary. Better yet, he'd impose 10pm curfew on the whole team.

* * *

LUKE

Luke was wedged between Jason and Cassie, trying to enjoy the show. The fireworks were mind-blowing, but for some reason he couldn't get comfortable in his seat. Yeah, he hadn't gotten too much sleep last night, but that had never bothered him before. He stole a glance at Cassie. She was watching the ceremony, totally enthralled. Her hair was flying around her face and he had to hold himself back not to run his fingers through it. Cassie. Boy, he really, really liked her. Underneath that tough exterior, she was really nice–sweet, and even surprisingly vulnerable. Luke never dated before and knew that this was not the right time or place, but he didn't care. He closed his eyes and leaned back in his seat. He was exhausted. Probably just nerves, with the Tournament starting tomorrow. It was still sometimes very unreal to him that he was actually here, part of the team. He glanced over at the "team spirit" trio and laughed under his breath. Max looked like some kind of elf. Even after a week, the tips of his ears were still blue. Luke had thought they might get told off for pulling this on the team's star striker, but instead it had become a thing. Now even Jason had thought about dyeing his hair. Cassie had almost fallen on the floor when he said that, and Luke had a hard time keeping a straight face, too. Jason had no idea why they collapsed into giggles.

Luke looked at his friend. Jason seemed to be scanning the crowd. Knowing Jason, he was probably assessing his opponents and masterminding some killer strategy. Seemed like Jason hardly ever relaxed anymore. Luke willed himself to take a deep breath and enjoy the show. He could *not* be getting sick. He couldn't let his team down. That would be really terrible timing. Maybe he should go see the nurse after the ceremony, just to make sure. Maybe he could get a double dose of the vitamins or something to help him feel better. After refusing the pills for the first few weeks, he saw how the others were improving, so he started taking them, too. He didn't like the pills, but he could see the benefits. He had gotten stronger and taller in just a few months and his game had never been better. And now this. He felt suddenly very cold, even though he could feel sweat running down his back.

Chapter Twelve

JASON

It wasn't butterflies in Jason's stomach, more like bats or something with much stronger wing power. Their game against Brazil was about to start and Luke was still in the locker room. Jason wanted to go back in and check on him, but there wasn't time. Luke had missed the game against New Zealand two days ago because of what the nurse said was a nasty cold. Everyone knew it would be an easy match even without their best center back, so Coach had made the decision to let Luke rest.

This morning, Luke had come into the cafeteria for breakfast pumped up and ready to play, but by the time they left the table, Luke's energy seemed to have dissipated. He didn't even have a blue joke for Reed when he walked by. Luke had spent the last two weeks asking Reed if he felt blue and suggesting that various other parts of his anatomy might be blue. Watching Luke slowly wilt over breakfast made Jason wonder if he should even play against Brazil. This was a very important game, and they needed him on the field, but only if he had the energy for it.

"You made it!" Jason shouted as Luke appeared on the field. "I was beginning to wonder if you needed an engraved invitation," Jason joked.

"Yeah, he was just sending me over to see what I can do to persuade you to join us," Cassie joined in.

Luke was still a little pale, but his grin was as wide as ever.

"I was just making sure I looked my best for all the cameras," he said, running his fingers through his short hair so it stood up ridiculously on end, and striking a male model-type pose.

"Are you really feeling okay?" Jason asked quietly, looking around to make sure that Reed and his buddies were out of earshot.

"Better than ever, Captain!" said Luke, and did couple of jumping jacks and performed a perfect standing somersault to prove it. "The nurse gave me meds, and I feel awesome."

"Hey, stop horsing around. We need you with all your limbs intact. Are you sure you're okay?" Cassie asked, pulling him toward the bench where the team was gathering.

"If I was any better, vitamins would be taking me!" Luke grinned. Cassie and Jason laughed along with Luke, but Jason wasn't convinced.

"Seriously, I am so pumped up, I could take the whole Brazilian team on by myself. I don't even need you guys." Jason glanced at Cassie, who shrugged her shoulders. She didn't seem convinced either, but what could they do? All the players gathered around Coach Andrews.

"This is it, gentlemen! And lady. That last game was just a warm-up. This is the game we need to win. We trained hard and I have total confidence in you. Focus, think, use your teammates. Don't lose your head. This is a big game, and I want you to leave everything on the field. Everything, got it?

Good! Now, let's show everybody what Alaska is made of! Let's do it!"

They all put in their hands to the center of the circle.

"Go Alaska!" Jason yelled and all his teammates joined in. "Alaska!"

As Jason headed to his place in the goal, he heard Coach call him. He jogged back toward the bench. Coach was standing with his arms crossed, watching the players take the field.

"Jason, I want you to keep an eye on Luke. If he starts fading, don't keep it to yourself. I can move Dan to center, and send Evan in as left back, if we need to. But Luke's our best, and he has experience against Ronaldo."

"Okay, Coach," said Jason, and turned to head toward the field. He looked up at the stadium. It was completely packed— even high up into the stands he could see people cheering and waving blue flags and green and yellow flags.

Luke came over and gave him a fist-bump.

"Let's do it!" Luke headed for his spot, about 15 meters in front of Jason.

"Luke," called Jason. Luke turned.

"What?"

"If you start feeling tired, tell me, okay?" Jason kept his eyes toward the stands. He didn't want Luke to see his concern.

"What, and Coach is going to bring in Evan to replace me?" Luke was scornful. "Evan's great, but against Ronaldo I know what I'm doing. He doesn't. I'm fine. Seriously. It was just a cold or something, it's done. Don't worry so much," Luke cracked a smile. Jason smiled back. Luke was fine.

The whistle blew. It was on. From the goal, Jason watched the blue jerseys surge toward the opposite goal. His defense, Luke, Jack, Dan, and Yoshi, looked solid. The midfield players, Cassie, Max, Josh, and Akim passed flawlessly up the field. Josh kicked a beautiful long one to Max, who did a give-and-go with Sam before booting a strong cross in front of the goal. Score! Reed headed it in perfectly, and ran with his arms raised to the corner, where the entire offense piled on him. A great start to the game. Jason checked on Luke, who was jogging back toward him. He looked good. When the whistle blew for the kickoff, the Brazilian offense took off, running up the field. Luke deftly intercepted a pass, controlling the ball and kicking it up the field to Cassie before the offense was on him. Jason breathed a sigh of relief, and settled into the goal. This was going to be a great game.

Then, in the 21st minute, Reed got a yellow card for tripping Ronaldo with 'excessive force' in the box. Jason had a perfect view of the trip, too, and he couldn't argue with the ref. Reed had totally intended to wreck Ronaldo, jamming his leg in front of him so that the kid did a flying somersault on the field. Ronaldo was lucky he hadn't broken a leg.

"Thanks a lot, Reed," Jason muttered, as he prepared for the penalty kick. As Reed passed by, Jason couldn't hold in his anger.

"Just had to do it *in* the box, didn't you?"

"Hey, that was totally fair!" Reed called back. "Not my fault Ronaldo has always had trouble with his balance." Max and Sam snickered.

Jason looked at Luke, who just grinned and shrugged his shoulders. That was Reed being Reed.

Jason sized up Ronaldo, and decided that he was probably going to go right. He was left-footed, and his right foot was pointing toward the right corner. Right before he kicked, Ronaldo raised his head (a lowered head usually means a cross-body shot) and looked into the right corner, a dead giveaway. Jason was ready. When Ronaldo's foot connected with the ball, he leaped, stretched out his arms as far as they could go, and felt for the ball. He curled his fingers around it, and managed to bring it to his chest as he fell to the ground. The crowd cheered. Jason took the goal kick.

"Nice save!" panted Luke, as he jogged up the field after the ball. He looked a little pale.

"Luke," called Jason, "You okay?"

"Awesome!" Luke called back, and headed toward the action. In a few seconds, Luke was running toward Jason, with Ronaldo just ahead of him. No one ever outran Luke. Ronaldo must have gotten faster since their last "friendly" match. Jack swooped in from the side to support Luke, but left his man open for the pass. The shot bounced off the top bar, and Ronaldo got it on the rebound, but overshot and the ball flew into the stadium seats behind the goal. Lucky.

Over the next 20 minutes, the play went back and forth. Reed made several fast breaks, and he, Max, Sam, Josh, and Cassie all made solid shots but the Brazilian goalie was very good, and only let one more shot in. Reed played a very physical game, and Jason heard Coach yelling warnings to Reed. He grinned to himself. Ahead two goals *and* Reed getting yelled at, a pretty good game. Cassie and the rest of the midfield were blocking passing lanes and denying plays, frustrating the Brazilian offense.

In the last three minutes of the half, Ronaldo seemed to sprout wings on his feet, and started hammering Jason with shots. Jason was ready for him. He felt like he was in tune with the universe, as he anticipated every move and saved every shot.

In the locker room at half-time, he felt good about their chances. Jason handed Luke some energy gel and water, and raised an eyebrow in question while Coach was going over their strategy for containing Ronaldo. Luke looked wiped, but insisted he felt great, just a little tired after his cold, so Jason decided not to have Coach pull him. They were up 2-0, after all.

* * *

There were three minutes left in the game. Brazil had tied it up, 2-2. Jason felt like kicking himself instead of the ball. In the first 10 minutes of the second half, things had gone rapidly downhill. First, Reed had gotten himself a second yellow card for grabbing a player's jersey and pulling him down. At least it wasn't in the box this time. But two yellow cards meant Reed was expelled, and Alaska had to play down a man for the remaining 35 minutes. Playing a man down was somewhere between a massive bummer and a death sentence. Coach switched them from a 4-4-2 to a 4-4-1 formation, leaving Sam as the sole forward.

Without Reed to lead the offense, Sam and Max had trouble converting their breaks into goals, even with Cassie and Josh passing like crazy to compensate for the missing man. On defense, Luke was becoming a liability. Ronaldo and the rest of the Brazilian team exploited the soft spot, and nearly all the shots came from Luke's side. Ronaldo had made a crazy breakaway run, leaving everyone else in the dust, and shot at Jason. Jason leapt toward the ball, which hit him solidly in the stomach. It had been impossible to breathe for a few long seconds, and when he could breathe, he felt a sharp pain in his lungs. Luke knelt down beside him, breathing hard. He tried to pull Jason up, but couldn't hold his footing. Luke needed to get out.

Even though their four-man defense hadn't changed, everyone was feeling the effects of playing a man down. Having Luke at less than 100% was becoming a real problem. Jason was bombarded with shots. He blocked them as fast as they came, his body responding to the player's stance and balance before his brain could process it. But with so many shots, it was only a matter of time. After two shots found their mark in the 66th and 78th minutes, Coach finally pulled Luke from the game, and sent in Evan. Luke had seemed relieved.

Jason had put Luke out of his mind. He needed to be razor sharp and focused. Three more minutes. Playing a man down stunk. He felt like smacking Reed. He kicked the ball hard up the side to Cassie, who dribbled around two players, and passed to Sam. A Brazilian player slammed into Max, dropping him to the ground. When Sam paused to scream at the ref, a Brazilian player stole the ball from under him. Josh and Cassie converged on the player, and Cassie managed to steal with ball away. Two minutes left now.

Coach was standing on the sidelines, screaming his instructions.

"Max, wake up! Sam is open! Cassie, send it now, do it!" Less than one minute left. Max executed a perfect pass and Sam took a shot with his left foot.

"GOOOOOOAL, GOOOOOOOAL!!!!" People in the stadium were standing up, screaming, stomping their feet.

Thirty seconds were left to play, and Jason knew Brazil could score. They could score twice, even. It had happened. Brazil's players were hungry. They needed this win to stay in the Tournament. At the midfield line, the ref blew the whistle, and Ronaldo tore into a breakneck run down the field, right toward the goal. Evan was caught napping, as Ronaldo deftly dribbled around him. Evan recovered, and hurtled toward the ball as Jack closed in on Ronaldo. Jason lost the ball in the shuffle of feet. Then, before he had time to think, he saw the ball skimming the ground to his right and dove for it. He tipped it out of the goal with his finger, and sent it to the side of the goal just as the whistle blew. Jack was the first to reach him, jumping on Jason's back like a monkey. Cassie, Josh, Evan, and the rest of the team were soon high-fiving, hugging, and slapping each other on the back. Reed ran onto the field and joined in the group celebration. As Reed high-fived him, Jason couldn't help it.

"You are such an idiot," he yelled at Reed over the din of his teammates. "You're so lucky that they changed the suspension rules, or you'd be out for the next game."

"Yeah, I know," grinned Reed, and then slapped Jason on the back. "But I knew you could handle it."

Jack and Josh were standing next to Jason, and they all broke into laughter. It was a close one, but they had pulled off another win and were going to the next round.

Jason noticed Cassie scanning the field for Luke, but he must have gone into the locker room already.

The team headed to the locker room, chattering noisily and reliving the last plays. Anton clapped Jason on the back.

"Bro, I thought they had you at the end, there!" said Anton.

"No way!" said Jason. Now that it was over, he could bask in the glow of their win, and enjoy the fact that Coach had finally come down on Reed. Maybe Reed getting expelled from a game early in the Tournament was a good thing. Maybe he'd be more careful. At least it wasn't a direct red, so he wasn't disqualified from any future games in this Tournament. Suddenly, the team stopped at the door to the locker room and Jason heard someone yell, "Help!" He and Cassie ran around the group to slide in the door.

Luke had collapsed on the floor by his locker.

"Luke!" Jason took a few steps over to his prone body, and kneeled down with Cassie. Luke's face was gray and his hands were clammy. His pupils were large and unfocused, and he was breathing hard.

"Luke, what is it? What's wrong?" Cassie was trying to raise Luke's head and put it in her lap.

"Call the ambulance and get Coach!" Jason yelled. He saw Jack nod and run out the door. The team was standing around Luke watching Cassie's and Jason's efforts to get some response from him. Reed came and kneeled next to Luke's side.

"Can't. Breathe," Luke wheezed. Reed and Jason together tried to boost Luke's upper body, and leaned him on Cassie's knees.

"Don't worry, you'll be fine," Jason was holding Luke's hand. "Just hold on, breathe slowly." Jason's voice cracked.

"Coach called the ambulance," said Jack, coming back in.

"Give him some space," said Reed, as the team crowded around them. Cassie held Luke's head and brushed his hair from his forehead. Then she leaned down and gave him a little kiss. A tear streaked down her cheek. Luke smiled.

"I would have. Fainted. Much earlier." Luke paused. "If I knew. I would. Get. A kiss." His voice was barely audible. Reed looked around uncomfortably and walked to the door.

"They're here," he said to Jason.

"Just hang in there, ok?" said Cassie to Luke. The locker room was flooded with emergency medics, who moved everyone out of the way. They surrounded Luke, hooking him up to various machines, taking his pulse, and inserting a tube into his nose. Cassie and Jason found themselves pushed back against the lockers. The medics had just put Luke onto a stretcher when the team doctor rushed in, and followed Luke into the ambulance. Jason, Reed, and a few others watched as the medics strapped him down, and then closed the doors. The ambulance drove carefully across the field, turning on its lights and siren when it hit the road.

Reed and Jason stared after it, not sure what to say. The excitement of winning had evaporated. The stadium was still full of people trickling out after the game. Reporters with microphones and cameras approached the team, and Coach was there to meet them. Jason decided this was a good time to disappear.

He headed back to the locker room and decided to check on Cassie. He found her leaning against the wall in her locker room, crying. He put his arm around her, and hugged her tight while she cried.

"C'mon, we better escape before they start asking us questions," he said, wiping away a tear on her cheek, and leading her toward the exit area.

"Yeah, okay." Cassie wiped her eyes, and half-smiled at Jason. "Thanks."

They were surprised to see that Reed was still there, standing by the bulletin board near the door. The rest of the team had gone, presumably to shower and try to enjoy their win, despite Luke's condition.

"I need to talk to you." Reed ignored Cassie, whose arm was still twined around Jason's, and looked only at Jason.

"What's up?" said Jason.

"Okay, look, I think I know what's wrong with Luke." Reed glanced around, looking uncomfortable and fidgety. The locker room had emptied out. It was just the three of them now.

"What?" asked Cassie, tears welling up in her eyes again.

"Those aren't vitamins we're taking." Reed said.

"What do you mean?" Jason demanded.

"Those pills are some kind of new growth hormone combined with a slow-release form of adrenalin. It's never been used before, so it's not something that the drug tests will pick up," explained Reed.

"What do you mean it's never been used before? How do you know?" asked Jason.

"I overheard the President and some other people talking to my dad at a party at our house," said Reed.

"The President was at your house?" Jason was surprised that Reed knew the President personally.

"Yeah, it was a party celebrating the beginning of the Tournament," said Reed. "My dad told me the drug was developed not even a year ago, just to help us win. But there are some side effects they didn't know about, and I bet that's what's happening to Luke," he finished.

"Luke went to see the doctor this morning, and he said they gave him some extra pills to help him get over his cold," said Jason.

"That explains why he was bouncing off the walls before the game. Do you think we can go see him at the hospital?" asked Cassie.

"Let's go ask Coach where they took him," Jason said. They headed back to the Coach's office, around the corner from the locker room.

From outside the office, they could tell Coach Andrews was talking to someone on the phone. Coach sounded pretty upset.

"I never signed up for this! Nobody told me that I'd have kids falling on the field or fainting in the locker rooms. The dosage is clearly too high. I think we should take them off the pills, at least until we see what happens with Luke. We can't risk the whole team falling apart like that."

There was a pause, as Coach listened.

"Yes, well, you talk to the President about it then. But do it tonight. I know he wants to win, and we can't win without a team. Losing Luke at this crucial time is definitely not good for the team, you tell him that!"

Jason and Cassie looked at each other. Reed was right about the pills. Jason felt sick. He knocked on the door of the coach's office.

"What do you want?" shouted Coach. Cassie, Jason, and Reed opened the door and walked in.

"Oh, it's you." Coach suddenly sounded very tired.

"How's Luke?" Cassie asked. "Can we go see him?"

"It's not a good idea tonight. They're trying to stabilize him. We won't have practice in the morning. You can go see him in the hospital then. But for tonight, I want you all to get some rest, relax, and stop worrying. He's going to be fine."

"What's wrong with him?" asked Reed.

"The doctors think it might be a strong virus," said Coach, not meeting their eyes. "We'll know more once they finish running all the tests on him. You kids go back to the dorms and rest up. We have a big game against Argentina day after tomorrow." He shooed them out the door.

Cassie, Reed, and Jason stood in the hallway for minute. Then Reed said, "See ya," and took off down the hall. Jason looked at Cassie.

"Let's go the cafeteria and get some hot chocolate or something," he said. "You look like you need some sugar."

Chapter Thirteen

NATE

Nate and Nikko were sitting in the first row of seats directly in front of the enormous widescreen TV, watching the Alaska-Argentina pre-game show. The TV room was packed. Some kids were sitting in between the rows of the seats on the floor; some were standing by the wall. Nate got the seat of honor because his brother was playing in the Tournament.

"We're gonna whip their butts," Nikko mumbled, stuffing his face with popcorn. Nate loved popcorn but his stomach felt like it was the size of a raisin. He was watching the screen for his brother. All the music stopped suddenly.

"Tonight's game is going to be slightly delayed. We have some sad news to report about a member of the Alaska national team," said an announcer. "Alaska's star defender, Luke Petrov, passed away unexpectedly early yesterday morning due to a sudden illness. We are all mourning his loss, not only to our Alaska team, but to the sport of soccer worldwide. Luke Petrov was not only an upcoming bright soccer star, but also a great friend and team member. We will never forget him. Please join us for a moment of silence in his memory." A close-up of Luke's smiling face appeared on the giant screen hanging above the field. The cameras zoomed on the stunned audience. In the TV room, you could hear a pin drop. Nate felt a cold shudder run up his body. Luke was Jason's roommate and best buddy on the team. He had been playing just two days ago. How could he be dead? Whatever this illness was, he hoped it wasn't contagious.

"That really stinks," Nikko said, "To lose our best defender at the beginning of the Tournament."

"Yeah," said Nate, "This is going to be tough. I hope Jason's okay."

"Those players have had all the good stuff, so they're strong and disease-resistant. It must have been something bizarre, like a traumatic brain injury," said Nikko. "Or maybe hypertrophic cardiomyopathy or a torn pericardium."

Nate wasn't paying attention to Nikko anymore. Alaska's team arrived on the field to subdued cheers from the spectators. The TV cameras showed close-ups of the players' faces, and Nate saw Jason's face on the screen. He looked terrible. Most of the players looked worn out and tired. This was going to be a much tougher game than anyone had expected.

"Can I take it back?" asked Nikko.

"Take what back?" said Nate, distracted.

"My prediction. I don't think we're gonna whip their butts. Not today." Nate silently agreed. He had never seen Jason look so dispirited.

Argentina took an early lead, scoring a goal on Jason in the first 10 minutes. It was a hard shot that bounced off the top bar. When Jason stepped out to grab it, an Argentinean player jumped over him to head it into the goal. Nate groaned.

"I don't think I want to watch this," said Nikko. He was so agitated he actually stopped stuffing his face with popcorn. Nate was squeezing his fists so tightly he was losing circulation in his hand.

"This is really getting to him. He should've had that ball on the rebound." Nate was frustrated for Jason. "C'mon Jason, get it together. You can do this!" he yelled at the screen. Argentina was using their momentum, pushing forward; most of the game was being played on Alaska's side of the field. Nate could see Cassie, Josh, and Max struggling to create opportunities for Reed and Sam to score.

"Look at that girl!" Nikko yelled.

Nate and Nikko watched in admiration as Cassie dribbled up the field, running around one player after another. She ran the entire length of the field, her face fierce in concentration, her ponytail flying behind her like a sail.

"Kick the ball, just kick it!" Nate yelled. As she got close to the goal, two Argentinean players charged her, but Cassie snuck a shot by them to Reed, who faked out the goalie with a left-footed shot. The stadium erupted in cheers. People were jumping up and down, flying Alaskan flags, flashing huge "We love Reed" signs. The noise in TV room was deafening. Kids were yelling, stomping, high-fiving each other. The screen focused on the shot, showing it from every imaginable angle.

"Did you see that pass?" Nate could not hide his awe. "That was incredible foot work. But that ref should have called those guys for charging. At least an indirect."

Nikko looked at him blankly. Nate forgot that Nikko had spent his last four years immersed in high tech science and math, and had just learned about penalty kicks and yellow cards during the last game.

"Yeah and look at those legs." Nikko was grinning from ear to ear. Nate couldn't agree more. Those were some fine legs on that girl. He grinned. There was still hope.

* * *

Two hours later, Nate and Nikko were still in the TV room, hanging around with their friends, talking about the game. It was a nail-biter that finally ended in a 1:1 draw.

"That's still ok," Nikko said for the fifteenth time. "We're moving to the next round. Two wins, one tie. That's a good record."

"Yeah, and Argentina is coming with us to the Round of 16," Nate said, with a worried expression. "They're going to be a tough team to beat. And we might have to play them again in the quarterfinals, if we make it that far."

"Sure, but they have to beat Australia first," said Nikko, looking at playoff schedule on the screen.

"No contest," said Nate. "Argentina is ranked #2. What is Australia, like #6?

"Yeah, but we did really well, all things considered." Nikko was much more understanding now that the game was over. The last hour and a half that he had spent yelling at the TV screen in frustration was forgotten. "They did just go through a big shock, with Petrov dying. They'll be much better next time."

"Let's hope so," Nate muttered under his breath, thinking about Jason. Now that the post-game euphoria was wearing off, he could not stop worrying about his twin. He decided to try him online.

"I'm going to the computer room for a while. You coming?" Nate asked Nikko, even though he really wanted to go alone.

"No, I'm exhausted. Watching this game was hard work. I'm gonna hit the sack. Remember, we've got that special training tomorrow," Nikko stretched and yawned.

"See you later, then." In the heat of the game, Nate had totally forgotten about the new training program. He just hoped it was on dry land, and possibly indoors, for a change. Well, whatever fun they had planned for him, he'd find out soon enough.

He logged into the game but Jason wasn't there. No surprise. It was too early. They were probably just getting settled after the game. Coach was probably going over the mistakes they had made in this game and pointers for the next one. He really missed soccer. He decided to try again tomorrow. Nate figured that Thursday would be an off day for the team. It would be so much easier if he had a phone. The government kept sending out announcements about cell phone towers that were being rebuilt and added to the network, but cell phones were expensive and coverage was spotty. No one in the soccer training center had access to a phone. Web was the most reliable way to communicate, but you both needed to be there at the same time. For all the good he was doing Jason right now, he might as well be on Mars.

* * *

The next morning, the 20 kids who'd been chosen for special training were seated in the meeting room at 0600. Colonel Gladov was already there, pacing back and forth. He was waiting for something or somebody and getting very restless.

"He makes me dizzy, marching around like he OD'd on coffee or something," Nikko was yawning, still half asleep. Nate smiled. Nikko was not a morning person. Unlike Nate, who jumped out of the bed any hour during the night or day and was ready and awake in an instant. Nate tried to temper his early morning perkiness since Nikko really hated morning people. Apparently his "genius" brain couldn't function until he had breakfast.

A short, pudgy man entered the room. He had gray hair, funny looking old-fashioned glasses with thick rims and was dragging a big briefcase.

"Sorry I'm late," the man said to Gladov, "It's not so easy to find you all the way out here."

Nate whispered to Nikko, "Yeah, well that's kind of the idea, isn't it?"

Colonel Gladov shook the man's hand and turned to the lined-up kids.

"Gentlemen, this is Mr. Kraus. He used to work for the Department of Nuclear Advancement before the War. He has come to help us in the next step of your training. You've noticed that there are only 20 of you here. You were selected based on the IQ tests you took when you started in this program. You have the best minds here, and we want to make use of them. I don't have to tell you that what you're going to see and learn now is more than classified. I hope none of you talks in your sleep, because you are not allowed to breathe a word of this to anyone outside this select group."

Nate looked at Nikko.

"Department of Nuclear Advancement?" Nikko asked.

"Well, nothing surprises me anymore. I didn't think there were any guns or grenades left, either. And now I'm using them every day," replied Nate.

"I guess Alaska was better stocked than we'd ever imagined."

"Yeah, no kidding." They turned their attention back to Gladov.

"Gentlemen, we are going to proceed to a very secure underground bunker where you will learn how to protect our country with the best technology at our disposal."

They followed Gladov outside where a bus was waiting for them. Gladov motioned them in. They headed north, a direction their training hadn't yet taken them, through a wooded area on a dirt road. After 15 or so minutes, the bus got off the dirt road and stopped in the middle of an empty field.

Gladov led them away from the bus, and then stopped. They were in the middle of a large meadow. Gladov looked at their puzzled faces.

"You are standing on top of it, gentlemen." They looked down. Gladov reached into the grass, and opened a concealed trapdoor. Nate noticed that if he dragged his boot, he could feel the metal plates camouflaged by the dry grasses.

"After me," said Gladov. They followed him down a narrow ladder in a metal tube, and into the bunker. The narrow, claustrophobic passage opened up into a huge space, about the size of half a soccer field. There were desks and monitors positioned along the walls, and in the middle of the room there was an enormous, round metal container.

"Come closer, everybody." Gladov pressed a series of buttons on the closest computer and large round metal hatch opened up. Kraus was almost jumping up and down in excitement. His glasses steamed up, and he had to take them off to wipe them down.

"Have you ever seen anything so beautiful?" he asked, leaning over the opening. "I didn't think I would live long enough to see them again."

Nikko looked at Nate.

"That guy is really creeping me out." They leaned over and looked in. The huge, rounded tips of several dozen nuclear warheads came into view.

"Holy cow!" Nate couldn't believe his eyes. Nikko looked at the warheads, his eyes like saucers. Everyone was muttering.

"How did these get here?" asked one of the other kids.

"These little beauties have been here since before the War, camouflaged by the glacier. They were a lot harder to access and only very few people knew about their secret location," said Kraus.

"Finding them was the result of many years of outstanding work by our intelligence forces," continued Gladov. "There are very few people who know how to operate them, and that is why we were fortunate to be able to recruit Mr. Kraus back from retirement to help us out. He will teach you all that you need to know. Starting today, your new schedule will focus on learning how to use these nuclear weapons. As far as the rest of the base is concerned, you are working in our intelligence division and your work is top secret. No indiscretion will be tolerated. None. Keep that in mind. Your instruction begins now. I will leave you to Mr. Kraus. Do your utmost to repay the trust we put in you. Remember, your country's safety depends on you. Do not disappoint us. Any questions?"

Nate had millions of questions, but none that he could ask. To even think about using nuclear weapons was complete insanity. Who were they going to use them on? He didn't want any part of this, but it didn't look like he had any choice. The moment he got injured flashed in his mind. If only he had been a split second faster, the idiot who'd fouled him would've missed, and he'd be with Jason worrying about the next game instead of learning how to use nukes. If he ever got his hands on that guy, he would give him something to remember him by. This was insane.

Kraus turned to them, gave a broad smile to the group, and said, "Everyone sit down at a computer and turn it on. We will start with the basics."

Chapter Fourteen

CASSIE

Cassie was lying in her bed, wide awake. The last four days had passed in a blur. Luke's collapse, and then his death, still seemed surreal. It was hard to accept that he was gone. His smile. The warm pressure of his hand. Gone forever. She felt like a zombie. She went from her room to practices and meals and back again. The first three nights after Luke's death, she had skipped the computer games, and gone immediately to her room after dinner, where she fell asleep almost as soon as she peeled off her clothes. Sleep was a refuge.

After Coach broke the news to the team, he had given them the morning off. He told them that they had no choice but to soldier on. He said he'd be watching their performances on the field carefully, and would not hesitate to pull them from the games if he didn't think they were psychologically fit. Here he looked directly at Cassie. She had managed to put everything out of her mind for the game against Argentina, and Coach had given her a little pat on the back after the game and said, "good job," to her. Tears welled up in her eyes again. She had cried more in last four days than in her entire 16 years. She lay in her bed, unable to sleep, letting the tears fall.

She was lost in the memory of that crazy night in the cafeteria when she was interrupted by a knock. She looked at the clock. 1:31am.

Cassie wiped her eyes, swung her feet over the edge of her bed, shrugged on an old hoodie, and opened the door a crack.

"Can I come in? I know it's late, I just can't sleep," Jason was standing before her door in pajama bottoms and a hoodie of his own. He looked exhausted, his eyes were as red and puffed up as her own

"Sure. I can't sleep either." Cassie glanced down the long corridor, making sure that coast was clear. "Did anyone see you?"

"I don't think so. Quiet as a tomb out there." Jason sat down on the chair by her desk. Punishment for being out of bed was usually strict, but during the Tournament, Cassie guessed they would be lenient. They needed Jason.

"You look awful," said Cassie. She and Jason had barely talked since the news of Luke's death. They still sat together at meals, but neither could figure out what to say. Jason looked at her and flashed her an unexpected grin.

"Yeah, well, I don't think you're exactly in the running for beauty queen either," he said.

Cassie threw a pillow at him. Jason's grin disappeared and he sighed as he looked around her room, avoiding her eyes. Not that there was anything to see. Unlike Reed's room, she had little in the way of decorations, and certainly no life-sized posters of herself. On her dresser, there were a few pictures of her family and the washed out pudding cup with the bedraggled remains of a few dandelions Luke had jokingly picked for her the day before he died. Cassie looked at the dandelions, and felt the tears start again. She took a deep breath, sat down on her bed, crossed her legs, and waited for Jason to say something.

"I'm so mad," he said, his voice was barely above a whisper. "I keep thinking about Luke and what they did to him and what they're doing to us. I want to scream. Or kick someone. Or leak a story to the media. Just something, anything, so I wouldn't feel so helpless," he said.

Cassie understood. She looked down at the quilt on her bed, an ancient multi-colored quilt that her great grandma had made before the War, when materials were plentiful. Her eyes ran over the familiar patterns of triangular quilt pieces. There was one fabric that had tiny black and white line-drawings of cats in it. That was her favorite. She loved the way the few lines came together and so clearly made you think of a cat, even though the lines by themselves didn't look like anything in particular. She looked up at Jason, and found his eyes on her.

"You know, he had nobody that would actually miss him, no family. Just us. He was 17 years old and he's dead!"

Cassie got up from the bed and knelt down next to Jason. She had thought about that too. She had wondered if Luke's orphan status had allowed them to experiment a little more with him than they might have with her or with someone like Reed. She tentatively reached out her hand to Jason, who took it, lightly, looking down at their hands.

"I'm so angry I could explode. First they take my brother away and now Luke..." Jason's voice rose, and he dropped her hand, walked over to the wall, and slammed his hand hard against it. He pulled it back, shaking it.

"Here, use this, it'll be quieter and probably less painful," said Cassie, handing him a soft stuffed ball with soccer-ball markings on it. "Slam it against the wall. It helps," she said, thinking of the many times that Karen had told her the same thing when she was angry about bad calls in games or mean things other kids had said about her.

Jason slammed the ball against the wall. It bounced a little, and fell to the floor. He picked it up and threw it again. And again. Each time, with such force that he was breathing hard from the exertion. Cassie just watched. Seeing Jason so out of control shook her out of herself. The next time the ball fell, she picked it up. Jason sat back down in the chair, breathing hard. He put his head between his hands, covering his eyes.

Please don't cry, thought Cassie. I can't handle that. She leaned over and patted his back, like she had done with her brothers when they were little.

"What are we supposed to do?" asked Jason.

"I guess we just get up and do what we're supposed to do," said Cassie. "Breathe. Eat. Play soccer. What else can we do? We're in the middle of the Tournament." She sat back on the bed, and looked at Jason.

"At least they stopped drugging us," said Jason.

"Do you think it could happen to us? Do you think those pills could kill us?" asked Cassie.

"I don't know. But we haven't gotten sick like Luke did, so maybe the rest of us are okay." Jason didn't look particularly convinced. She'd been thinking about that, too, and almost wished that the whole team would get too sick to play to punish the government for being so ruthless.

"It's just wrong. People have to know that they're using us like guinea pigs, and it killed Luke," Cassie said. She had no idea what they could do. She felt powerless.

Then, suddenly, she heard footsteps in the hallway. Jason swore.

"Quick, in there!" she whispered. Jason dove into the bottom of the closet, and tried to pull the few dresses and coats in front of his face. Cassie threw one of her extra blankets in after him, hoping he could cover himself in that, and closed the closet door quietly.

Cassie dove into her bed, and flicked off the bedside table lamp. The footsteps stopped in front of her door. She closed her eyes and tried to even out her breathing. She heard a key in the lock, and peeked through her closed eyelashes at the door. She watched as it swung open. Of course, she knew the lock and her supposed "privacy" were just for show, but she didn't think anyone had done a bed check on her in years. Or if they had, she had been asleep. Her heart started beating faster, but she tried to keep her breathing even. She kept her eyes firmly closed.

The footsteps came toward her bed. They stopped. Cassie kept her breathing as even as she could. Another step closer. She felt the urge to scream. She could say it was a nightmare. No. It had to be the Miss Farrow, the Dorm Monitor, but the footsteps sounded too heavy for a woman. Someone must have heard Jason slamming his hand against the wall. Or maybe it was just a random bed check. It seemed like hours, but it must have been only seconds, and then the footsteps moved toward the door. The person's shadow blocked some of the hallway light, and Cassie took a risk and opened her eyes just a sliver. The person was standing in front of her dresser. She couldn't tell who it was, but possibly male. She got a glimpse of track pants with stripes down the sides. That could be anyone. Then the person walked out the door. The door clicked closed. Cassie opened her eyes fully, but lay still. The person was still outside the door. She checked the clock. The luminous blue display read 1:57 a.m. There was no movement from the closet. She willed Jason to stay still. She kept listening. The minutes ticked by. Finally, at 2:13 a.m., the footsteps started again, walking away from her room toward the main hallway. She forced herself to wait another fifteen minutes before moving. Who was that? What were they doing? Were they going to check on Jason next? Did they already know Jason was out of bed?

At 2:28, she sat up in bed, and whispered, "Jason."

She fished around her nightstand and found the flashlight she used when the power was out. She tiptoed over to the closet, and opened it.

"Jason," she whispered again. She heard a faint snore from a lump at the bottom of the closet under her blanket. She poked the blanket.

"Jason, you have to go back to your room!" she whispered, more urgently.

Jason's eyes opened.

"Did I fall asleep?" He sat up, and started crawling out of the closet. "I was waiting for you to give the all-clear. Who was that?"

"I have no idea. I don't think it was Miss Farrow, but I couldn't tell who it was. I kept my eyes closed until they left. Maybe it was a bed check?" Cassie said.

"What are we? Five years old?" Jason swore under his breath again. He unwound himself from the blanket and tossed it to her. "Look, I actually came to talk to you about something besides Luke, but I guess it'll have to wait 'til tomorrow."

"Yeah, you better go. We can talk in the morning," said Cassie. Her flashlight swung toward the door, and Jason put his hand carefully on the handle, stopping to listen.

"Jason!" Cassie whispered.

"What?"

"Jason, look," she pointed the flashlight at her dresser. "Whoever it was took pudding cup with the dandelions Luke gave me."

"Probably just cleaning up. They were pretty dead," he said.

"Yeah, maybe," said Cassie. That was weird. Why would someone doing a bed check take that? Jason turned to leave, and then turned back.

"They came and cleaned out his stuff today while we were at practice," he said. "That's one of the reasons I came here tonight. I couldn't stand looking at the bare mattress."

"Oh," said Cassie. She hadn't thought about Luke's stuff. There was no family to come get it. She wondered what they did with it.

"See you later," said Jason, and he disappeared out the door.

Cassie crawled back into bed. Her other night-time visitor freaked her out. Was someone removing all traces of Luke? Or was it just someone looking at dead flowers, and thinking they should be thrown out? Luke had loved conspiracy theories. She wished he were here to puzzle over it with her. She wished she had really kissed him. Of all the stupid things to be sad about, that was probably at the top of the list. And now, that would never happen. She closed her eyes, but the tears leaked out anyway.

* * *

They spent the next day in preparation for the game against Chile. Coach took them through merciless drills to make sure their minds were focused. Chile was tough, and beating them was going to take everything they had. Chilean soccer players were known to play dirty, and Coach had been preparing them for how to avoid being called for their fouls, and how to play squeaky-clean themselves, because the refs would be watching closely.

She looked around at her teammates. Jason was blocking shot after shot that the goalie coach threw at him. He didn't look at all like the guy who had been in shambles in her room last night. His anger and his sadness had taken her by surprise. So had his ability to nap in the bottom of her closet. Cassie was working on a drill with Reed, Akim, Josh, Sam, and Max. Jason passed by Cassie retrieving a stray ball, and stopped.

"Let's meet tonight in your room." He jogged back toward the goal, and then turned, "I asked Reed to come, too." Cassie looked at Jason, with her eyebrow raised. "Yeah, I know, but I think we need all the help we can get," he said.

"Okay," sighed Cassie. Reed was a jerk, but a well-connected jerk.

After dinner, Jason and Cassie walked back to her room. Reed knocked on the door a few minutes later. Just a week ago, Jason, Cassie, and Luke had been hanging out in her room. Now, Luke was dead and it was Reed who was sitting on her bed, looking around her room, fiddling with her stuff.

Jason was pacing back and forth.

"What I have to tell you can get all of us into huge trouble. All of us, but especially my brother." Reed looked up from the bed.

"Your brother? What does he have to do with anything?"

Jason told them everything he heard from Nate: About Alaska building up its military, training kids to be soldiers with traditional weapons, and now nukes, all because of some power-hungry country.

"That can't be true," said Cassie. "All the regular weapons were destroyed after the War, and nobody has them anymore. And the Global Government has control over all the nuclear weapons."

"All the nukes they know about," said Jason. Reed got up from the bed and started pacing around the room. He was quiet. Cassie looked at Jason.

"It's true," said Reed. Cassie's jaw dropped. "There's more. I probably shouldn't tell you this. I shouldn't even know this. But the country that wants to take over the Global Government...it's Alaska. Remember when I told you about overhearing the conversation in my house about the drugs? That was only part of the conversation. We need to win the Tournament so the President can get the control of the Global Government peacefully, but if we don't win, they're ready to use weapons. I had no idea they were talking about nukes, but it makes even more sense now."

Cassie shook her head in disbelief. This was not happening. But she realized that if it was true, some of the changes in the training program, the need to drug them, the pressure coming directly from the President, all made sense.

"But we can never go against the Global Government, even if we have some nuclear weapons. We'll just end up obliterated," Jason said.

"I wonder how many we have, and do they still work after all this time? And if we have some, how many other countries do?" Cassie said.

"I'm guessing nothing good would happen if Alaska even threatens another war," Jason answered. "If other countries decide to fight back, then we're probably toast."

"This stinks," said Reed.

"No kidding," Cassie and Jason said at the same time.

Chapter Fifteen

JASON

The next day dawned cool and clear. It was a beautiful sunrise, orange with streaks of bright pink clouds. Very pretty, but Jason was annoyed he was up to see it. It had been a bad night. His dreams had been vivid and terrifying, with explosions and limbs flying everywhere. Watching a sunrise was probably more restful, actually, and with any luck the adrenaline of a big game would kick in.

He looked over at the empty bed, and a familiar lump rose in his throat. For a minute, he let himself imagine what the day would be like if Luke were here. He'd probably throw a pillow to wake him up after he pushed the snooze alarm over and over. Then they'd jog down the hall to breakfast, hoping not to be too late. They'd sit with Cassie and maybe Carlo, Jack, Evan, and Anton, talk trash about the Chilean players. Luke would keep them all from getting too tense with his jokes. He would probably still be teasing Reed about the blue hair, which was now returning to its normal blond color, but that wouldn't stop Luke. The call of a robin outside interrupted his fantasy, and reality came crashing back. He turned over and tried to go back to sleep until his alarm rang.

The birds were making a racket. He hardly ever noticed the birds in the morning, but for some reason today, of all days, the birds were incredibly noisy. He got up and looked out the window. Sure enough, the air outside was filled with squawking robins, apparently engaged in a feeding frenzy on the white berries in the tree right outside his window. Jason slammed the window shut. That muted the noise. Stupid birds! He went back to bed and tried to sleep. If he could just get another half hour of sleep in—preferably a half hour with no terrifying explosions—he knew he would feel better.

He felt like he had just drifted off to sleep, when he heard knocking on his door.

"Go away," he called, and tried to recapture his dream. It was a nice dream. He was walking along a riverside with Nate. Nate was saying he was all wrong, there were no nukes, just fireworks and sparklers, like the fourth of July. Jason was so relieved.

The knock interrupted his walk again.

"I said go away!" he screamed.

"Jason, get up!" came a muffled voice from outside.

"Why?" called Jason back, grumpily.

"You're missing breakfast! Coach is looking for you!" It sounded like Jack.

"Okay, I'm up," groaned Jason. He sat up, trying to clear the haze from his head.

In a few minutes, Jason was showered, dressed in his workout clothes, and on his way to the dining hall, when he was stopped by Coach.

"Jason, I was looking for you," he said. "Are you feeling okay?"

"Fine, Coach. Just overslept. Haven't been sleeping well, since, well, you know." Jason felt that familiar lump rise again, and cleared his throat. "I'm fine. Ready to go."

Coach smiled. One-on-one, his usual harsh exterior softened. Jason liked him as a coach. Not that he still didn't wonder what had happened to Coach Chip, but this guy was okay. He had given them some time to deal with Luke's death, and he was obviously shaken up by it, too.

"I wanted to talk to you about Carlo." Jason's surprise must have showed on his face.

"What about Carlo?" asked Jason. Suddenly, he had a sinking feeling. At the end of yesterday's practice, Carlo's knee had started to hurt after a particularly tough play and he had limped off the field.

"The MRI scan came back, and it looks like Carlo really did a number on his ACL. It's a severe tear, and he'll need surgery, so he'll be out for the rest of the Tournament."

"Oh boy," said Jason. "Does Anton know?"

"I told Anton at breakfast. He's a great goalie under normal circumstances, but he seems to have more trouble under pressure," said Coach.

Jason nodded. Luck didn't seem to be on their side. After having lost Luke, Ted seemed to have the same signs of 'illness' Luke had shown, and then Demetri hurt his ankle in the game against Brazil. Without Luke, Ted, and Demetri, they were short on defenders. And now down a goalie.

"Jason, I don't want to tell you to be careful out there, but if Anton has to play against Chile, I'm probably going to pull out what little hair I have left by the end of the game."

"Got it, Coach," said Jason, and headed down to the cafeteria, where he grabbed two bananas and a yogurt as the food service line was shutting down. He found Cassie and

Reed waiting for him, the last two of his teammates in the cafeteria. Odd that they were sitting together.

"Hey," Cassie and Reed said in unison. Jason raised his eyebrows. When did they get so chummy? "We were starting to wonder if you were okay."

"Well, I'm here. I just overslept. Stupid birds woke me up early, and then I guess I fell back asleep and never heard my alarm," said Jason, shrugging. "No big deal. So what's up?"

"Nothing much," said Reed, scanning the tables around them, which were nearly all empty. Just a few other stragglers, mostly staff at the training center. "I was talking to my dad last night," Reed dropped his voice very low, "and he was asking me how you were doing, and if I thought you were really strong enough to face that Chilean offense. Some of those guys are all beef. "

"We were just talking about how to protect you," said Cassie.

"Protect me?" asked Jason. "This isn't American football, you guys don't protect me. That's what the ref is for. And red cards." Reed and Cassie exchanged a look.

"At least Carlo is a really solid goalie," said Cassie, "You know, if you get injured by one of their goons."

"Uh, about that," said Jason, "Coach told me Carlo tore his ACL last night. It's pretty bad, and Carlo'll be out for the rest of the Tournament. He has to have surgery. So Anton might have to come in, if something happens to me," Reed started to break in, but Jason continued over him.

"When's the last time anyone took out a goalie? I don't think it's ever happened in the history of the World Cup. I'll be fine."

"Yeah, well my dad told me about this goalie that broke his leg during the game, so it could happen," said Reed. "And

I wouldn't put anything past Chile, from what my dad says about them."

"And we're down three defenders," said Cassie. "This is going to be tough," she said, shaking her head.

"But Evan and Jack have been doing great on D, and I'm fine," said Jason.

"Yeah, they're both big guys, and can probably handle whatever Chile dishes out. No offense, Jason, but you're not the biggest guy on the field and if they have one of those super-big guys like that Chinese dude from the last Tournament, you'll probably crumple like wet tissue," said Reed.

"They don't have anyone as big as Zhang this year. Coach said. And anyway, Shorty, what if they mow you down?" retorted Jason.

"Hey, you only have about an inch on me," said Reed, "and plus, I'm solid muscle. You could use some meat on your bones."

"Lean and mean," said Jason. "I can take you anytime. You wanna try?"

"Boys, boys," said Cassie, rolling her eyes, "Chill out. You're both incredible specimens of manhood. Now, can we move on? I think we need to talk to Jack and Evan about making sure they protect Jason," Cassie said to Reed. "Agreed?"

"Yeah, I guess we gotta protect el Capitan," said Reed, poking Jason with his foot as he got up from the table. "I'll go find them."

"What a jackass," said Jason, after Reed had left the table. "So, you think he's an incredible specimen of manhood?"

Cassie grimaced.

"Sure, if I was into guys who had egos the size of Mt. McKinley," she said, but she seemed to see what he was getting at. "Before you got here, Reed was telling me about what his dad was asking. I told him how political some of the games were, even before the War. You know, how Argentina convinced Peru to lose in 1978 by giving them an interest-free loan of $50 million. There was an actual war between El Salvador and Honduras in 1969 during qualifications for the 1970 World Cup. And before that an Italian dictator called Mussolini essentially hired the refs to be on his team's side—one of the referees even headed the ball back to the Italian team. I guess it's never been just a game," said Cassie.

"Well, that's depressing. Thanks a lot, Ms. Encyclopedia of soccer history," said Jason.

"Sorry," Cassie shrugged. "C'mon, time for practice."

* * *

Cassie was already at the field when he got there for the early afternoon game. She was juggling and practicing her tricks on the sidelines. Jason noticed a group of middle school girls watching Cassie from the stands. A dark-haired girl called out, "Cassie!" and Cassie looked up and ran over to her. The girl gave Cassie a big hug over the barrier, and then Cassie was engulfed by the mob of girls. Cassie signed balls for them, chatting with them and accepting their good wishes for the upcoming game.

He noticed some teenage boys calling her name, and waving signs with "I love Cassie," on them. That pissed him off. Not that she didn't deserve the attention, thought Jason, just that it was too soon after Luke. Jason walked over to

Cassie, grabbed her ball, and said gruffly, "C'mon, I need you to help me warm up."

"Jason, this is my best friend Karen Chigliak, and her team of U10s. Girls, say hi to Jason Carey, our amazing keeper," Cassie said, ignoring Jason's rudeness

"Uh, hi," said Jason, reluctantly, to a chorus of hellos from the group, and then tried to surreptitiously tug Cassie's shorts. She got the hint.

"Okay, bye girls! We have to go warm up. Bye, Karen," she gave Karen a last hug, and then fell in step beside Jason.

"What's up?" Cassie said, grabbing her ball back.

"Nothing, I just thought we should do some shooting practice, if you can leave your fan club." Jason started walking toward the goal.

"Jason," said Cassie, stopping. "Seriously."

"Look, it's stupid, okay? I just saw those guys looking at you, and…" Jason trailed off. Cassie turned around.

"Those guys?" she said, pointing to the exact clump of teenage boys that had triggered Jason's protective instincts.

"Yup, those guys," Jason answered. Cassie looked at Jason like he was crazy.

"Come on! You think I'm going to get distracted by a bunch of boys right before this game? *This* game?" Cassie's face was turning red, and she started speaking very softly but with great intensity. "I didn't get here without being strong and without being focused, Jason. You don't need to protect me. Now, go get in your goal and worry about yourself for a change. Go!" Jason went meekly into his goal. Cassie started bombing balls at Jason, left, right, and center, and it was all Jason could do to block about a third of them. He wasn't diving, though–he wanted to save that for the game.

In a few minutes, Coach called them to the side for their pre-game talk.

"This is Chile," he said. "They drill, drill, drill. They are big, they are fast, and it's going to be all you can do to keep up with them. But we can beat them. They play a very traditional, very scripted game. You will have to be creative, independent, and inventive. Do the unexpected, keep them on their toes. Cassie, put that fancy footwork to good use. Reed, cross that ball! Don't keep it to yourself. Evan and Jack, I want you to keep an eye on #10, he's their main scorer. And everyone, especially you, Jason, watch out for your bodies. These guys are going to bring it hard."

Then they were on the field. The ref blew the whistle, and it was on. Jason watched the passes from blue jerseys get intercepted by red and white-striped shirts, and then vice versa. Back and forth. Neither team was able to make any real headway, and most of the play was happening in the middle of the field. Then, there was a sudden breakaway by the Chilean team. Before he knew it, two Chilean players were bearing down on him. He kept his eyes glued to the ball, looking for signs of which way it would move. With only about 10 meters separating Jason and the ball, Evan came charging in from the left and used his momentum and size to intimidate #10, so that he had to pass it and Jason was able to position himself for the shot. He caught it, punted it out, and yelled a grateful, "thanks," to Evan, as Evan took off down the field. The next 30 minutes sped by. Jason made several good saves and one really amazing one. He didn't think he would get there in time, but he just managed to tip the ball, and was lucky that it bounced off the outside of the post and out.

After that first breakaway, Evan kept on #10 like white on rice. But Alaska hadn't been able to score either. Reed and Sam were having a hard time getting the shots in, though Cassie, Josh, Akim, and Max were reliably feeding them passes. At half time, Reed was red-faced not just from exertion but from anger, Jason realized. Coach talked strategy to the strikers, while Jason drank his water and looked around the stadium. It was enormous. The top of the stadium was open to the sky today, and it was a giant patch of baby blue as far as you could see. The people in the stands were a colorful mass of humanity, with some clumps of blue for Alaska and red and white for Chile here and there.

He could see the President and some other dignitaries in one of the VIP boxes. The President had sent a message to the players through the Coach at half time. He had said, "The eyes of Alaska are on you, rooting for you to win and bring glory to our country." Jason looked at Cassie as Coach relayed the message and rolled his eyes. Reed just looked grim.

All too soon, Coach was sending the team back out on the field, and Jason had to refocus. He jogged to the goalie box.

Almost as soon as the ref blew the whistle, Jason saw a wave of striped jerseys coming toward him. He watched the ball, repositioning himself as it moved toward him. Evan, Jack, and Yoshi were shadowing the offense carefully. A midfielder kicked the ball high up in the air, and Jason ran to catch it before it could bounce in front of him. As he leaped up to grab the ball, #10 came barreling out from behind Evan, leaped up into the air and kicked the ball right out of Jason's hands, catching Jason's ear in the process. Jason was blasted to the ground, but he dove backward, ignoring the pain in his ear, and tried to grab the ball before it slid into the goal. He heard the whistle blow and saw the ball roll over the goal line, but didn't know which was first. Goal. It was a goal. Blast! He had just gotten up, when he saw the medical team running toward him.

"I'm fine," he said, to the team doctor as soon as he was in earshot.

"No, you're not," said the doctor. "You're bleeding."

"I am? Where?" By now the team had gathered around him.

"Your ear. He got you pretty good. You can't play if you're bleeding. The refs are pretty strict about that."

"What's going on?" asked Reed. Then he saw blood running down Jason's neck. He looked over at Anton, who was stretching on the bench and looking a little green. He kicked the turf with his shoe and muttered under his breath.

"Are you okay?" asked Cassie, as she leaned in for a closer look at Jason. "It doesn't look too bad, just a torn earlobe."

"Sorry, man, I thought I had him blocked. He got a yellow card, if that helps at all," said Jack, as the doctor cleaned off Jason's ear.

"Jason, can you play?" asked Coach, leaning down to look in his eyes.

"I can play, Coach," said Jason, "I don't feel bad at all."

"You sure?" Coach was looking at him intently.

"I'm sure. I'm fine," said Jason.

"Okay, doc, let's keep this game going. We've only got a few more seconds in this time out. Wrap it well, though, because if any blood shows, he's out."

"Got it, Andrews. I'll be done in a sec." Jason felt gauze being attached to his ear with tape, and the doctor was trotting off the field.

Jason stood up to applause from the stadium, and the team took their places. The next 40 minutes passed in a blur, with Jason alternating between standing at the edge of the goalie box to see what was happening at the other end of the field, to jumping crazily around the goal blocking and catching shots. He was yelling encouragements to his teammates. He completely forgot about his ear.

And then, while he was alone at his end of the field, he saw his teammates screaming and jumping up and down. Reed had scored, on a sweet pass from Max. Jason knew that Chile would be coming at him fast and furious to even the score. And they did. With three minutes left to play, Chile shot on him three times, and he saved each shot. A few seconds before the whistle blew, Reed came out of nowhere and scored a spectacular winning goal. Wild cheers erupted from the stadium.

Chapter Sixteen

REED

Reed was coming out of the shower when Coach Andrews approached him after practice the next day.

"Got a minute? I need to talk you," said Coach.

"Sure, Coach. Just give me a second to dress." Reed hoped Coach wasn't mad at him. He was thinking about his performance during yesterday's game against Chile. It wasn't until the last minute, but he had scored the winning goal. Coach couldn't complain about that. He hurriedly pulled on his clothes and headed to Coach's office

"Reed, sit down. This next game is against Australia," Coach paused. "If we win, we'll make the semifinals. Did you have a chance to look at the videos of the Australian team I left in the video room?"

"No. I was planning to watch them tonight," he said.

"Take a good look at #24. Kevin Mullins. He's scored goals in every game so far, and three against Argentina. He's a real threat, especially now that we don't have Luke," said Coach.

"Okay, Coach. I'll watch the videos tonight." Reed got up to go.

"Watching him won't be enough," said Coach.

"What do you mean?" asked Reed.

"Up your physicality in the game, Reed. I know you love it." Coach smiled at Reed. "There's no need to hold back tomorrow, just be smart about it. We need to win the game, and Mullins is the only player on that team who could stop us. Nobody expected them to beat Argentina, and it was all thanks to him. I can't stress enough how important this is."

"Do you have anything specific in mind, Coach?"

"You know I don't condone violence, Reed. It makes the team look bad. If we had to play a man down, we'd be in real trouble. So whatever you do, make it subtle. I've seen you do it plenty of times."

"Ok, Coach. You got it." Reed almost bounced out of Coach's office. Finally! He loved physical games but coach had been keeping him in check. He was wondering if he should enlist Max and Sam. They were meeting later to watch the videos anyway. He wouldn't have to tell them that it came from Coach. He would just paint a nice big target on #24's back for them. They'd take the bait, happily, he was sure.

On the way to his room, Reed saw Jason and Cassie coming out of the video room. He felt a little twinge of annoyance, seeing them together. His hands went to his hair. As he ran his fingers through it, he reminded himself it was back to its normal color. Revenge was still on the menu. He hadn't decided where or how. But it was definitely coming.

"Hey," Reed called out to them. "Did you guys watch the videos?"

"Yeah, we just finished," said Jason.

"What did you think? Anything I should know?"

"It's a tough team, with one guy who has some serious moves," Cassie said.

"That guy's not gonna be a problem," said Reed.

"Oh yeah? Why's that?" asked Cassie.

"He's going to have *me* to deal with," said Reed smugly. He headed back toward his room.

"What did he mean by that?" asked Jason as Reed walked away.

"Well, he's back to his old self, being a jerk," said Cassie. Reed smiled to himself. He didn't care what she thought.

Max and Sam met Reed at the video room a couple of minutes later. They were stuffing their faces with some junk food from the concession stands.

"Still eating non-stop, huh? I haven't been that hungry since the Tournament started," said Reed.

"Yeah, well, we're always hungry." said Sam, wiping his greasy hands on his pants.

"You guys are disgusting. Why do I put up with you?" Reed sighed.

"You put up with us cause we're the best! And because I pass balls to you with such incredible accuracy, that you can step in and be the big hero," said Max, showing off a teeth covered with powdered sugar.

"Yup, without us feeding you those precision passes, you'd be nothing," said Sam, high-fiving Max. Reed flashed them a grin.

"Someone has to take all the glory," said Reed. "Might as well be me."

Reed flicked the console on, and chose the video from the onscreen menu.

Kevin Mullins dribbled, passed, and scored, outsmarting the defense time after time. He was good. If Reed was honest with himself, he had to admit that this guy was as good as he was. And therefore, dangerous.

"Watch #24."

"Damn he's good," Max said.

"This is going to be a tough game," Sam said. "I hope Evan and Jack watched these games very carefully."

"Without Luke, Ted, and Demetri they are going to be stretched thin. No offense to Evan, but he's just not as good as Luke was, and we need really strong D," replied Max.

"The D will be fine," said Sam, "but if something happens to Jason, we're screwed. You're not going to tell me Anton could cover for Jason."

"He could probably do a decent job, if he had to. And if he had Jack and Evan managing the defense," said Max.

"Are you kidding me? He's decent and he can block some tough shots, but Jason is the best. Anton just can't touch him." Sam was shaking his head.

"Luke was kind of a goofball, but we could sure use him tomorrow," sighed Max.

"Yeah. We should probably help Jack and Evan out tomorrow," said Reed, with a significant look at Max and Sam.

"But we're offense," said Sam, confused.

"No, you loser. We might have to 'help' Jack and Evan, get it?" said Max to Sam, nudging him.

"Ohhhhhhh," said Sam. "You mean that kind of help. The kind of help we can do so well."

"Yeah, just no fouls in the box. That would really screw us over. Whatever you do, just make it count. We need this guy out of the game, and early on," said Reed. "And we need all of us in the game, so no red cards."

They watched the videos a couple more times, and talked about the opportunities that might present themselves during the game to take #24 out discreetly. It felt almost like old times.

* * *

Reed waved good night to Sam and Max, and headed out to the training center's entrance. It was raining. He hadn't been outside all day, and had not even thought about the weather. A small gray sedan was waiting for him. The driver got out and opened the door for him. As they pulled away and passed the enormous sign that said in foot-high blue and white letters "Soccer Training Center" and "Home of the Alaska National Team," Reed felt himself start to relax for the first time all day. He didn't know this driver, and he was glad. He was too tired to field questions about the team.

He looked out the window. Rain streaked down the windows, distorting the lights and street signs. It was past 10 p.m., and the streets of suburban Fairbanks were deserted. They passed the high school that Reed would have gone to if he hadn't been in training. It was a long flat brick building that predated the War. It looked sturdy and dull. The thought of going to school and sitting in classes all day made Reed shudder.

As they drove into Reed's neighborhood, the houses got larger and farther apart. His house was all the way at the end of a cul-de-sac on the top of a hill, and was right up against conservation land. He remembered sneaking out of the house to an open field that was just a short walk away. He must have been five or six, and he knew he wasn't allowed to go out of their yard by himself. He did it anyway. His mom was sick and didn't have the energy to take him out. His dad was busy with work. And Rosa was busy with his mom.

He would take a soccer ball and play by himself. He remembered spending hours kicking the ball as hard as he could and retrieving it, and then doing it again, back and forth across the field. He practiced headers by sending the ball into the air as high as he could. Sometimes it made him dizzy, but he kept going. He was pretty sure the ball knocked him out at least once. He dimly remembered the fuzzy face and cold nose of their chocolate lab, Duke, hovering over him as he lay on the ground wondering how he got there. Duke would come by and check in on Reed, but he never stayed to play. Duke chased squirrels and chipmunks, not balls. Fetch was not his thing.

Sometimes on particularly hot days, Reed and Duke headed down to the river together. It never seemed to him like Duke was his dog or his family's dog, it was more like Duke was his own dog. Duke seemed to have his own agenda.

Now 15, Duke spent most of his time sleeping. Reed had once asked his dad about getting a puppy, but they both agreed that since only Rosa was home on a regular basis, it should be her call. Rosa said Duke wouldn't appreciate a bouncy puppy around the house, and that was the end of the discussion.

As they pulled up to the house, Reed noticed that the light was on in his father's study. He felt a twinge in his stomach. Reed thanked the driver and got out, ducking through the raindrops to the front door. He turned the handle and was relieved that it was unlocked, saving him from scrambling around the bottom of his gym bag for the key. Duke was sleeping on his dog bed in the living room, but opened one eye and thumped his tail a few times to let Reed know his arrival had been noted. Reed looked down the hall toward the kitchen. All the lights were off, so Rosa was probably in bed. He walked across the living room, stopping to give Duke's head a quick pat, and was rewarded with a few more small tail thumps. He stopped at his dad's study, not sure if he wanted to talk to him. He could hear his dad talking. Must be on the phone. Good. He could go straight to bed. He was not going to hang around any more doors listening. He had learned that lesson.

Reed brushed his teeth, got on his pajamas, and slid into bed. He turned out the light, and turned over, willing himself to sleep. But he couldn't help himself. He was listening for his father's steps. A few minutes later, he heard the familiar steps coming toward his room. He heard the door creak open.

"Reed, are you asleep?"

Reed thought about answering. After a few seconds, his father closed the door. Reed almost sat up and called to him. But he didn't want to. All he wanted to do with focus on tomorrow's game and how he was going to beat the crap out of Kevin Mullins. Using the most sportsmanlike conduct, of course.

Chapter Seventeen

.

NATE

Nate couldn't sleep. It was stifling in the barracks. He tried to kick away his blanket to get some cooler air on his body, but he was wrapped in the stupid thing like a sausage in casing. He struggled against the blanket and finally managed to untwist himself. All the windows in the barracks were open, and he caught a little cross breeze. It felt good on his exposed skin. Nate closed his eyes, trying to take long, deep breaths. In-two-three-four, hold, hold, out-two-three-four. In-two-three-four, hold, out-two-three-four. He couldn't remember which coach taught them to relax before big games this way, but it worked. In-two-three-four, hold, out-two-three-four. Slowly. Let all the trouble go. Nate blew out one big exasperated breath and swore.

He sat up on his bed, looking around. The quiet in the barracks filled his ears like cotton. No sounds but the occasional rustle of sheets or a light snore from fellow trainees.

On the next bed, Nikko was out like a light. Lucky guy. Nate kept going over what Jason had told him when they met on the online game site earlier in the evening. It was Alaska trying to take control of the nuclear weapons. Alaska. Not China or some other major world power from before the War, but Alaska–trying to regain the position of the former United States. It all felt so unreal. It reminded him of spy thrillers from before the War. Nate and Jason had seen a few of those old movies where the intelligence agent discovers the plot of an evil criminal to take over the world, and has to stop the madman single-handedly because no one will believe him. Nate felt like he was in the middle of a movie like that, only without the stunt doubles and cool special effects.

"Yeah, just call me Bond. James Bond," he laughed to himself. When Jason told him about the team being doped and Luke's death, Nate felt sick. All the kids in the military camp were taking daily supplements, and now he was wondering if it was the same stuff. Nate knew he had built some serious muscles, but he had stupidly thought it was due to the never-ending drills.

The Global Government could probably stop this. Nate could just imagine trying to call someone in the Global Government–if he could get a working phone number or access to a phone, which would be a trick in itself–and say, what?

"Hey, did you know Alaska is trying to take over the nuclear weapons and world? You didn't? Well, my brother and I discovered a plot, yeah. How old are we? Uh…"

Nate wondered if Gladov knew, and Kraus, and Jason's soccer coach? Were they part of the conspiracy or just pawns like him, Nikko, and kids on the soccer team?

Finally, around 3 a.m., when the sun started to rise, it came to him. Nate realized that, while there wasn't anyone out there to turn to for help, there might be something he could do himself. He was here with the nuclear weapons, and he was learning how to use them. Were there more weapons and other training facilities around the country? Maybe, but he doubted that there were other nuclear warheads. Kraus was practically wetting himself with excitement about these, so there probably weren't, Nate decided. He would break his word to Jason and talk to Nikko. Nikko could be trusted. Nate needed him since Nikko seemed to instinctively understand the commands and controls, and was way ahead of the rest of the class in the mathematics they needed to program these old machines. If anyone could think of a way to disable or sabotage the nukes, it would be Nikko. If Nate could just convince him to do it. They would have to find a way to disable the system without it being obvious. If they were caught, they'd probably be executed for treason—or maybe they would just disappear and their bodies would never be found. Urghh. Nate wished someone would hit him on the head and give him selective amnesia. He longed for the old days, back at the training center, playing soccer with the guys, hanging out with friends, knowing nothing about any of this.

Nate finally drifted off to sleep, thinking about soccer and dreaming that he was playing in the game against Australia. He and Jason were unstoppable together.

* * *

On their way out to the bunker the next morning, Nate stopped to tie his shoe and Nikko waited for him.

"What's up with you, Nate? You've hardly said a word all morning." Nikko stood over Nate, his shadow blocking the sun. "Even *after* I had my breakfast."

"I've just been thinking," Nate stood up.

"Ha! Good one. Just be careful so you don't hurt yourself." Nikko chuckled, and pushed Nate in the direction of the group.

"We better catch up, or we'll get locked out. I don't know about you, but I'm way ahead of Kraus now, and I just want to see how much control I have over those things." Nikko's enthusiasm made Nate smile. But then he remembered he was about to ruin the fun for him.

"Nikko, I really need to talk to you. But you have to swear that you won't tell anyone else," Nate was looking at Nikko's face, waiting for reaction.

"Geez, what's up with you today? Had a bowl of paranoia for breakfast? You know that I don't go around telling people stuff. What's going on?"

"I talked to Jason last night. Again. Do you want to take a guess at who is threatening us?" Nate asked.

"You talked to your brother? How? Wait. I don't want to know. What we do here is supposed to be classified, remember?" Nikko's voice dropped.

"Just answer the question. Your best guess at which country is responsible for all of this—us being here, training with weapons." Nate was standing still, waiting for Nikko to say something.

"China, I'd bet, or maybe Argentina—they hardly got touched by the War," said Nikko.

"No. Not China. It's us, Alaska. We're the country 'going rogue.' If you think about it, it makes sense. We have kind of history of it." Nate kept his voice low as they walked to catch up with the group.

"Nate, that's insane. You heard Gladov and Kraus. We're just trying to protect ourselves. There's some mad crazy country out there," said Nikko.

I wish," Nate mumbled under his breath. Then he stopped and took hold of Nikko's arm, forcing him to stop and look at him.

"Look, that's not what Jason told me, and he heard it from Reed, the Security Minister's kid on the soccer team. I think he might know what he's talking about. And there's more. The President has this grand scheme. If our team wins the Tournament, we'll take control peacefully. If not, that's where we come in. You remember Luke? The kid who died? Apparently, the team has been doped to make them stronger and bigger. Some experimental drug went haywire in his case," Nate said.

Nikko raised his eyebrows. He looked at Nate.

"Okay, we need to talk more. But not now. I'm not saying I don't believe you, but it sounds crazy, you have to admit."

Nate nodded.

"I'll see what I can find out today—maybe there's a trail in the system to who we're after or what we're preparing for. But I'll bet your brother's wrong. I bet that Reed kid is just trying to wind him up. I'll see what I can get out of Kraus, though. C'mon, we better hurry." Nikko trotted ahead.

"Just be careful. If somebody catches on what we're doing, we're toast," warned Nate.

"Of course I'll be careful, you idiot. This is *my* life on the line, too," Nikko replied.

"Kraus is probably in on it, if it really is us, you know. He's got to know. He has to set the targets, right?" Nate asked.

Nikko looked at Nate thoughtfully.

"Maybe. Depends on who is at the top and who is telling who what. But look, Nate, you better not be telling anyone else about this crackpot theory of yours either. It's probably not true, and if it is, you'll probably find yourself wandering around some incredibly remote part of the Alaska wilderness, if you're lucky. Whether you're right or wrong, I don't think Gladov is the kind of guy who is interested in your opinions." Nikko looked concerned.

"Yeah, I kind of get that feeling," Nate agreed. He felt a wave of relief wash over him. At least Nikko was willing to take this seriously. And maybe Jason had misunderstood, and there really was some other crazy country out there. That wasn't exactly a reassuring thought either, though. Nikko and Nate arrived at the bunker entrance just as the last kids were disappearing down the hatch.

* * *

That afternoon, the whole training camp was released from their duties early to watch the Alaska v. Australia game. Crammed into the TV room with 200 other kids, there was no way to talk. Nate kept looking at Nikko for a sign. Had he found anything? Nikko just shook his head, and mouthed "later," to him. Nate didn't know how he would be able to sit and watch this game, but his attention was immediately captured in the first 30 seconds, when Australia's striker had the ball at Alaska's goal. Jason barely got a finger on the shot, but it was just enough to deflect the ball up and over the crossbar. The corner kick that followed was sent right in front of the goal, with #24, Kevin Mullins, perfectly positioned to shoot the ball into the goal at close range, but luckily Jack happened to be in the way, and the ball glanced off his shoulder and off the field. Corner kick. Soon Nate had forgotten anything else and was sitting at the edge of his seat.

Nikko was plowing aggressively through a bag of chips, as if eating chips would somehow keep the ball out of Alaska's goal.

"They better get that ball out of there," Nate muttered.

"This stinks," agreed Nikko, emptying the bag, blowing the air in and popping it. Bang. Nate jumped in his seat at the sound.

"Nikko, you're such an idiot!" People around them started throwing things at Nikko's head.

Nate pulled his chair farther away from his bombarded friend. The TV camera did a close-up of Jason, who looked sweaty and red-faced, but still focused. Good thing, too. For the first 10 minutes, Alaska couldn't keep Australia out of their half, and Jason was barraged shot after shot. Nate's knuckles were white as he watched the Alaska team get beaten to the ball time and again by Mullins.

"That guy is good. Too good. Our defense has no chance." Mullins was everywhere. Sooner or later, he would score. It was inevitable. And then, there it was, a perfect pass into the middle. Nate knew that this was it, even before Evan started to sprint towards the ball. Mullins was faster, and the shot went right into the upper left corner of the goal. The whole room moaned, echoed by the moans of the thousands of people in the stadium. 0-1. Jason had dived for the ball, even though there was no way he could have blocked it. Not good. Nate knew how easy the team could crumble after an early goal like that.

They watched as Jason got up and started yelling instructions to his teammates. His face looked grim but determined.

"There was no way he could have gotten it," said Nikko.

"Yeah. That one was impossible. But it's only one, they can get it back," said Nate.

He looked at Nikko. Their eyes met in understanding. If the team lost the game, their time to act might come sooner than expected. For the first time in his life, he really did not want to watch a soccer game. He wanted to hear what Nikko found out. And then some decisions would have to be made. He already knew what he wanted to do, but could he ask Nikko? This could be a matter of life and death.

Chapter Eighteen

REED

Reed was looking at the perfect shot to the left corner and knew this was the real deal. He swore loudly. He watched Jason dive for the ball. It was a pretty sick dive, but there was no way he could have stopped it. Mullins just earned himself a "man of the match" if they did that in Australia.

Reed held in a scream of frustration. He kicked at the field with his cleat, making a dent in the turf. He wiped the sweat off his face and fixed the bandana on his head. It was soaked. Yuck. Maybe he should shave his head.

He watched as Jason picked himself up, grabbed the ball, and punted it hard toward the middle of the field, where he, Max, and Sam were ready to position the ball for the kick-off. Jason had done the best he could, but Evan and Jack just couldn't keep up with Mullins. He was like that stupid Energizer bunny. They had to bring some heat. At the whistle, Max sent the ball down toward the goal. Reed and Mullins both sprinted after the ball. Reed braced himself for impact with Mullins, but Mullins suddenly fell just before Reed took possession of the ball and started heading toward the goal. Then he heard the whistle. Foul. Reed wasn't sure exactly what Sam had done, but he earned himself a yellow card. Reed groaned.

"Stupid!" he mouthed to Sam. Subtlety was definitely not Sam's strong point. Mullins was back up. Reed realized Sam had temporarily interrupted his target, but hadn't delivered the knock-out blow they needed. Australia got the ball and quickly orchestrated a new attack. Taking advantage of their momentum, the Aussies strung together a series of quick one-touch passes. Reed was frustrated as he watched his team's defenders respond slowly to Australia's attack.

This is when games were lost. Well, not on his watch. Australia's offense was heading dangerously close to Jason again. Reed sprinted back, but Cassie beat him to it and made a tremendous tackle as she stole the ball and passed it to Reed. He flashed her a grin. In that split-second of distraction, an Australian player took the ball from him and Reed felt like the world's biggest idiot. How could let himself get distracted? He did a quick pivot, and chased after the ball. Some quick footwork and the ball was his again. He barreled toward the goal. Then, Mullins was bearing down on him. Reed executed a quick pass to Max, who was coming up on his left. He tried to position himself to shoot, but Mullins was in his way. Max sent a beautiful pass high in front of the goal. Reed ran towards it as hard as he could, but Mullins was there, too. Instead of aiming for the ball, Reed decided to aim for Mullins, and rammed his 160 pounds as hard as he could into Mullins' left side. He heard a crunch, but couldn't tell what it was. When the two players came to a stop, Reed waited with his eyes closed for couple of seconds. When he opened them, and looked up, Mullins was doubled over in pain. Sweet, thought Reed.

A team of medics ran onto the field with the stretcher. Reed thought they were coming for Mullins, but they brought the stretcher next to him. Reed waved them off, sat up, and slowly got to his feet. The stands broke into applause. He looked around to see what had happened to his nemesis, and saw him already standing on the field, looking fine. Unbelievable! Reed ground his teeth. His whole body was sore from the impact. That guy had to be made of rubber or something.

Play started again, and Alaska finally seemed to come alive. Cassie and Max both had shots on goal quickly, but neither went in. Evan easily deflected a few attempts at shots on their end of the field, and Jason looked more relaxed. The rest of the half passed quickly, with Cassie finally getting a beautiful shot in the last minute to even the score: 1-1. The guys ran to her and Cassie ended up in the middle of the sweaty mob. Reed saw Jason give her a quick hug.

"Great shot, Palmer," Reed said.

"Thanks," she said with a skeptical look on her face.

At the half, Coach called Reed over.

"Are you okay?" Coach looked at him. "That was a hard hit you took."

"I'm good, Coach. And I'm going to get him." He lowered his voice.

As Reed ran onto the field, he signaled to Max and Sam. They looked at each other and nodded.

At the whistle, Australia started their assault, stronger than ever. What were they on? Mullins seemed to be all over the field, dribbling and passing, and his energy infected his team. In the first few minutes, they were pummeling Alaska, and Evan, Yoshi, Dan, and Jack were struggling to just keep the ball out of the box. Reed was keeping a close eye on

Mullins, waiting for the right moment, while at the same time trying to keep open for a possible run up the field.

The Aussies took advantage of Alaska's disorganization, and shot one at close range, right into Jason's face. Jason tried to get a grip on the ball, but it popped out of his hands and fell right behind him into the goal. 1-2. There was an enormous groan from the stands.

Cassie and Reed huddled around Jason, who was slowly getting up, holding his hand over his face. When he removed his hand, they could see the skin around Jason's eye turning an interesting shade of purple, and his nose looked a little swollen.

"Is your nose broken?" Cassie asked. Reed looked around at the ref. His attention was on his little notebook, where he was marking down the goal. Jason quickly felt around his nose.

"Maybe," Jason said, "but I think I'm okay to play." Reed felt sick to his stomach. If Jason got injured, it would be Anton in the goal and that would be the end of their road to the semifinals. Jason seemed to sense Reed's fear.

"I'm fine, get out of here! We've got to get it back." He looked at Reed. "You go get him."

"Yeah, smart ass. What else do you think I've been trying to do?" Reed muttered under his breath.

They all headed to their positions, except Cassie.

"Are you okay?" Reed heard Cassie ask.

"I'm freakin' awesome," Jason barked back at her. "Just score!"

The whistle blew and Mullins was fast off the mark, barreling towards Jason again. Reed kept his shoulder tackles clean, with his arms close to his body and his feet on the ground, but Mullins had no such reservations. As soon as

Reed had possession, Mullins charged full force into him, bowling him over. Reed landed hard on his back, and couldn't catch his breath. The ref called the foul on Mullins, awarded Reed a direct kick, and called both of them in for a chat. He told them both in no uncertain terms the next foul he saw from either of them would be a red card. It was obvious to Reed that he wasn't the only one who got some instructions from his coach.

The game resumed with Alaska scrambling to block the Aussie players. Cassie stole the ball and took a great shot that deflected off an Australian defender. Out of bounds, but at least they got a corner kick out of it. Reed glanced at Max, who was setting up the kick, and nodded. Sam and Reed positioned themselves a few feet on either side of Mullins. Max kicked another ball beautifully on target, right to Reed. Reed was ready, watching Mullins lunge to head the ball. Instead of aiming for the ball, Reed decided again to aim for Mullins. Disabling Mullins would do more for them than this one goal. He saw it in slow motion...his head, the ball, Mullins' head all on a collision path, and then, out of nowhere Sam's head got in the way, blocked Reed, and crunched right into Mullins' head. There was a cracking sound, and both boys fell down. The ball bounced up into the air, and fell right into the goalie's hands. The ref blew his whistle to stop play, as both Mullins and Sam were on the ground and not getting up. Reed was beside Sam.

"That was truly awesome, dude," he whispered. Sam gave him a lopsided smile. His pupils were dilated, and there was blood pooling at his hairline.

"Did I get him?" he whispered back. Reed looked over at Mullins, who was now surrounded by a medical team.

"Yup, I think so—but you're out, too." The medics surrounded Sam, and took him off the field on the stretcher.

"Score a goal," Sam called to Reed. Reed watched Mullins being taken off the field and didn't even feel a twinge of remorse.

Without Mullins on the field to set up the plays, Australia lost all their momentum. Xavier came in for Sam, and he along with Reed, Cassie, and Max, shot relentlessly on Australia's goalie. Reed got a perfect shot in from the right side at the end of official time, and Cassie followed it up with a beautiful rebound shot in the 91st minute, giving Alaska a nail-biting victory, 3-2.

* * *

The shower felt good. Reed was exhausted. Every inch of his body was sore from his run-ins with Mullins. If Sam hadn't taken him out, they would have probably lost. He was glad Sam was okay. He was checked by their team doctor right after the collision and passed the concussion test. They were told Sam would remain under observation for the next 24 hours, but then should be good to go. Mullins, on the other hand, had a hairline fracture of the skull. And Australia was out of the Tournament. A good day.

Reed took the shampoo, carefully checking the bottle. He smirked, thinking about Cassie and her prank. He would definitely never take a shampoo bottle for granted again. He shampooed his hair, thinking about the game. Cassie had been amazing. She more than stepped into Sam's shoes and actually scored two of their three goals today. He would never admit it out loud, but that girl could run and control the ball like nobody else. He could easily see her replacing Max or

Sam if need be. In fact, he thought the only reason she was a midfielder and not on the front line was because of the relationship he, Max, and Sam had. They had played together for so long knew each other's moves so well. The triangle they formed with Max in midfield passing to Sam and Reed in the front was exactly what Coach meant when he was talking about synergy.

He finished his shower and wrapped a towel around his waist. No point in lying to himself. Reed liked Cassie. Really liked her. Like a girl. If Max and Sam got any whiff of this, he would never live it down. Never. He put his clean sweats on and towel dried his blond hair. He needed to get over it. It seemed she was with Jason, anyway.

But he still owed her one for the blue hair. It had been about a month since she pulled her prank. He had probably lured her into a false sense of security by now. Ha! Like he would ever let something like that go unpunished. He could hear the shower in the "girl" section of the locker room. Hmm, Cassie was still there, taking a shower. Places of great vulnerabilities, showers. He grinned to himself.

"Reed, hurry up and let's get out of here!" Max was standing with Evan and Anton in front of the locker room, waiting. "We wanna go see that suicidal maniac."

"You've got to hand it to him, he really did a number on Mullins," said Evan.

"That was pretty sick, wasn't it?" Max said to Reed, and Reed was suddenly worried that Max had told Evan and Anton about Coach's instructions. If word got out that they had deliberately gone after Mullins, they would be in big trouble.

"Yeah, um, pretty lucky for us," he said, emphasizing the word lucky. "Let's stop by the caf. I'm starving. Maybe we can take him an apple or something." Reed followed the others, and as he was leaving, he heard Cassie's shower turn off. Oh, he knew exactly what his revenge would be. He just had to wait for the opportunity.

Chapter Nineteen

NATE

At the training camp, the room broke into cheers when Cassie scored the last goal. Nikko and Nate were jumping up and down and yelling along with everyone else. After watching the highlights and talking about the game for a few minutes, it was back to business as usual, and Nikko and Nate headed to the bunker with the rest of the nuke team. Nate nudged Nikko.

"So?" he asked quietly.

"Maybe," said Nikko. "I'm not sure, but maybe. I'll have to look again tomorrow." Nikko looked troubled, and Nate almost felt bad for ruining Nikko's day.

* * *

"Hey Nikko, wait up," Nate called as he left the dining hall after dinner. The nuke team had put in another five hours of computer training after yesterday's game, plus a full day today. Nate had been trying to find time to check in with Nikko, alone, but he was constantly surrounded by members of the nuke team who followed him everywhere thanks to his new "nuclear genius" reputation.

"Wanna go for a run?" In the height of the Alaskan summer, you could have a sunset jog for several hours.

"Yeah, sure. We've been sitting at those computers for days. I feel like a lump," said Nikko. Nate poked his stomach, and realized it felt a softer than it ever had. For the first time in his life, he wasn't spending six to eight hours a day in physical training, and it was starting to show.

"Let me get rid of these guys, and I'll meet you outside in 10 minutes," said Nikko.

Nate did some stretches while he waited. He tried to focus on extending his muscles and holding the stretches as long as he could. But he found his mind drifting back to the nukes.

If anyone could dig out the truth, it was Nikko. What was taking him so long? Finally, Nikko emerged, alone.

"Sorry, I couldn't get rid of them. I had to sneak out."

"Gave me plenty of time to do every stretch I could think of. But I've been going crazy. Did you find out anything?"

"Jason got it right, from what I could find," said Nikko, as they started jogging around the outdoor track. Nikko was panting already, so Nate slowed down. He forgot sometimes that Nikko had never been an athlete.

"It was pretty easy to get into Gladov's files," continued Nikko. "He's obviously a military guy, not a computer genius. Either they don't think they need much protection, or he's just an idiot. The stuff wasn't even protected beyond a stupid password, and I mean really stupid."

"What was it?" asked Nate.

"It was NUKES, if you can believe that," Nikko was laughing. "My guess is that he didn't think there was any need for security, since we're all on the same side here."

"Brilliant. And he's one of the guys trying to take over the world? We are so doomed," said Nate. "But seriously, tell me what you found."

"It looks like our unit would be activated only if we lose the Tournament. If we win, there's no need for any immediate action, we'd just be a back-up in case some other country doesn't want to cooperate with our government. But if we lose, then we're it. We'll launch the warheads on specific targets and it'll be 30 years ago all over again, or maybe even worse. Gladov is supposed to get a set of targets from the government a few days before the final game, and we'll program them in, in case we have to launch." Nikko sounded very matter-of-fact at the discovery of plans for World War IV.

Nate felt the gnawing anxiety in his stomach kick up a notch.

"What do you think we should do?" Nate asked.

They ran in silence again. The sky was a dusky blue, with occasional streaks of pink or orange, as the sun moved around the horizon, not setting, not rising, in that odd continuous twilight of a summer evening in Alaska.

"We could just forget what we know and just do what we're told. That would probably be the smartest thing for us to do," said Nikko.

"Yeah, I know," Nate agreed. He had spent most of last night considering that option, and coming to the conclusion that he couldn't do that.

"We can't stay out of it," Nate finally said. "Not to be overly dramatic or anything, but it's the fate of the world we're talking about. We can't just sit back and watch some crazy guy blow what's left up."

"Yes. We can." said Nikko. "We're just kids."

"We aren't just kids, Nikko. We're soldiers now. And if there's one thing I've learned from military history, it's that the people at the top don't always know what's right or wrong. This is wrong. What if, 30 years ago, you knew what was going to happen, had the chance to stop it, and you didn't? What if a billion people hadn't been completely obliterated, along with all their houses and cars and dogs, and what if another four billion hadn't died from radiation poisoning, starvation, and dirty water? How would you feel?" Nate was on a roll now.

"Think of how different the world would be without so many people dead from the bombs and from radiation sickness, so much of the world uninhabitable, some of the most amazing places on Earth completely bombed to smithereens. Don't you ever wish you could have seen New York City? Or Paris? Or elephants? Or monkeys? Or the Pyramids?" Nate was talking louder and running faster with each lost thing he thought of.

"Hey, slow down," Nikko was panting. "We're just talking, relax."

"Oh right, we're just talking about another nuclear disaster, and you want me to be calm?" But Nate slowed down.

They didn't talk for another lap.

"Nikko, I understand if you don't want to have anything to do with this, but I need to do something."

"I get it," sighed Nikko. "I knew your overdeveloped sense of morality would never go along with Plan A. And I want to help."

"So do you know what we could actually do to disarm them?" Nate hoped it would be something simple, like snipping some wires or changing some part of the code to say "off" instead of "on."

"I have an idea," said Nikko. "I found some old Cold War documents online, and I think I found a way to do it. Inside each warhead, there's a pit–sort of a hollow sphere where the plutonium or uranium is. Anyway, there's a tiny tube that allows tritium and deuterium–those are radioactive isotopes of hydrogen that generate fusion neutrons–to enter the pit. Once they're in the pit, a small particle accelerator drives deuterium-tritium fusion, and the particles bounce around the pit in all directions and will strike the nuclei of the plutonium or uranium, which is what triggers the nuclear chain reaction."

Nate stared at Nikko astonished.

"Nikko, I can see your lips are moving, but I have no idea what you're talking about," said Nate.

"Yeah, well I did a little extra research while the rest of you were stumbling around like babies trying to write code. So, anyway, what you can do is fill the pit with steel wires. It's called 'pit stuffing.' You just have to carefully thread the wire through the tube into the pit. And then there just isn't room for the nuclear reaction to start. The weapon can't go off, and there's no way to pull the wire out through the tube, especially if you fray the ends before you stuff it. The only way to use the weapon after it's been stuffed is to deactivate it, remove the pit, cut the pit open, take the wire out, make a new pit, and put it all back together." Nikko looked thoughtful. "It might not stop them permanently, but it would definitely slow them down. They also wouldn't know that the pits had been stuffed unless they x-rayed them before they tried to fire them. The computers won't know, since there aren't any sensors in the pit."

"Sick." Nate was impressed. Nikko had really done his homework. "How did you get all that information so fast?"

"Well, I had already finished all our work for the day before the game, so I just kept those files open on my screen while I ran some searches in the background. I cleared all my history, but I don't know how close an eye they keep on our monitors. I asked Kraus a few questions during the afternoon so he wouldn't be suspicious. That is definitely one thing I love about our new gigs—so much Internet access!"

Nate remembered some of the things he had found when he had a few moments to web surf today. He had been looking at some images of New York City. His father had grown up there, in a part called Brooklyn, and Nate had been checking some maps to see if he could find his dad's home town, to see what it had looked like. New York City had taken a direct hit in the War, so the current images showed a large, round sandy-gray rim of dirt, stone and chunks of metal, filled in with ocean water. No signs of life, according to satellite pictures. But in the old pictures, there were closely-crammed shops lining sidewalks, people dressed in suits filling the sidewalks, elegant couples eating at outdoor cafes. It all looked so vibrant and energetic. Fairbanks was okay, but it was nothing like that.

"Okay, so we'll stuff the pits with wires. How long will that take? And then what?" Nate was impatient to get a plan.

"The stuffing should only take a minute or two per pit, so, what, we've got 30 to disable? If we can find time to do it without anyone around, we could get it done in an hour or two. But if we have to try to sneak it in while everyone else is working, it'll be tougher. And, then, once we've done it, we need to figure out what's next."

"What do you mean? If we stuff them, we're done, right? They're disabled, and no one will know until they try to fire them, right?" Nate asked.

"I think if we do this, we have to get out of here after we've done it. If there's a problem, you know they are going to come looking for me. And I really don't think Gladov and Kraus would take it too well."

"Yeah, I don't think this would make us very popular with Gladov," agreed Nate.

"Or the President, for that matter," said Nikko. "And I have a feeling they wouldn't just ground us or send us to jail. I think it would be much worse than that."

"Right. We'll need an exit strategy." Nate agreed. "How long do you think we have before they could figure it out?"

"I think we'd have a few days after we do it. If everything goes as planned, they won't have any idea we did anything until they are ready to program the targets in. The best thing would probably be to make it look like we died in some kind of 'accident.' Funny, I never thought I'd be planning my own death," said Nikko.

"A fake accident. Hmm." Nate was thinking. "I guess we'll need a big explosion, if they're going to expect to believe we're dead and our bodies are gone. Or water, some kind of accidental drowning might work, with our bodies swept out to sea or something." Nate wondered. Nikko looked at Nate.

"The only small problem being that there is no big body of water around here, unless you are planning to drown in a bathtub." They both started to laugh.

"Well, I'm still working on it, cut me some slack," Nate felt better even though what they were planning was crazy scary.

"Well, think fast!" said Nikko.

"We'll have to ditch these uniforms. And we'll need food and supplies. We're pretty far from any towns or cities, so we might be out there for a long time." Nate looked out across the horizon. There was no sign of human activity anywhere beyond their camp. Not a flickering light in the distance, just darkness as far as the eye could see.

"Do you think we could make it to Canada? We might be able to hide there. I read about some new settlements right across the old borders. We could lay low there for a while, and see what happens," suggested Nate.

"Our families will think we're dead," said Nikko.

That seemed kind of cruel, but it was probably the best solution, thought Nate.

"I wish there was a better way, but I can't think of anything else. If they find out those nukes were disabled, they'll know it was you. They know none of the rest of us would even have a clue."

"Sad, but true," joked Nikko.

"We need to start preparing. It's only about 10 days until the final game," said Nikko.

"I have to talk to Jason," said Nate.

"You can't say anything to Jason! You never know who might be listening." Nikko warned. "If we're going to pull this off, it's going to take us being really careful and very prepared. For anything."

"I know. But I have to talk to him. Plus, maybe he'll have more information for us. I'll be quick and careful." Nate thought they might need someone who knew what they were doing, just in case.

"So to recap: we're going to stuff 30 nuclear warheads without anyone knowing, and then we're going to blow ourselves up in a fake accident, and *then* we're going to spend months camping out in the wilderness in search of a place to hide. Brilliant," he said.

"We can do it," said Nikko. "I'm a genius, remember? Would I steer you wrong?" Nikko grinned his crazy grin, like he was talking about some school project or giving dating advice.

"We better get back to the barracks. It's almost time for lights out." Nate checked his watch.

"I hope I have enough time for a shower."

"Me too. You stink."

"Ha ha."

Watching the sun still bobbing along the horizon, Nate felt hopeful. Their plan definitely had some holes in it—holes you could send a nuclear warhead through—but he thought it would work.

Chapter Twenty

CASSIE

Cassie was in the shower at the gym, sluicing off the sweat and grime of another practice in preparation for the semi-final game. Now that they were in the final four, there was an incredible energy to the team. Coach kept telling them to take it easy, but with the semifinal game coming up in less than a week, she found herself kicking harder and making riskier plays, and pulling them off. The Canada-Albania game would be played tomorrow, and then they would know who they would be up against. Cassie was hoping for Albania.

With her eyes closed, Cassie rinsed out the rest of the conditioner, and then stood there, enjoying the feeling of the warm water. When she turned it off, her hand groped for the towel, but felt only air. Ugh, she thought, hoping it wasn't lying soaking on the ground. But it wasn't. Did she forget to bring her towel again? Oh well. She squeezed out her hair, jumped up and down to shake off the water, and opened the shower curtain.

Her bag was gone. Her towel was gone. Her locker door was hanging open, empty.

"You little jerk!" she yelled, but there was no response.

She stood there dripping water onto the cold cement floor.

She saw her cleats and socks in the corner. Wonderful. Not like she could get dry off and run down several hallways in just two sweaty socks. She opened the other lockers, but there were no forgotten towels or sweatpants to save her. She checked the cabinet under the sink. A few rolls of toilet paper. Not helpful. She sat down on the bench, put her hands in her head and tried to relax. She would not cry. It was just clothes, after all. It wasn't that far to her dorm room–maybe 60 seconds if she sprinted the whole way.

She sat still, listening. There were no showers running or lockers slamming in the boys' locker room. She had done some extra stretching after the game, so had gone in late to shower. It was dinner time. They were all probably stuffing their faces. Good. She could sneak in their locker room and grab something to wear. Jason was probably just as messy in the locker room as he was in his own room.

Cassie peered into the hallway. It was empty. Slowly she crept toward the boy's locker room door, and quietly pushed it open. She walked in and started scanning all the surfaces for anything wearable. Nothing on the floor or the benches. Really? They were this neat? She checked the showers. Nothing. Did they all suddenly have a neatness attack?

She started opening lockers. The boys' names were above the lockers. Jason's first. Some shin guards, that was all. Come on, Evan, she thought, please. Nothing. Fine, she thought, I can't be picky. Reed? Nothing. Sam? What was that? Ew. Max? Empty, except for power bar wrappers. She kicked a locker in frustration. The metal reverberated in the silence.

She heard footsteps coming out of Coach's office. Oh no. Coach couldn't see her like this. She'd die. On the spot. She ran back to her locker room, not caring if he heard her, and slammed the door. She leaned against the door, her heart beating fast. She swore under her breath.

There had to be some way out of this. Think. Think.

She walked back towards her shower. Maybe that little rat had missed something. The shower curtain! White plastic. It was hanging by metal reinforced holes on metal loops attached to the shower curtain rod. Easy. She had them all unhooked in less than a minute, and started fashioning a toga out of the unwieldy material. She folded it over to make it a little harder to see through, but then it got pretty short. Well, better than nothing. Ha, she thought to Reed. Ha bloody ha!

With cleats and socks in hand, she headed into the hallway, crossing her fingers that she wouldn't see anyone and have to do any explaining. She paused before turning every corner, listening for footsteps. Almost there.

As she turned the corner, she saw her worst nightmare come true. Immersed in a hand-held videogame with a half-empty bowl of popcorn next to him. The nerve! She started to back away, but suddenly Reed looked up and gave a wolf whistle.

"Palmer, I am impressed, that is one nice dress. Seriously. You should think about going into fashion design or something," said Reed, grinning widely.

Cassie felt tears prick her eyes, tears of anger and humiliation. But she held herself together. She wouldn't give him the satisfaction.

"Oh, shut up," she muttered and headed right toward her door, turning the handle in one swift move. Locked. She turned back to Reed, eyes blazing

"Where's my bag, you jackass?"

Reed pulled her gym bag out under him.

"What'll you give me for it?" he taunted.

"You have *got* to be kidding me. Give it now, or I'll kill you. Literally." She glared at him. Was it her imagination, or did he look a little scared?

"Fine, Palmer, no need to get all upset. Geez. It was just a little joke." He slid the bag over to her. He watched as she fumbled around in the bag looking for the key. Why didn't he leave? Where was that stupid key? Her hand finally found the key ring.

"Leave, you idiot! You had your fun, now go away!" Reed held up his hands and backed away.

"Whoa. Can't you take a joke? Seems to me I remember someone turning my hair blue not that long ago. Don't dish it out if you can't take it, Palmer." He gave her his trademark 'I'm so wonderful' grin. Cassie's blood hit its boiling point.

"I'm sick of it, Reed! You have been giving me the business since day one, and I am just plain sick of it!"

Reed's mouth dropped open. Cassie walked toward him, poking her finger into his chest.

"I'm every bit as good as you are, and you need to get that through your big thick macho skull. You need me on that team, you moron. No one else passes you that ball like I do, and you know it. This ends now, got it?"

"Wow, you can be kind of scary, you know that?" Reed pushed her finger away from his chest, still grinning. Cassie put her hands on her hips and continued to glare at him.

"This stays between us, got it? We're even. If I hear one word out of Max or Sam or anyone else about this, I will never pass you another ball as long as you live, do you understand? Never."

Reed's eyes got wide.

"Okay, Cassie. Calm down. It was just a joke."

* * *

At dinner that night, Cassie was still seething. Reed was such a colossal jerk.

"Earth to Cassie..." said Jason.

She looked up from her plate, where she had been carefully shaping her mashed potatoes into a mountain, and dotting the edges with peas.

"What?" Jason was looking at her.

"You didn't hear a single word I was saying, did you?" asked Jason.

"Oh sorry, no," replied Cassie. "What were you saying?"

"Just that Reed stopped me in the hall earlier and said he had something to tell us. So he's going to meet us tonight in your room, okay?" Cassie felt her face get hot. He had some nerve! Coming to her room!

Before Cassie had a chance to respond, Anton and Evan came up to their table, carrying their trays.

"You guys want to join us for some foursquare in the gym? Though we'd blow off a little steam before bed," said Anton. Jason looked hesitant, and Cassie was in no mood to go play.

"C'mon, it'll be fun," said Evan. "We need to get sleep tonight, and I don't know about you, but all I can think about is enormous Canadians running towards me..." Evan trailed off. At 6 foot 4, Evan didn't normally worry about the size of other players, but Cassie knew the Canadian team had a couple of forwards that topped 6 foot 6, and she could understand why Evan looked a little green.

"It might be Albanians, Evan. We might get lucky," said Jason. Evan gave him a weak grin.

"So, you guys coming?" asked Anton.

"Sure, we'll join you. Sounds like fun," said Jason. Cassie just nodded.

"Wow, that's some serious enthusiasm. You guys don't have to. We just thought it would be fun." Anton was looking at them with narrowed eyes. "Are you two okay?"

"Yeah, fine. Just, you know, nervous about semi-finals," Cassie figured the semi-final game was an all-purpose excuse. Sure, she was nervous about the game, but right now she was still thinking about all the things she should have said to Reed.

"Okay, let's go, then." Jason and Cassie pushed their chairs back, grabbed their trays, and headed over to the trash/recycling/compost station behind Anton and Evan. Cassie looked up and noticed they would have to pass right by Reed, Sam, and Max, who were laughing hysterically about something. Cassie decided she wouldn't even look at Reed as she went by. If he was telling them, she would punch his teeth out.

As she passed, Sam let out a hyena-like laugh, and Reed caught her eye and winked at her. Before she knew it, she had emptied her mashed potatoes and peas on Reed's head, and he was staring at her in complete surprise. He stood up. The cafeteria was suddenly quiet. Then Max and Sam burst into braying laughter, as the potatoes starting sliding down Reed's head, leaving a trail of potato-y residue. Uh oh. Jason's jaw had dropped open, and he was staring at her and Reed.

"You did not just do that," said Reed in a menacing voice, taking a step toward Cassie. Cassie took a step back. "You really should NOT have done that." A glob of cranberry sauce hit her on the cheek. She looked over and saw Sam wiping his hand on his shirt, leaving a trail of pink. Jason got between Reed and Cassie. Then, splat, a spray of bright yellow mustard hit Jason's back. Cassie looked over, and saw Anton holding the yellow bottle and laughing. Within 10 seconds, food was flying all over the cafeteria—more mashed potatoes, peas, red and green jello cubes, cranberry sauce, wheat rolls, carrots and broccoli. The potatoes and cranberry sauce were the best, as they left colorful tracks and hit with satisfying smacks—until Sam and Max came back with a load of ketchup bottles from the condiment counter, and started spraying everyone with streams of red. They started slipping on the floor with all the food, and soon Cassie found herself in a messy pile of her teammates, laughing crazily while trying to massage cranberry sauce into Anton's hair while Sam squirted her with a nearly empty ketchup bottle that was just making farting sounds. Reed had a huge untouched tray of red jello that he was dipping his hands into and throwing up to the ceiling, where it stuck for a second before falling onto people's heads. A sharp whistle interrupted the fight.

Coach was watching them, whistle in hand and a very dismayed look in his eyes.

"We're in for it," whispered Cassie, even as she popped a piece of broccoli down Anton's shirt.

"What is the meaning of this?" he screamed at the team. "This is what you do to get ready for the biggest games of your lives? I can't believe you!" Coach was getting into full rant mode, Cassie could tell. And then one of Reed's thrown globs of jello fell from the ceiling onto Reed's head, where it sat, mesmerizing everyone, until it slid quietly down Reed's back.

Coach started to laugh. Reed wiped his neck off, and picked up a fresh tray, but Coach held up his hand.

"Okay, gentlemen and lady, you've had your fun. But you have created a disaster area. I want everyone down to the showers, and back here in 15 minutes ready to clean this mess up. Do you understand me? No dawdling. "

Cassie jogged back to her room, dunked herself into the shower after piling her sticky, food-covered clothes in the corner to deal with later, and pulled on her sweats. Most of the team was already hard at work when she get back. The dorm monitors were handing out garbage bags, sponges, brooms, and small dustpans to scoop up the food. Jason and Evan were sweeping up large swaths of food with long-handled brooms, while Sam and Max were wiping the walls free of ketchup and mustard. Reed had a long-handled mop and was waving it haphazardly around the ceiling, removing bits of jello. His path of jello removal brought him close to where she was picking up mashed up food bits from under the table legs. He didn't look at her, and Cassie felt herself again get flushed. But she could ignore him, too.

"I swear I didn't say anything to anyone," he said quietly, so only she could hear. Cassie felt her shoulders relax.

"And?" she said, looking up at him. His eyes were focused on the ceiling. He finally looked down at her.

"And I need you on the team. I really do," he said, giving her a wink. So full of himself. But this time, she smiled before turning her attention back to the messy task at hand.

It took at least an hour to clean up the sticky devastation they had caused in less than five minutes, but everyone was in a good mood, and reliving their best hits. Sam was awarded "Best Use of a Condiment" for his farting ketchup bottle, while Reed won "Most Artistic" for his jello ceiling art.

Jason and Cassie were the last to leave. As they headed back to their dorm rooms, Jason asked, "So, what made you dump the potatoes on Reed's head?"

She definitely wasn't going to tell him.

"I don't know. He just deserved it. He was sitting there smirking, and I just lost it, I guess." Cassie laughed. "It's Reed. Do I need a reason?"

"Yeah, if he didn't do anything particular to deserve it, I'm sure he will soon," said Jason.

"I guess he can have his okay moments," said Cassie.

Jason looked at her with a raised eyebrow.

"Oh really?"

"Well, he did come to us with that stuff he heard from his dad. Without him we wouldn't know what was going on, and Nate wouldn't know either," said Cassie.

"Don't remind me. I had almost forgotten about all that. We should do food fights more often," said Jason.

"Somehow I doubt that would go over well," said Cassie, smiling. "Beat foursquare, though, didn't it?"

"Sure did. See you later, Cass." Right, they were meeting Reed later. Way too much Reed in my day today, she thought.

Chapter Twenty-One

JASON

Jason was lying on the empty bed in Cassie's room, his legs propped up on the wall, his hands behind his head. Cassie had moved the extra bed so that it formed an L with hers, creating a sofa-like corner of the room. In Jason's room, Luke's bed just sat there, mattress bare, a reminder of his friend. He didn't even throw stuff on it. It would seem wrong, but now looking at Cassie's arrangement, maybe he should use it. Life is for the living, and all that. He was looking up at a funny-looking crack in Cassie's ceiling, squinting his eyes, trying to make it into different shapes. Like Reed's face with a big shiner. Ha! He wasn't convinced by Cassie's change of heart. Reed was still the biggest jerk on the team—always making sure *he* got the credit for their wins.

Boy, he was tired. He looked over at Cassie, who was sitting on her bed, propped up on her blue and green throw pillows, but her eyes were closed.

"What's keeping him?" Jason asked. Cassie opened her eyes, startled.

"Sorry, did I wake you, sleeping beauty?" Jason poked her playfully with his foot.

"No. Yes. I'm just so tired. I feel like my grandma, who was always dozing off in the middle of conversations." Cassie looked like she barely had the energy to sit up. "What did you say?"

"I said, what's keeping him? He said he'd be here at 10 and it's almost 11. I have to be up at 5 a.m. tomorrow, so I was kind of hoping to get some actual sleep tonight." Jason was yawning and talking at the same time.

"Why do you have to be up at five? No practice until 10. Coach is letting us *sleep in*, remember?" Cassie was looking at him like he had lost his mind.

"I'm supposed to talk to Nate tomorrow morning. No one's up that early, so it's easier to avoid any questions," Jason replied.

"Yeah, maybe, but if anyone sees you they are going to wonder what the heck you're doing up," Cassie said, skeptically.

"I can always claim nerves," said Jason.

"True." said Cassie, yawning.

Jason saw Cassie's eyes close again. His own eyes felt sticky, and he rubbed them. His eyes went back to the crack in the ceiling. It looked more and more like Reed's face, but maybe with two big shiners this time. What a jerk. Jason woke with a start. He looked at the clock. 10:59. He must have just dozed off for a second.

"I wonder if he forgot about us." Jason said grumpily.

Cassie's eyes fluttered open. She looked at Jason, and shrugged.

"Yeah, maybe. We're not exactly VIPs to him so he probably doesn't think it matters to keep us waiting, Mr. Big Shot."

"What's that about Mr. Big Shot?" Reed strolled in.

"Don't you ever knock, jerk?" Jason considered punching him in his self-satisfied, well-fed face. But he'd have to get up from the bed, which seemed like too much effort.

"Am I interrupting something, lovebirds?" Reed was wearing his usual smirk as he sat down on Cassie's spare bed, nudging Jason to the side.

"Hey, watch it!" Jason grumbled.

"We were just discussing your personality traits," Cassie replied.

"Oh, you mean my extraordinary charm, charisma, intelligence, say nothing of handsome physique?" Reed asked innocently.

"Actually no, it was more like self-centered, arrogant, insensitive, jerk. That kind of stuff," Jason yawned.

"Oh, well, that's what you think. Hardly the universal opinion. According to the media, I'm pretty awesome," Reed said, unscathed and smiling.

"You shouldn't believe everything you see on TV," said Cassie, stifling another yawn.

"So, why did you want to meet us? And make it quick, 'cause I am just barely keeping my eyes open here."

"I went home for my dad's birthday, and after we had cake, I went to my room to get some stuff. I overheard them talking. My dad really needs to do something about how sound travels in our house."

"Thanks for that fascinating glimpse into your home life. Get to the point." Jason snapped. The thought of cake made him hungry. And grumpy.

"The President is very happy with how we're doing. They're all very optimistic about our chances. He said that all the other plans are on hold, as long as we keep winning. So the longer we keep winning, the better," Reed finished.

"More time is good, but then what? It's not like we can do anything to stop their plans, can we?" Cassie seemed awake now. "I can't believe that they might start another war. If we have old nukes, don't you think other countries might, too? We could win this Tournament and then be globs of dust in a week."

Jason just looked at Cassie. Then at Reed. They were both looking at him for some kind of answer. Jason let out a swear that raised Cassie's eyebrows.

"I'm so tired I can't think of anything. To think that I'll start another nuclear war if I let in a goal is just crazy. Talk about pressure." He covered his face with his hands.

"Reed, you aren't by any chance leaving a crucial part of the conversation out, are you? Like, maybe someone mentioned that launching a war against the Global Government was suicide?"

"Didn't hear anything like that, unfortunately. They seem deadly serious about it." Reed paused. "Do you think I should talk to my dad? About how insane this is?"

"Don't you think he knows? Didn't he live through it the first time?" Cassie was twisting a hair clip so hard, it snapped in half.

"Nate left me a message. Maybe he has an idea," Jason said to Reed.

"I hope he does," Reed's face was grim, "because I'm out of ideas."

The three of them sat in silence for another minute.

"And what if we lose?" Cassie finally asked.

"Well, about that," Reed seemed hesitant, "I think there are some plans in place to help us with that."

"What do you mean?" Jason asked.

"I heard the President saying something could be done, like a little food poisoning. Nothing drastic–those were his actual words," Reed replied, ducking his head.

"That would suck," Jason said.

"Yeah, hardly feels like winning if the other team is puking their guts out," Reed agreed.

"But I guess if they are actually considering another war, who cares about a little food poisoning?"

Cassie had a point, Jason realized. If food poisoning helped put off nuclear catastrophe, it was probably worth it. Maybe this was all about buying time.

"It's past 11. We better get to bed, or we'll be useless tomorrow, not to mention that we're violating curfew," said Jason, slowly getting up to leave. Ugh. Maybe he could just sleep here. But then he saw Reed looking at Cassie, and heaved himself to his feet. "Let's see what Nate has to say in the morning."

"Like they'd really do anything to us for being out of bed in the middle of the Tournament," said Reed, rolling his eyes. But he got up, too, and followed Jason toward the door.

"Night, Cassie," said Jason.

"Yeah, good night and have sweet dreams," said Reed, grinning at Cassie.

"Oh, shut up," said Cassie, grumpily. She fluffed her pillow, took off her sweatshirt revealing the pink tank top she slept in, and climbed under the covers.

"What?" she said, looking at Jason and Reed, who were both staring at her. "Go, good night, leave, and turn off the light by the door, okay?"

"Right," said Jason, and flipped off the light and closed the door.

Jason and Reed headed down the darkened hallway quietly. It was just a short walk to their hall. Jason decided this was the perfect to time to have a little chat with Reed.

"Okay, Reed, what's going on?"

"What do you mean?" asked Reed a little too innocently.

"I mean, what's going on with you and Cassie, idiot." Jason hissed.

"I could ask you the same question," he whispered back.

Jason opened his door, and motioned Reed inside. Reed hesitated and then walked in. He sat down on the empty mattress that had been Luke's bed.

"What's your issue, dude?" Reed asked, speaking normally now that they were inside.

"We have the biggest games of our lives coming up and we've got all this stupid crazy stuff going on, like maybe blowing up the world, you know, just a minor detail, and now I see you and Cassie acting weird around each other. You guys need to be able to work together on the field, so if she's pissed at you or you're pissed at her, you need to get over it." Jason paused. He wasn't sure how to say this next part. "And, if it's something else, where you guys, I don't know, like each other or something, well, you know the rules about that stuff."

"I know all that," said Reed, angrily. "This Tournament is something I've been working my whole life for, and I would never mess that up over some stupid girl, believe me," he finished.

Jason felt like hitting Reed.

"Stupid girl? That's what you think of her?" Jason hissed again. "She is our teammate and a really good one. If not for her, we wouldn't even be in the semi-finals, and you know it."

"Well, what about you? You guys are always together. What's up with that?" Reed challenged, with some flash in his eyes. Jason thought for a minute.

"I guess I feel responsible for her, in some way. I'm not sure why. You were such as a colossal jackass to her, and that just pissed me off. She is a great player and you were an idiot to treat her like that. Someone had to stand up for her," Jason replied.

"Yeah, she's one of the best on the team, I'll admit it. I just didn't believe a girl would actually be so good." He paused, like he was deciding something. "But she's also, well, kind of hot, don't you think? If you ever tell anyone I said that, I'll deny it," said Reed, turning a little red.

Jason just stared across the room at Reed. That was not at all what he was expecting. After all the torment he had put Cassie through at the beginning, he would turn around and admit to, well, what exactly? Not a crime to think a girl was pretty, after all. Jason sat down.

He grinned back at Reed. He wasn't attracted to Cassie that way, but that didn't mean he couldn't appreciate a nice body.

"Yeah, she kind of is. I mean, that tank top definitely showed off some…" Jason trailed off, then he stopped himself and gave himself a mental shake.

"I think we're both losing it," said Reed, flopping back on the bed and laughing.

Jason started laughing too.

"Besides, she hates you," said Jason, flat on his back, looking up at the ceiling, wondering if that was still true.

"I know," Reed said, still laughing, "She really hates me."

"Yeah, I'd hate you, too, if you ever tied my shoes to the bench." Jason said seriously, but then he started laughing again.

"Boy, you should have seen the look on her face," said Reed, nearly falling off the mattress.

"But seriously," Jason said, sitting up and taking control of himself. "Even if you like her … I mean even if you *like her* like her, she's our teammate, and we have a lot to deal with, so we should just try to keep it all…" Why was he having so much trouble finishing his sentences? Must be exhaustion.

"Professional?" asked Reed.

"Yeah, that. We have a job to do and we need to focus on that. And I need to get some sleep." Jason checked the clock. Great, 11:30. If he fell asleep fast, he could get almost six hours in.

Reed glanced at the clock.

"I better get going. My driver's probably getting bored waiting for me," said Reed. He stood up and walked toward the door.

"I thought you were staying here tonight," said Jason.

"Nope, I can sleep better at home and I get a home-made breakfast, not that crap you get here," said Reed, cheerfully.

"Oh, kiss off," muttered Jason.

As Jason brushed his teeth, he shook his head. They were in the middle of the Tournament, and instead of getting the rest they needed, they were up late talking. About a girl. He really needed to have his brain examined.

Grudgingly, he thought to himself that Cassie might not be completely crazy. Reed could be human. He'd try to remember that next time Reed acted like a total moron.

Chapter Twenty-Two

NATE

It was time. Nate got quietly out of bed and started to shake Nikko, who was snoring. The guy had nerves of steel, Nate thought. He hadn't been able to sleep at all.

Nikko sat straight up. He looked at Nate with none of his usual sleepiness, swung his legs quietly over the edge of his bed, and grabbed his boots. They had both gone to bed fully dressed. Quietly, they made their way through the dark barracks to the door, boots in hand. When they reached the door, they swung it open slowly, and stood in the quiet hallway for a moment, listening for strains of movement from anywhere. All was quiet. Nikko nodded to Nate, and they walked carefully outside the barracks, staying under the overhang along the walls.

Nikko had pointed out two video surveillance cameras that they needed to steer clear of, and they had plotted their route to avoid those lines of vision, as best as they could. They could be wrong. If they were caught, they were going to plead hungry teenagers in search of a snack. This was convenient, since the route the bus took out of the camp to the bunker was past the kitchens.

Nate's heart was beating fast. Nikko looked at him, and nodded toward the dining hall. They walked through the middle of the camp, through what they hoped was a video blind spot, keeping their eyes peeled for any signs of movement. Their socked feet made almost no sound on the grainy gravel.

They passed the dining hall, and then the kitchen. Now any cover story would be blown. Nikko flashed Nate a grin, and Nate realized Nikko was actually enjoying this. Nate started to relax as they rounded the last corner of the camp. The tall chain-link fence surrounding the camp presented a small problem, but Nate had brought along a set of wire cutters that quickly snipped through some rusted-out links near the bottom where weeds provided natural camouflage, and they were outside the fence.

"Let's go," whispered Nate, as they stuffed their feet into their boots and jogged down the dirt road toward the bunker. It was only a 15-minute bus ride, but it took an hour by foot. By the time they reached the bunker, both were sweating.

"It's midnight. We only have four hours before the sun rises," whispered Nate. "Let's get going."

They dropped into the hatch. Once inside, Nikko pointed toward the surveillance cameras. There were two: one pointed toward the entrance to the bunker and one focused on the keypad security system next to it. Nate held out the laser pointers he had swiped from the lecture hall. They hoped that these lasers were powerful enough to temporarily blind the cameras. All that time they had spent listening to Kraus drone on about his supposed role in the invention of the laser was finally paying off. If what Kraus had told them was correct, the tiny beams of light pointed right at the lens should make the images unreadable.

Nikko took one of the lasers and approached the camera with the laser held out toward the lens. He walked slowly toward the camera, keeping the laser focused tightly on the camera, and Nate did the same. Even if this didn't work, with their hats and uniforms, they would be difficult to distinguish from any other soldier, but Nate had confidence in Kraus's mastery of scientific principles, even if his grasp of morals was questionable.

"That should do it," said Nate after a full minute of pointing the laser at the camera. Nikko turned his attention to the keypad, coded in the numbers he had watched Kraus code in every day, and the bunker unlocked.

Nate opened the door to the control room, where the slumbering machines were humming quietly.

"There aren't any cameras in here, right?" asked Nate, nervously.

"I couldn't find any, but keep your eyes out," was Nikko's not exactly reassuring response.

"Right," said Nate, as they walked quickly down the hall and then down the metal stairs that led into the belly of the bunker.

"So far, no alarms," said Nikko cheerfully.

"At least none that we can hear," muttered Nate.

When they reached the base of the pit of the first warhead, Nikko started pulling tools out of his small backpack. A drill. A long spool of wire. A long metal rod. Gray plasticine. He held the drill out to Nate, who shook his head.

"You do it," he said.

"No, it will be faster if you do the drilling. I'll do the stuffing. I think you want a spot right in the center here," said Nikko, marking an X on the body of the missile where the pit was located.

"What if I miss?" asked Nate.

"You really don't pay attention, do you? You aren't going to trigger a nuclear reaction with this tiny little thing. You need much, much more power to get it going," said Nikko.

"Here goes nothing." Nate drilled a tiny hole in the metal casing.

"Perfect," said Nikko. "You do the next one, while I stuff this one."

"Okay, boss," said Nate.

When Nate had finished drilling all the holes, Nikko handed him the gray plasticine to cover them up. If anyone looked very closely, they could see evidence of tampering. But the holes were tiny, just 3/8 of an inch wide. And with the gray plasticine, practically invisible.

When they were done, they scattered the fine metal dust under the drill holes with their hands. There was so little, Nate couldn't imagine a little scattered dust would cause any concern. Though it was very, very clean down here, he noticed.

"Uh-oh," said Nikko.

"What?" asked Nate, his heart taking up its now-familiar pounding rhythm.

"It's been two hours. We better get outta here." Nikko dumped the tools back into the pack, and they ran up the stairs, and through the control room. The opened the security door just a crack and pointed the lasers at the cameras. They counted to 100, and then climbed up the ladder to the hatch lid, and ran for it. The hatch lid clanked down after them, but they hoped that no one was listening. With adrenalin fueling them, they made it back to camp in 45 minutes, still well before sunrise. They slid along the walls and dashed across open spaces until they were back in their barracks. They headed for the bathroom, where they collapsed on the floor, exhausted but giddy with success.

* * *

"You did what?" Jason didn't seem to understand what Nate was saying.

"Look, we stuck some wires in the–oh, never mind. Nikko could explain it better. He's the genius behind the job. The important thing is that we took the nukes out. They won't explode. It actually took less time than we thought it would."

"What are you still doing there, then?" asked Jason.

"We figure we have a few days before anyone figures out what we did, so we're still working on our exit strategy. It will probably involve C4. Don't believe anyone from the Security Ministry if they come knocking on your door and tell you I died in an accident," said Nate.

"You're going to explode? C4 is crazy stuff." Jason sounded really worried.

"Nah, it's actually pretty stable stuff, until you put a blasting cap on it. We were working with it before they put us into the nuke training. You can play with that stuff like play-doh. Don't worry, we've almost got a plan."

"Just almost?" asked Jason. "You better work fast."

Suddenly a blast of sound interrupted them, blaring over the speakers. Nate got a sick feeling in the pit of his stomach.

"I gotta go!" Nate took off.

"Nate!" yelled Jason, but Nate couldn't stop.

* * *

Nate ran to the barracks to get Nikko and their survival backpacks, which they had packed yesterday. Nikko was, amazingly, still asleep, even with the alarm blasting throughout the entire compound.

"Get up! Get up!" Nate shook Nikko, and grabbed their backpacks. He threw Nikko's shoes at him. "We have to get out of here right now!"

Nikko got out of the bed still half-asleep.

"What is it?" He pulled on his pants over his pajama bottoms, and stuffed his feet into his boots.

"I'm not sure what, but I have a bad feeling about this. We have to get out NOW!"

All around them, people were running around, pulling on their clothes, and trying to figure out what was going on. It was bedlam.

"Back door," Nate pulled Nikko behind him. Once they got outside, Nate pulled his arm and they ran close to the buildings, avoiding people, trying to stay out of sight, and headed towards the forest. Even though it was not quite 5:30 a.m., the sun was up and casting long shadows on the trees. When they hit the woods, they sped up. They weren't sure where they were going, but they were just trying to put as much distance between themselves and the barracks as possible. After running steadily for half an hour, they slowed down, breathing hard. The woods around them were completely quiet.

"I think we did it," said Nate, "I don't hear anyone following us."

"Yeah, well, they probably just figured out we're missing. What if this wasn't about us at all? Now they'll know something is up, when we're not in the line-up. Crap. It's too bad I was still asleep when you got me." Nikko looked annoyed. "How would they know we did anything? It was the middle of the night, and I double-checked all the security stuff. We shouldn't have run. It was probably some new stupid drill."

"I doubt it, but either way, there's no going back." Nate pulled out an old paper map from his backpack. "Let's just take a look. We need to head towards Canada. It's not too far. If we can hitch a ride part of the way, we can get there in couple of days."

"Right, I'm sure there are lots of people passing by who would give us rides out here in the middle of freaking nowhere." Nikko said, still fuming.

"We need to head east," said Nate. Then, off in the distance, he heard the sound of an approaching helicopter.

"Run!" They headed toward a stand of dense bushes.

"Get under, quick!" Nate dove into the bushes, with Nikko right behind. Panting, their hearts beating fast, listening to the helicopter hover over them, Nate whispered, "You still think it was some stupid drill?"

"Sorry I ever doubted you," Nikko whispered back. They tried to flatten themselves against the ground, waiting for the helicopter to pass over.

"I think we're in the clear," Nikko whispered a few minutes after the helicopter had moved on.

"Do you think they'd give up so easily? I bet they'll be back. Let's cover some ground." They took off running again, heading east, keeping to the wooded areas. As nervous as rabbits, they stopped still a few more times when they heard noises of any kind, but especially when they heard the helicopter. Each time, the sounds disappeared after a few minutes.

At one point, Nate stopped Nikko because he thought he heard footsteps following them. They hunkered down in rock crevice, pulled some branches over themselves, and sat, hearts racing, as they heard the crunch-crunch-crunch of steps on the branches and fallen leaves. Even in the summer, the leaf litter crackled. The steps came toward them, slowly, stopping every now and then. They could barely breathe. Nate's brain raced as he thought about whether they would be shot immediately, or whether they'd be taken back for torture and interrogation. Why didn't they pack any weapons? He just hadn't thought of that. There were plenty of weapons he could have grabbed. The steps came closer and closer, shuffling in the leaves. Nate was holding his breath, eyes wide, waiting for the soldiers or whoever was after them to come into sight. As they watched, a large grizzly bear lumbered past them, and a sigh of relief escaped Nikko.

"Shhhhh," Nate shushed Nikko, who was having a hard time containing his relief.

"It may not have an automatic weapon, but it could kill us just the same." Nikko nodded, and put his hands over his mouth, stifling any noise. They watched as the bear stopped to scratch itself, eat some more berries, and then shuffled off. After it was gone, they picked up their packs and kept heading east.

"You should have seen your eyes. I thought they were gonna fall right out of your sockets," Nate teased Nikko.

"You weren't scared at all," Nikko said sarcastically. "Your heart always beats so loud they can hear it in Fairbanks."

"Yeah, okay, I thought I was going to lose it." Nate admitted.

"That totally freaked me out, too. What do you think they would do if they caught us?" asked Nikko.

"The bear?" asked Nate. "Eat us, I guess."

"No, stupid, Colonel Gladov and company," said Nikko.

"Same," said Nate, causing Nikko to crack a smile.

After another hour, they came across the river they had spent so many hours in during training drills. It was not that wide, but they knew from their experience with the river in March and April that it was deep.

"Cross or go down the side?" They leaned over to check the temperature.

"Actually, it's not that bad. Feels a lot better than when we were swimming in March," Nate was sweating from all the running. "I think we have to cross it if we want to get to Canada. Otherwise we'll just go in circles."

"Let's go." They stripped down and stuffed their clothes into their backpacks. Carefully balancing them on their heads, they stepped into the currents. A few feet from the edge, the bottom dropped off, and both boys were swimming.

"This actually feels pretty good," shouted Nikko, holding his backpack above his head as he dog-paddled toward the opposite shore.

"Throw-in!" shouted Nate, and tossed his backpack over his head, like he would a soccer ball, to the opposite shore. It landed with a thud a few feet up the bank. Nikko tried to imitate, but he didn't have Nate's years of experience and his backpack barely made the water's edge.

Nate flicked water toward Nikko. Nikko dove down and pulled Nate's leg until he was under the water too. Suddenly ecstatic at having made their escape, they splashed and horsed around for a few minutes, enjoying the cool water and the afternoon sunshine. The chop-chop sound of a helicopter in the distance interrupted their game. They bolted out of the water, grabbed their packs and ran for cover. After tugging on their clothes under the bushes, they peered up through the bushes. The helicopter banked, and then left abruptly.

"Do you think they saw us?" Nikko wondered.

"Nah," Nate said. "Probably just the end of their shift."

When it became too dark to safely move in the woods, they decided to make camp. They assembled their small tent, and then sat under a rock outcropping, chewing some dried jerky.

"I never thought I would miss our cafeteria dinners," Nikko was chewing laboriously, "I'd rather lick my shoes than eat this. I think I just lost a tooth." Nate smiled, but didn't quite have enough energy to muster a laugh.

"Go to sleep. I'll take a first watch. I'll wake you up in couple of hours."

"Do you think they're still looking?" Nikko was rolling out his sleeping bag.

"They're probably back at the camp. I bet they won't fly at night since they can't see much. But they'll be back tomorrow. Get some sleep, we should get an early start." Nate was exhausted, but knew it would be foolish not to keep watch.

He leaned against the rock, making himself more comfortable. It was a cloudy night. If it rained tomorrow it wouldn't be any fun to hike through, but low visibility would help their escape. Nate stifled a yawn. He thought longingly of his bed. His pillow. It might be a while before they slept in bed again. He was thinking about today. It seemed like they had covered much less ground than they were hoping for.

But then, you can never outrun a helicopter. He was so, so tired. In the dark night, his eyes closed before he realized it.

The sound of dogs barking in the distance jolted Nate awake. He could hear people running, crashing through the woods. He had no idea if he had slept for a few minutes or hours. He jumped up and started to shake Nikko.

"They're coming, Nikko, get up!' He pulled Nikko to his feet and they started running away from the sounds, towards the river, leaving their tent and everything else behind. "They have dogs, we need to get into the river so they lose our scent."

Nate was still holding Nikko's arm trying to help him. The sound of feet running was getting closer.

"Come on, wake up Nikko!" Why did he choose the one guy who was like a zombie when he woke up as his accomplice? He jumped into the cold water, pulling Nikko behind him. They tried to run and then swim towards the other side. This wasn't the same place they had waded through earlier. The river here was deeper and faster. The strong current ripped their hands apart. They were bobbing downstream like twigs. Nate was a strong swimmer, but this force was more than he could handle. He was being jostled about, bumping against rocks, trying to keep his head above water. Nikko's head was bobbing to his left, closer to the middle of the river. Nate wanted to call out to him, but every time he tried, he got a mouthful of water. He was trying to swim out of the current to the other side of the river where ferns and bushes provided at least some cover.

Then there were shouts along the riverbank, dogs barking, people running. A blinding spotlight shined over the water. Then a voice:

"Come out with your hands up! We know what you did!" It was Gladov on a megaphone. Nate's blood ran cold. He was almost on the other side, partially hidden by dense tree trunks at the water's edge.

"If you don't come out immediately, we will shoot you," said a higher, but extremely angry voice. Was that Kraus? Through his waterlogged ears, he thought it might be. So they knew. They knew that Nikko and Nate weren't just runaways. He heard a shot. Then another. They were firing.

"C'mon Nikko! Come on!" Nate yelled when he managed to hang onto a low growing tree trunk. A barrage of bullets hit the water, splashing noisily. Nate pulled himself almost all the way from the water, concealed by the darkness and the vegetation.

He heard another volley of shots, a piercing scream, and then Nikko's head was gone, under water. Nate scanned the water in the silence that followed the bullets, but he couldn't see Nikko's head. Where was he? He could hear the faint buzz of conversation across the river, and the static of a two-way radio. The spotlight shined where Nikko had been. In the weak light of early dawn, he could just make out a dark streak blossoming in the water.

Nikko was hit. Nate frantically scanned the river, looking for signs of him. The sharp "ping" of a shot stopped him, as it bounced off the dirt just a yard away. The spotlight swung in his direction, blinding him. He pulled back behind a tree trunk.

Another barrage of bullets hit the ground and water all around him, showering him with pinpricks of water and mud, but he was lucky. He saw only one way out of this. He slid slowly into the water, trying not to splash, and went under, letting the river drag him downstream. He stayed under for as long as he could, holding his breath until he thought he might explode. He breached the surface as quietly as he could and took a slow breath. He could still hear voices, and then gunfire. He could see the spotlight scanning the riverbank. Nate went under again, drifting in the fast currents. He repeated this maneuver 10 more times before he allowed himself to raise his head completely above the water. This time he couldn't see anyone or hear anything. No dogs, no helicopter, no people, just the gentle whoosh of the river.

He pulled himself out of the river, and sat, winded, on the riverbank. He was dripping wet. What now? He had nothing. He had no backpack, no food, no water, no map, and no Nikko.

He scanned the river again. No sign of Nikko. He hoped Nikko was alive, somewhere downriver. But, he had to face the possibility that Nikko had probably been shot. And in this water, wounded, losing blood, he probably was dying, unless he had been lucky enough to die quickly.

It felt unreal, like a nightmare. If he hadn't fallen asleep, maybe they could have gotten away. His stomach was heaving. He emptied himself out and collapsed in the mud. He was alone.

They would find him if he stayed in one place. Exhausted as he was, he knew he had to keep moving. At least he had ended up on the other side of the river. He picked himself up, and stumbled off in the direction of the hills, tripping over the rocky ground.

Chapter Twenty-Three

REED

The door to the study opened, and group of five men and two women in smart dark suits walked out, with Reed's dad following them. Reed was watching their reflection in the bathroom mirror, which, if you sat on the edge of the tub, gave you a perfect view of the door.

Yeah, my bathroom Spy Center, Reed smirked to himself as he glanced at the nearby toilet. Where you can spy while 'taking care' of business.

He'd have to remember to tell Cassie and Jason that one. Reed's mind flashed to his pony-tailed, long-legged teammate, and he immediately shook his head to derail that train of thought. He had to stop thinking about her. Pretending to not notice her was getting harder and harder. Sam and Max seemed to be picking up on something, and were teasing him more and more about her.

His attention turned back to the group: The President, the Vice-President, the Minister of Games, the Secretary of State, the Media Secretary, some small squirrelly guy with funny looking glasses he had never seen before, and a tall military guy who walked like he had something permanently lodged up his butt. And then his dad. They were all walking down the corridor. The squirrely guy cracked some joke, and the rest of them actually laughed. These guys were planning a nuclear war and they were cracking jokes? Reed stood up from the edge of the tub and stretched his aching back. Hmm, if this was going to be his spy center, some major improvements to comfort would have to be made. He looked at himself in the mirror above the sink. Intense blue eyes with dark circles were staring back at him. Tired, but still handsome. Ha! If only Cassie would notice. He splashed his face with cold water.

Reed waited a couple more minutes before heading back down to his room, where he had left a videogame going on automatic play. He could overhear conversation from his room, but he didn't recognize some of the voices. That seemed important, so when it sounded like they were getting ready to leave, he headed to his lookout spot again.

Afterwards, he wished he hadn't. He wasn't sure what do about what he overheard. It seemed that Jason's brother and his brother's friend had been shot while attempting to escape the training camp. The President was livid when somebody from the group recounted the whole story. Now Reed knew it was the something-lodged-up-his-butt guy in uniform. The President didn't exactly yell at him, but his voice was pretty chilling when he threatened grave consequences unless the "situation" was fixed quickly. They agreed that the official story would be that the boys had drowned in a river during a training exercise. They would tell the families it was a training accident. Eventually. But not now. Probably not for months.

Reed knew there was no way he could keep this to himself. Jason needed to be told that his brother had died, and it sounded like he had done something to sabotage the weapons, so Jason should be proud. But hell would have to freeze over before Reed would be the one to tell him. It's not like Jason was his best buddy or anything, but Reed still remembered all too well the pain of losing his mom, and he didn't wish that on anybody. After their conversation in Jason's room, Reed decided that he was actually a pretty good guy. Even if he guarded Cassie like a well-trained Rottweiler.

But the good news in this horrible situation–the really amazing news–was that the nukes were all "compromised," whatever that meant, and it was going to take months for the military guy and the squirrely guy to figure out if they could still be used. But the military guy didn't sound hopeful, and the squirrely guy reminded Reed of Gollum in *The Hobbit*. He half-expected the guy to refer to the nukes as his "precious," since he had sounded so in love with them. What a wacko.

Reed had no idea what Nate and Nikko had done to the nukes, but whatever they did was really clever and had totally caught the military guy off-guard and looking like an idiot. He could tell he was embarrassed to have been outsmarted by a pair of teenagers. The bad news for him and the rest of the team was, that now that Plan A was out, there would be even more pressure on them to win. The even worse news was that the President was willing to go to great lengths now to ensure their win, and it sounded like there would be some serious dirty pool going on. That really pissed Reed off. This was *his* chance to win the Tournament fair and square. He thought they could win without any outside "help." But this was well beyond a soccer game now. It always had been, Reed realized.

Fifteen minutes later, when his father knocked on his door after his guests had all left, Reed couldn't control himself. He didn't even pretend he didn't know what was going on.

"How could you all be so stupid?" He blasted at his father before he had even come all the way into his room. "What are you trying to do? Start another war?"

Reed's father closed the door. He opened his mouth. And then closed it.

"Yeah, I overheard, okay? This wasn't the first time. I know what the President is plotting. And I can't believe you're going along with it," Reed was disgusted with his father.

"Reed," his dad said, in a calm voice. "You're too young to understand. I'm sorry, I don't mean to belittle you, but it's the truth. The President only wants what's best for Alaska. He wants to bring our country more opportunities and more resources, like food so that no one has to go hungry. Reed, over 50 percent of our population lives under the poverty level. You can't even imagine, you've never lacked for anything, but people are dying every day. Even after all those years, most of the soil is still contaminated. Our people deserve more. The U.S. was one of the most powerful countries in the world before the War. We led the world in all things. And look at us now. Other countries, like China, took advantage of our moment of weakness and stacked the deck in their favor. We have every right to get some of that back. He's been trying to negotiate with them for years."

"Oh, wait. So you think the way to do it is to start another war? Yeah, let's kill off whatever population remained and genius, no more poverty problem, right? You can't really believe that?" Reed was shocked to hear what came out of his father's mouth. "Seriously, Dad? Don't you remember what it was like? What about Mom? She died because someone like him put his finger on the button and blew up half the world and poisoned the other half!"

Reed looked at his father, and saw him for the first time as an old man. He was past 50, now, and the radiation had obviously taken a toll on his health. Reed had outgrown his father by a couple of inches, thanks to the drugs, and was strong from all the training. His father looked worn down and tired. He was standing close to Reed, rubbing his eyes and face.

"Reed, nobody wants to start a war. You just need to win the Tournament and everything will be fine. And that's what we'll focus on now. You winning. You have our full support. Life isn't simple. There's not always a right and a wrong. Sometimes there are gray areas, and you have to choose the best option out of some bad choices."

Reed started to interrupt, but his dad held up a finger signaling him to wait. With great effort, Reed kept his mouth shut.

"Look, Reed, this is not something you need to worry about. You need to focus on playing in the Tournament and beating Canada. The game against Albania showed us what they've got, and they're a serious threat, Reed. Regardless of what the President's plans are, you have a duty to your country to do your best. And if you need help doing your best, I'll see to it that you get it. We will all see to it. You just let me know what you need. Are we clear?"

Reed nodded.

"The rest of this is none of your concern. Let me worry about this. I promise you, everything will turn out fine. And don't listen at doors anymore, okay?"

"Okay, Dad, whatever." Reed looked at his dad. The man who raised him, who had been his mom and dad, and sometimes his best friend. What happened to him? Where did he disappear to? Did he really think everything would be okay if the President bombed the heck out of China or Brazil? This did not sound like the father he had grown up with, the guy who told him countless times how important it was to know right from wrong, and to take action when you see wrong. If someone had just taken action to stop that crazy prime minister, he always said, we would all be living entirely different lives. And here it was, his opportunity to do something, and he was just going to let it slide.

His father left, closing the door behind him. Reed checked that his alarm was set, turned off the light, and lay on his bed in the dark trying to figure out what his father could be thinking. His father may say there's no right and wrong on this one, but to Reed, the right and wrong were right there, staring him in the face.

Take a player out physically in a game: Right. Take a team out through food poisoning: Wrong. Simple. Stop another nuclear war: Right. Not do everything in your power to prevent another nuclear war: Wrong. Simple.

Reed propped his head on the pillow. He was thinking about Jason and his twin. Somebody would have to tell him the truth. Maybe he could tell Cassie and she could tell Jason. That would give him an excuse to get Cassie alone, which he had to admit was pretty appealing, even though it would be awful. And Cassie had to be the one to tell Jason. They were close friends. Just friends, though, Jason had been very clear. She would know how to do it. He would have to find Cassie tomorrow.

Chapter Twenty-Four

NATE

Nate spent part of the day hiding in a shallow cave close to the river. Curled up in the shadows, he was wet and cold, but he hadn't wanted to start a fire in case it gave him away. Who was he kidding? He couldn't start a fire even if he wanted to. His backpack, tent, food and matches were miles upstream, if they hadn't been taken by the search teams. He really wished he had watched those survivalist shows that Jason loved so much, instead of spending his down-time reading. Jason would probably know how to start a fire with rocks or something, but Nate was clueless. He was shivering from his damp clothes, and his teeth were starting to chatter. It would be much warmer in the sun, but he was scared to venture out. He hadn't heard any helicopters or search teams in hours. If he didn't get his butt moving soon, he would probably freeze to death.

Nate sat up, and moved into the bright afternoon sunshine. That was better. He took stock of his situation: Nikko was gone, probably badly injured or possibly dead. He had no supplies. He didn't know where he was or where he was going. A hopeless situation.

He closed his eyes and turned his face toward the sun. The woods around him were quiet, the silence broken only by the occasional bird call. The sun seared into his closed eyelids. He was alive. He was tired, cold, bruised, and scratched, but not badly injured. Nikko might be alive.

Nate decided to take a chance and go back to see if there were any signs of Nikko and their supplies. He started moving back towards the river, his senses on high alert. The woods were quiet. Late afternoon sun bathed everything around him in warm orange colors. It seemed like such a nice, normal day. It was hard to believe it was just a few hours ago that people were shooting at him, and he had been close to drowning. Nate started to jog up the river, hoping he could find their camp before it got dark. Since the sun didn't set until around 10, he had some time, but he had no idea how far he might have drifted downstream.

After a few hours, he thought he recognized some landmarks. A funny rock here, a bend in the river there, but it was hard to know. Then he saw patches of sand along the other side of the river that were all torn up, grasses flattened, paw prints and footprints all over the place. The quiet was odd, after the commotion and terror of last night. He stared at the spot, looking for signs of any soldiers or guards, but all he could hear was the occasional bird song. They were gone.

He found their camp from last night. Their tent was gone. So were their sleeping bags. The dirt was pockmarked with bootprints. The rock outcropping was deserted. He could survive without a sleeping bag and tent, but the backpacks would be key. Nate slowly approached the cluster of trees about 100 yards from their camp where they had hung the packs on a high branch. After they met the bear yesterday,

Nate had enough sense to store the food away up high, in case that bear or any of its friends were in the neighborhood.

Yes! The backpacks were hanging on the tree, hidden by the thick green leaves. Nate felt a glimmer of hope. He climbed up the tree, grabbed the backpacks and tossed them down.

His first order of business was to peel off his wet, torn, sweaty, smelly clothes and put on some warmer clothes and dry socks. That felt so much better. His boots were mostly dry, but he had blisters from his wet socks rubbing against his boots. He wasn't sure what to do with his clothes, so he decided to throw them in the river, and hope that the dogs or the search teams would be thrown off track. In the water's reflection, he could see that his face was covered with streaks of dried blood mingled with dirt. With his wet t-shirt, he tried to clean it off. Ouch. He had a pretty deep cut above his left eyebrow. Probably from his face hitting a rock in the river last night. The cut started bleeding again as he cleaned it. He rummaged through the packs, and found some antibiotic cream and a bandage. He covered it as well as he could. At least the blood stopped dripping down his face. The next order of business was food. Nate dug into the depths of the backpack, but all he could find was some jerky. They had meant to pack more food. He gnawed on the hard sticks as he headed back to the river. He decided to follow the river downstream until it got dark, and look for any sign of Nikko.

Nate stayed in the underbrush, but every so often he would go out to the river to see if there was any trace of his friend in the clumps of grasses or piles of rocks. When it got to be twilight, he decided to stop. There was no sign of Nikko. He gathered some fallen branches and built a little shelter, big enough to stretch under and sleep. He was too tired to think. He covered himself with Nikko's spare clothing and fell asleep instantly.

* * *

He woke up suddenly, not knowing why. It was very early morning. With green rolling hills, blue sky, and snow-covered mountains, it was another picture postcard day. Nate got out of his shelter and stretched his bruised, exhausted body. Off in the distance, he could hear a noise. He stood up, totally alert. It didn't sound like a search team—no running, dogs, people yelling to each other. No helicopters or airplanes overhead. It sounded like gravel. Or wheels on gravel. Was that a cow? Nate picked up both backpacks, scattered the branches of his shelter, and crept quietly toward the noise to see what it was. In couple of minutes, he came across a road. He had no idea his camp was that close to a road—he didn't remember a road from the map.

Well, calling it a road might be an overstatement, Nate thought as he looked down a narrow strip of pavement pockmarked with patches of weeds and summer wildflowers. Coming towards him was the strangest procession he had ever seen. Horses and oxen were pulling old-fashioned covered wagons that looked a lot like what he remembered from history videos. There were some men and women on horseback, and some kids running alongside the wagons.

Nate had the bizarre feeling that he had somehow walked into the middle of a documentary movie about Alaska's pioneers. Except there didn't seem to be any cameras or directors. If he could blend in with this group, he might be able to give the search teams the slip. As the group approached, Nate decided it was his only chance. He walked into the middle of the road, and approached a guy on horseback who seemed to be leading it. The whole caravan of people, animals, and carts stopped.

"Hi, my name is Nate. I was on a school survival camping trip and I got lost," he said with what he hoped was a convincingly innocent smile. "I feel so stupid."

"Hi Nate, I'm Shaun." He was a middle-aged guy wearing a floppy hat. "Well, as rotten luck goes, yours is not so bad. We're probably the only people to pass this way in 30 years. Where're you headed?"

"Fairbanks," Nate said without thinking. "My, uh, school is in Fairbanks. I think they left the area without me, so I think I should just head back there." Without Nikko, he had to find Jason.

"Well, you can tag along with us. We're headed that direction. We'll pass by the outskirts of Fairbanks in a few days, if the weather holds. A few of us will go into the city to get supplies, while the rest camp out, so you can go with them. You hungry?" Shaun took Jason's two packs and chucked them into the nearest wagon. People were looking at Nate curiously. Shaun made an announcement to the whole group.

"This is Nate. He got separated from his school group and we're going to take him back to Fairbanks. Margie, could you get the boy some food? Let's go everyone." The wagons started to move again.

"Well, go get some food from Margie, over there in that wagon," Shaun pointed to a tall, thin woman with long brown braids, who was holding a large bag that appeared to be full of odd-shaped loaves of bread. He grinned at Nate. "Don't worry, kid, we've got you covered."

"Okay, then. Thanks." Nate headed over to Margie, who pulled out a roll from her bag. He grabbed it, and then swung himself into the wagon with her.

Margie looked at him with an appraising eye.

"I think you're going to need a little more than bread," she said. She pointed to an older couple in the wagon.

"This is Jim, and this is Jan," she said. Like everyone else Nate had seen, they were sun-browned and wiry. They appeared to be taking some kind of inventory, as Jan had a checklist in front of her, and Jim seemed to be counting melons. There were supplies stacked on all sides: sacks of potatoes, barrels of apples, pears, corn, cucumbers, tomatoes, some smoked meats hanging from the wagon's ceiling, and a variety of other containers.

"This is Nate," said Margie. "He's joining us for a while. He got lost on a school trip, and he's hungry." Jan patted the floor beside her, where she had a large metal pot.

"Starving," said Nate, his mouth salivating at the smell coming from the pot. "All I've eaten for past two days is beef jerky." Jim looked him up and down, while Jan found a metal cup and a spoon, and spooned some still-warm stew.

"Beef jerky's better than nothing, but you need some real food. Looks like you've been through a lot, given the state of you," said Jim.

"Well, I ran across this big grizzly bear," explained Nate.

"You'll have to tell me about it sometime," said Jim, sitting down next to him.

Nate was in heaven. He hadn't eaten anything so good in the last ten years. His mom used to make delicious beef stew when they were kids. Jim and Jan watched as he inhaled the stew.

"That was delicious," he said, when he came up for air. Jan smiled at him.

"It's an old family recipe. Seconds?" she said.

"Oh yes, please," said Nate, handing back the cup.

"When you're done, I'd like to take a look at some of your cuts, son." Jim started rummaging around near the back of the wagon.

"Jim's a doctor," said Jan.

"Where are you all going?" Nate asked, in between mouthfuls.

"Well, some government guys came into town a few weeks ago, and told us we had to leave our town. They told us they had detected some dangerous radiation levels in the town. They said they had some apartments that we could move into in Fairbanks, but we just aren't really town people." Jan frowned, and Jim was shaking his head.

"So you just left?" said Nate.

"We didn't have much choice," said Jim.

Nate thought it was strange, but he didn't ask any more. They weren't asking too many questions of him, and he thought he'd return the favor. He finished his food and sighed contentedly. Then he felt guilty. Nikko should be here with him. He would have loved the stew.

When he was done, Jim said, "Come over here into the light, so I can get a better look at your eye. Looks like you're lucky you still have an eye."

Nate went to the back edge of the wagon, where bright mid-morning sunshine was streaming in. Jim dabbed some antibiotic cream on the scratches on his arms and legs, before turning to the bandage over his eyebrow. He carefully peeled it off, and then cleaned it out, which made Nate squirm. It hurt. Finally, he closed the wound with a butterfly bandage.

"That probably should get some stitches," said Jim, "But I'm not going to try that on the back of a moving horse-cart. Maybe if we stop. If not, you'll just look like a dangerous character for the rest of your days." Nate grinned at him.

After Jim had finished, Nate thanked Jan again for the stew, and jumped out of the wagon. He found Shaun sitting in the front of the first wagon, holding the reins of two huge brown draft horses.

"So where are you guys going?" he asked.

"South," said Shaun. Nate sat beside Shaun, and found himself relaxing. Shaun was an easy person to talk to. Nate asked him about their town, and learned that it had been founded after the war by a group of survivalists who wanted nothing more to do with the politics of the outside world. And over the years, the town had grown into a pretty sizeable and self-sufficient community. But now, being kicked out of their home, they were looking for a new place to live. Shaun and his group were going as far south as they could get before winter started to hit them, and after the winter, they would keep going. This was the first set of wagons, but there were a dozen others a week behind them that they would meet up with at the border. They seemed like people out of one of Nate's books from pioneer times.

"Why wagons?" asked Nate.

"Do you see any gas stations around here?" joked Shaun. "We have no idea what lies south of here, but from the satellite images, there doesn't seem to be much," he continued.

By noon, he had met about half the group, and even tossed a football with some of the older boys as they ran ahead.

"You look wiped," said one of the boys, a tall, skinny kid named Jared, who seemed to be about his age.

"I'm pretty beat," Nate admitted.

"Why don't you go take a nap? The third wagon is where we packed all the sheets and towels. Makes for pretty good sleeping," said Jared, pushing him in the direction of the wagon.

"You don't have to tell me twice," said Nate, and soon found himself dropping off to sleep to the gentle rock of a horse-drawn wagon.

Nate woke with a start. The wagon had stopped, and the sun seemed to be low in the sky. He must have slept all day. He heard voices murmuring, and then people walking by the wagons.

"No, there's just sheets and linens in this one," he heard Shaun's voice saying.

"We'll just take a look anyway," said a gruff voice.

"Go right ahead," Shaun sounded unconcerned.

"Dad!" Was that Jared's voice?

Nate rolled himself into the far left corner of the wagon, and flattened himself along edge, hoping that the piles of linens would shield him from view. He heard the wagon flaps being pushed aside, and then saw the beam of a flashlight bouncing around the inside of the wagon. He knew he should probably duck his head, but he was afraid to move in case movement attracted attention. He had sudden sympathy for animals that froze in headlights.

The flashlight moved on, and then the flaps were closing. He heard footsteps receding. Nate let out a sigh of relief.

A few moments later, Jared's head popped in.

"Nate!" he whispered.

"Yeah?" Nate whispered back.

Jared climbed over the piles to where Nate was still lying flat against the side.

"Good job hiding. I tried to tell Dad, but it was too late before I realized what was going on. Sorry."

"Luckily, I heard people coming in time to roll in here," said Nate.

"They have pictures of you and some other kid they're showing around. And they warned us that you're mentally ill, delusional and probably dangerous. Made it sound like you escaped from some kind of mental institution." Nate took that in.

"Did you?" Jared asked, after a few moments.

"Did I what?" asked Nate.

"Did you escape from a mental institution?" Jared asked.

"Uh, no. No, I did not. There were definitely crazy people there, but it wasn't a mental institution. Though you would probably think I was delusional and dangerous if I told you, so that was a pretty good cover story." Nate planted his face in the sheets. Then looked up at Jared. "If they found me, I think they might kill me."

"Why would they kill you?" asked Jared.

Nate decided to tell Jared what was happening. He needed to tell someone about Nikko. It felt like a heavy weight he'd been carrying. And, if Nikko was still alive and Jared's group spotted him, Jared would know who he was and would keep him safe.

The wagons had started rolling again. Nate had made it past the checkpoint. Jared and Nate made themselves comfortable on piles of towels, and talked as the sun went down.

Chapter Twenty-Five

CASSIE

It was an early morning and Cassie was in the gym, juggling the ball. Left foot, left foot, head, chest, right foot. 83, 84, 85…the ball was bouncing off her body flawlessly. This came so naturally to her, she didn't even have to think about it. Her mind was free to wander while her body was in the total control of the ball. It was a good thing, too, because her head was still reeling from what she had heard last night. She tried to keep her attention on the ball, and relax, but she kept coming back to the bleak look in Reed's eyes.

It has been late and she was in her PJs, ready for bed, when she heard a soft knock on her door. Jason? She stole a quick look at herself in the mirror before she opened the door.

She stopped at her door startled.

"Reed? What do you want?" She didn't mean to sound so snippy, but seeing him at that time of the night was unexpected. Reed never came to her room unless she or Jason specifically invited him.

Reed scanned the empty corridor and said quietly,

"We need to talk. Can I come in?"

Cassie held the door firmly between them.

"It's really late. You can't come in. Can't it wait until tomorrow?"

"No, it can't. It's about Jason's brother. Are you sure you want to talk out here?" She looked at him skeptically. He looked serious.

"You should've told me that to begin with," she muttered as she moved aside. Reed glanced both ways down the corridor and walked in, closing the door behind him. Cassie pulled a sweatshirt over her tank top and sat down on her bed, looking at Reed expectantly.

"You wanted to talk, so talk. What's going on?"

Reed sat down on the bed. He seemed awkward.

"Listen, I don't even know where to start or how to say it, but... Jason's brother is dead."

"What?" Cassie looked at his face. "Reed, if this is your idea of joke, I will never, never talk to you again, I swear," she said.

Reed looked at her and for once he didn't look all cocky and self-assured. He recounted the whole story of what he had overheard at his house. About Nate and Nikko being shot while escaping the military base. About them disabling the nukes. About the President's Plan B. He even told her about speaking with his dad, but getting nowhere. Cassie was shocked. Reed came to tell *her* first, asking for *her* advice. Reed, asking what to do. That thought just didn't apply to any universe she lived in. She asked questions and he answered what he could, but when he finally left her room an hour later, she felt shocked and confused. Nate was dead. Dead. Jason had no idea and somebody needed to tell him what happened.

Reed had been clear that he wasn't going to do it. She had been mad at him at first, but then it wasn't like Reed was Jason's friend. And she saw his point that she should be the one to tell him. After all, Jason was her friend, her really good friend. She had probed her feelings last night to see if there was more there. But no, he was just a friend, as if that 'just' was limiting instead of the opposite. Really, it should be 'just' a boyfriend—friends lasted a lot longer in her experience. Jason needed to know and she had to man up and tell him.

Last night she had been ready to do it, but as the morning progressed, her resolve was waning away. She kept juggling her ball, trying to relax.

Fifteen minutes later, Jason walked in, an easy grin on his face.

"Cass, here you are! I went to your room to wake you up, but it looks like you have been here for a bit. What's the count?"

"4, 5, 6," she said, catching the ball after six and grinning at him.

"Yeah, right, more like 404, 405, 406... am I right?" He teased her, as usual, and Cassie's heart felt like breaking. Should she tell him here? Now? The next chance she would have alone with him in the privacy of one of their rooms would be late tonight. She had to tell him sooner. She should tell him now. She noticed she was juggling again—she had dropped the ball on her feet while she was thinking, and her feet just took over.

"So, I wanted to talk to Prince Charming last night, but he wasn't in his room. Have you seen him? I wonder if he heard anything new," Jason asked, juggling his own ball next to her. He could make it to a couple hundred, but nothing like Cassie.

Cassie startled and dropped the ball. It bounced away, and she just let it go. She watched until it stopped at a corner of the gym, then she turned to look at Jason, who was concentrating on keeping his ball from bouncing out of control off his knees.

"You just need to use a little less power," she couldn't help saying. "Just keep it low, and you'll keep it under control."

"Yeah, I know, I just like to see how much power," Jason paused here to take a few steps to catch a high-bouncing ball with his toes, and get it back under control, "I can…" and the ball started to career away again, causing Jason to lunge after it, "use and still keep it …" he paused again to control the ball, "under control." And here the ball bounced away into the corner of the gym where Cassie's ball had gone. As they walked over to retrieve the balls, Cassie decided she had to get this over with. Like ripping off a Band-Aid. She looked around the gym. It was still early, and only a few kids were there. Reed wasn't. Anton was in goal, working against the automatic shooter that sent balls flying toward him at regular intervals. The light above him flashed a green 93%, a great blocking percentage. It was as good a time as any, she guessed.

"I saw Reed last night. He came by my room," she said.

"Oh really? I didn't know you two were so close," Jason's voice had a funny edge to it.

"We're not!" Cassie snapped.

"Fine. Whatever. So what did he want?"

Cassie took a deep breath.

"Jason, I need to tell you something and I'm really sorry. It's about Nate," she whispered. Jason looked at her in surprise.

"What about him?" he asked.

"There was another meeting at Reed's house two days ago. Everybody was there. The President, the Vice President and that guy from Nate's camp. You know—Gladov."

"So, what about Nate?"

"They shot them." Cassie's voice was barely a whisper. "Nate and Nikko. They were trying to escape the camp and they shot them. They're both dead," she said, tears streaming down her face.

Jason was standing there, totally still. He closed his eyes for a brief moment. Cassie wanted to do something, anything to make it better, to give him some comfort. She put her arms around him.

"Jason," she whispered into his shirt, "I am so sorry. So incredibly sorry."

Cassie was holding her breath, waiting for Jason to say something. Suddenly Jason pulled back.

"I don't believe it," he said. "No. It's not true!" he shouted as he pushed Cassie away from him.

"Shhh!" Cassie grabbed his arm, and pulled him close again. She looked behind him, to see if anyone had noticed Jason's outburst, but Anton was focused on the ball-shooter. Across the gym, she saw Max, Sam and Reed coming in. Jason noticed her eyes looking across the gym and followed her gaze. Reed started kicking balls at Anton. Max and Sam quickly joined in, making it impossible for Anton to keep an eye on the ball-shooter and the barrage of other balls coming at him. His score went from 95% to 54% in a matter of seconds, flashing red above him. Jason turned back to Cassie.

"Look, Cassie, Nate warned me this might happen. He said they would try to make it look like they died in some explosion or something. He said not to panic if I hear they're dead. It was just their exit strategy, that's all. He's not dead. I would know. I would just know. Nate isn't dead." Jason was almost shouting at the end.

"Okay, okay. Keep it down. You're probably right. But you need to calm down."

"I'm going to talk to Reed. I need to hear everything. Every. Single. Word." Jason turned on his heels and stomped across the gym toward Reed.

Cassie wiped her eyes on the back of her sleeve. Well, that went well. She was tired. Monumentally tired. Drained. Maybe Jason was right. Maybe it was an exit strategy. Those two guys were smart enough to disarm nukes, why not stage their own death? If Nate had warned Jason not to believe any rumors of his death, maybe he was alive. She kicked away her ball, picked up her sweatshirt, and followed her friend.

Chapter Twenty-Six

NATE

Nate woke to the sounds of roosters crowing. Roosters? Where was he? He sat up, looked around at the inside of the covered wagon, and remembered. He was with Shaun's group. Jared was sleeping next to him.

Nate got out of his borrowed sleeping bag quietly, and headed to the wagon opening. He sat on the edge and looked around. A few people were up, and the chickens were pecking the ground in a makeshift pen. The wagons were neatly arranged in a wide circle in a clearing off the road, with some tents set up in the middle near the remains of a large campfire. The sun was rising over the trees, and it looked like it would be another hot, sunny summer day.

Today some of the group would be heading into town. Fairbanks was a detour from their route, which was following the Yukon River to Canada, where the group hoped to settle. But they needed some additional supplies, and it was the only place they could get them. They had stopped about 10 miles outside Fairbanks for the night. Getting into Fairbanks would only take an hour or so, Shaun had said. That was the easy part, thought Nate. Shaun and a few others were going in to do the shopping, and then Nate would leave them and head for the stadium where Jason had told him the team practiced in the afternoons. Nate was nervous about being recognized, but Fairbanks was a fairly big town—about 200,000 people—and with the Tournament in town, that population probably doubled.

Nate hopped down from the wagon, and headed over to the campfire, where Jan was stirring the contents of a large metal pot. Jim, Shaun, and several other adults were up, drinking coffee and chatting. After he told Jared his story, Jared convinced him to tell Shaun. It had really helped to tell them about Gladov and Kraus, the nukes and Nikko. Shaun seemed less surprised that he would have expected, and mentioned that people in the town had noticed unusual activity in the area and suspected something was going on. Shaun had then gotten out his two-way radio and contacted the other group that was following them, telling them to keep a lookout for any signs of Nikko. Every time he heard the crackle of the radio, he was hoping for some news. But the last two days had passed without any reports, and now they were getting close to Fairbanks.

"Hi Nate, how'd you sleep?" Shaun asked, as he was going through an inventory and updating a list of supplies.

"Like a log," said Nate. Nate looked at Shaun's radio, but Shaun just shook his head.

"Coffee?" asked Jan, holding out a steaming mug.

"Thanks," said Nate. While he was doing soccer training, coffee had been prohibited, along with all other caffeinated beverages. He had avoided it at first at the training camp, but after Nikko had showed him how to fix it up with lots of milk and sugar, Nate had gotten into the habit of having coffee in the morning.

"Breakfast will be ready in a few minutes. Then we'll have to be on our way," said Shaun.

"What time do you want to be out of Fairbanks?" asked Jim. They stood around drinking coffee and talking about what needed to be done. Nate drank his coffee and listened. It was interesting to hear what they had to say about which shops to check for rope, tarps, smoked meats, and fresh, radiation-free vegetables. The group was discussing the merits of axes versus machetes, when Jared came up behind Nate, and offered him a bowl of oatmeal with raisins and brown sugar.

"Thanks," said Nate, and dug in.

Jared sat down on a log and started in on his own bowl. Nate noticed Jared's bowl was more like a mixing bowl than a regular cereal bowl. Jared noticed him staring.

"Well, there aren't that many cereal bowls and I always go back for seconds and thirds, so Jan just figured she'd save time," he grinned. They ate in companionable silence for a few minutes, listening to the grown-ups, who had moved on to debating where they might be able to find some two-way radios.

"So, what's your plan?" asked Jared, still scooping out mounds of oatmeal.

"I'm going to find a way to get into the stadium. My brother should be there this afternoon. It's a good thing they have a strict training schedule, or I wouldn't know where to find them."

"That's so cool that your twin brother's on the National team. When I was little, I really, really wanted to play on the team. I spent, like, a million hours practicing shots. I guess all little kids in Alaska want to. Those guys are serious celebrities. Plus, all those sweet benefits—the extra food coupons and school and stuff. Must have sucked when you didn't make it, huh?" Jared said sympathetically

"I had this knee injury, so I knew I wouldn't make it," explained Nate. "Up until last year, I probably would have. But yeah, it sucked. And then when they sent me to this strategic training camp, I was glad. At least I wouldn't be going home in disgrace. Boy, was I wrong," laughed Nate.

"Nah, you weren't wrong. If you hadn't gone there, who knows what would have happened. You and Nikko might have actually prevented a war, you know?" It sounded crazy to Nate, to hear Jared put it like that.

"Yeah, but I'm the reason that Nikko is probably dead. The whole thing was my idea. He wanted to stay out of it," said Nate quietly, looking down at the ground.

"No. You did the right thing. Look Nate, anyone can go along with what other people tell them to do. It takes real guts to stand up for what you believe in and risk your life for what you think is right. And that's what you and Nikko did. And besides, Nikko might be alive. You don't know for sure," said Jared.

"I keep trying to remember what I saw that night. They were shooting at us. It was dark, and there were dogs barking and people yelling. But I know I saw Nikko go under and I never saw him come up. And I looked for him, and I kept looking, but I never saw any trace of him," said Nate.

"But you don't know for sure," persisted Jared.

"Yeah," said Nate, unconvinced. "Anyway, we need to get going."

Shaun looked up, and walked over to Nate and Jared.

"What's up, boys?" Shaun asked, joining them on the logs they were using as makeshift chairs.

"Are we about ready to go?" asked Nate.

"Before we go, Nate, I want to say something to you. Just hear me out. I think you should consider coming with us. It's up to you, of course, but it would be safer. If the President finds out you're alive, well, you might not to be able to maintain that condition," said Shaun, with a smile that belied the seriousness of what he was saying.

"But," started Nate.

"Before you say anything, think about it. You've seen who we are and you know where we're going. It would be a better life for you. You'd be safe with us. And when this all blows over, you can come back and get your brother. Maybe we could even find way to get word to him that you're okay."

"So what do you think?" asked Jared.

Nate was quiet. He pushed his spoon around his empty bowl, scrapping the last little bits of oatmeal off the sides into a neat pile in the middle. The idea of going somewhere new where he wouldn't have to hide was tempting. But then he thought about Jason.

"I wish I could," he finally said. "But I have to go find Jason. I can't leave him alone in this."

"If you change your mind," continued Shaun, "just follow the Yukon River south. That's where we'll be."

"Thanks," said Nate. "I'll keep it in mind."

* * *

After he said his goodbyes and thanks to Jared and Shaun at a grocery store, Nate headed toward the concession area near the stadium. He bought an Alaska soccer team hat and sunglasses with some money Shaun had given him. It was not going to be easy to get in. There were security guards at every gate. Nate looked for a loading entrance, someplace with trucks bringing supplies into the stadium. Maybe he could hide in a delivery truck. That always seemed to work in the movies.

After some time, Nate was starting to get anxious. How could he get in? And if he couldn't get in, where would he sleep? The Fairbanks police didn't have a reputation for kindness, so sleeping in a park or under a bridge was a sure way to get into trouble. His skin crawled just thinking about it. He realized that even though he'd been training here for most of his life, he didn't have a friend or teacher or anyone that he knew in Fairbanks. No one he could ask for help.

Finally, he saw his chance. There was a group of tourists from Argentina going toward the gate. It was a big group, and they were all wearing soccer team hats like his. Nate casually attached himself to the back of the group, and walked toward the gate with them. They were busy chatting with each other, and didn't seem to notice him. The guard was counting the people in the group as they went in, and checking them off. Nate hoped he couldn't count too well. He held his breath as he went by the guard, and then he was in! The guard stopped the group leader to check off some paperwork, and they seemed to be going over the list. Nate kneeled down to tie his shoe by the large metal bleachers that stretched all the way around the stadium. He slowly edged his way over to the bleachers, still tying his shoe, and then slipped underneath. He found a dark corner and hid, waiting for the group to move off. When they finally did, he breathed a sigh of relief. He made it.

Chapter Twenty-Seven

CASSIE

Cassie was sitting in the bleachers, icing her left knee and watching the rest of the team run laps around the stadium as a warm-up. Her knee had gotten whacked pretty hard in practice yesterday. It had hurt like crazy at impact, but after a few minutes everything seemed fine and she had continued with practice. This morning it had been a little swollen, so Coach told her to ice it and rest.

Jason was still in denial, and believed his brother was still out there. She wanted to believe him, but Cassie thought that Nate was probably dead. Poor Jason. But she was seriously impressed that two kids had managed to mess up the President's plan.

She picked up the icepack to inspect her knee. She prodded the sore spot. Ouch. Well, that's what you get for prodding a sore spot. Even if it hurt, she was determined to make it into the next game. She had the rest of her life to sit on the sidelines.

She thought about the Canadian team. She had watched the prep videos with Jason and Anton a few days ago, and they were definitely going to be a challenge. Truthfully, no one who followed soccer thought that Alaska would get this far. She hadn't realized just what a long shot they were until she was watching some of the commentary on their games, and heard the announcers talking. Before the Tournament, the rest of the world thought it was a foregone conclusion that China would win. But now Alaska was a real contender, and suddenly she was getting a lot of media attention. They'd interviewed her parents, her neighbors, her school friends, all kinds of people who had known her as a kid. She was glad the team had a media agent to deal with all of this.

Reed was getting even more attention than she was. He proved himself again and again, scoring most of their goals. Like he needed that ego boost. Oh well. Cassie had to admit he actually deserved it. Reed was really a star. And not just on the soccer field. When Jason cornered him in the gym Reed had suggested they take a walk around the track. Cassie had caught up with them, and she was impressed. While Jason pressed him for answers, Reed had been calm and told him as much as he could. And done it all with none of his usual swagger and smart-ass comments. For an insufferable jerk, he had shown some surprising redeeming qualities.

Cassie resettled the ice on her left knee, and started to balance a soccer ball on her arm, then rolled it down to her shoulder, passed it behind her back, and up the other arm. She was concentrating so hard, she almost fell off her seat when a voice came from under her.

"That's pretty good," said a familiar voice. She looked around, trying to find it. Jason was looking at her from under the bleachers.

"What are you doing down there?" Cassie asked. She let the ball drop, and squinted into the shadows. It wasn't like Jason to take advantage of Coach being gone to slack off.

She looked down at him again. It was Jason, but not Jason. Same eyes, same hair, same body—only a lot more scratched up and wearing an Alaska soccer team hat, green army pants, and a camo shirt instead of their workout uniforms. Cassie jumped up, letting the icepack drop to the ground, her knee forgotten. She ran down the bleachers and around the back. It was Nate. She threw her arms around his neck, surprising them both, giving him a big hug.

"Nate! We thought you were dead. I've got to get Jason, hang on. Just stay here," she went running off.

"Uh, okay. Nice to meet you. You must be Cassie." Nate called to her vanishing back. Cassie turned, coming back over.

"Oh, right. I forgot we hadn't met. I feel like I know you. I'm Cassie." She held out her hand. "I'm sorry about jumping on you like that."

"That's okay. I feel like I know you, too. Jason told me all about you," said Nate, giving her hand an official shake. Cassie felt a little dazzled by his smile. "Looks like you got banged up a little."

"Just a knee injury. Pretty minor, I think." She looked down at her knee, twisting it. "Ouch. Still hurts."

"The knees are what got me," said Nate, ruefully. "Treat it kindly." He looked at her, and she noticed his eyes were blue, blue, blue. A deeper bluer than Jason's, with flecks of gold. She realized she was staring, and pulled her gaze away.

"I better go get Jason," she said. "Stay here, don't move!"

"Whatever you say," Nate leaned against one of the metal bars.

Cassie looked out from their secluded spot. Coach was still gone. The team was still running around the track.

Cassie walked toward the track, and as they came by in a big clump, Cassie called out, "Jason, Coach wants to see you!"

Jason peeled off from the others, dripping sweat and breathing hard.

"What does he want?" he asked, grabbing his water bottle.

"Nate's here!" Cassie whispered, jumping up and down a little.

"What are you talking about?" He streamed water into his mouth.

Cassie pointed to the bleachers.

"Under," she said, having a hard time formulating complete sentences, "Nate!"

"What?" Jason looked at her in disbelief. "And Nikko?"

"No Nikko. Just Nate," said Cassie. Jason looked in the direction she pointed, but couldn't see Nate in the shadows under the bleachers. He drank some more water, and started grinning from ear to ear. He turned back to Cassie.

"Okay, what do we do? Whatever happens, we can't be seen together," he whispered urgently.

"Right," said Cassie. "Right, of course. Okay, look, how about if you go in to ask Coach something, and while you've got him distracted, I'll take Nate into the girl's locker room. No one goes in there except me. And then we've got to get him to your room."

"I have extra clothes in my gym locker. I'll go talk to Coach about, um, telling Reed to do a little more passing and less of a solo show. He'll of course say no, so we can have a short argument about that, while you get Nate into your locker room. Wait until the team is on the far side of the track. And then when I come out, I'll leave the extra clothes by the door. Once Nate changes, he'll be a lot safer, as long as no one sees us together."

"Oh sure, as long as no one notices he has a big gash on his forehead," said Cassie.

"He does? Where?" Jason asked.

"Right along his eyebrow, here." Cassie traced a finger about two inches across Jason's eyebrow right where Nate's scar was.

"We'll just have to hope no one sees him. Everyone's at practice, so the dorms should be empty," said Jason.

"Sounds like a plan," Cassie headed back to the bleachers to tell Nate.

Jason headed into the locker room to find Coach.

As soon as he was inside, Cassie and Nate walked over the locker room entrance. Cassie went ahead to make sure that Jason had found Coach, and he had. She heard raised voices, and Jason saying something like, he's got to stop being such a ball hog! Cassie rushed Nate through the entrance and into the side door that led to the much smaller girl's locker room.

"Phew. I think we made it. How did you get that?" Cassie asked, pointing to his eyebrow.

"Kind of a long story," said Nate. "I'll tell you the whole thing when you guys come back from practice."

"We heard through Reed, you know, the Security Minister's son, that you and that other kid had been killed after you destroyed the nukes."

"You heard all that?" Nate seemed surprised news had traveled so fast. So Cassie gave him the short version about what Reed had told them and that Jason had been sure he was alive. When she was done bringing him up to speed, Cassie went out to get the clothes from Jason.

While Nate was dressing in the shower stall, Cassie looked out the locker room door into the interior hallway to see if anyone was there.

Nate appeared by her side, dressed in Jason's workout gear, down to his extra cleats.

"Wow. You'll fool everyone. I'd swear you were Jason," said Cassie.

"That's kind of the whole identical twin thing," Nate said, grinning.

"Except for that cut, I'd totally believe you were him." She looked Nate up and down. "This might actually work. C'mon." Cassie led the way through the maze of hallways that was the main gym, and across the empty lunch room. Twice they ducked into unused classrooms when they heard voices. Finally they were at the door to Jason's room.

"I can't believe I forgot to ask him for the key!" said Cassie, looking at Jason's locked door.

"Hey, we're not twins for nothing," said Nate, reaching above the door frame. He unlocked the door.

"How did you know there was a key up there?" asked Cassie.

"Jason's never been very good at keeping track of keys, so we always put a spare above the door," he explained.

He dropped his two backpacks and sat down on the empty mattress, looking around the room.

"Luke's," said Cassie, pointing at the bare mattress.

"Nikko's," said Nate, pointing to the extra pack.

"Where is he?" asked Cassie.

"I don't know. He was shot while we were trying to escape the river. It was dark. We got separated. I tried to find him, but he was gone," Nate's voice trailed off.

Relief at Nate's survival and the loss of Luke and Nikko suddenly hit her, and she felt overwhelmed. Her eyes filled with tears. Nate got up and wrapped her in his arms. He must think I'm a nutcase, Cassie thought, but she leaned her head against his chest, and took the comfort he offered. After a minute, she pulled herself together. But being held in Nate's arms felt so good, she didn't want to leave. She felt awkward, though, now that the tears had stopped. But he didn't seem to be in any hurry to let her go either.

"You better get back to the field before they start to wonder where you went," said Nate, not loosening his arms at all.

"Yeah, you're right." Cassie said, reluctantly pulling herself out of his embrace.

"See you later," said Nate, clicking the door quietly behind her.

Cassie headed back out to the field, but she barely noticed her surroundings, her mind on Nate and Jason. They looked the same, superficially, but she had lied. She could tell them apart. She knew Jason so well at this point that Nate might fool her at a distance, but close-up, it was easy. They stood differently. They walked differently. They definitely talked differently.

She was sitting icing her knee where Coach had left her when he came back out to the field. Whether any of the team had noticed her absence, she didn't know.

Chapter Twenty-Eight

REED

Something was going on and Reed was annoyed. Jason acted strange during practice. He was all over the place, practically bouncing off the sides of the goal, playing way too far out. And still saving everything. More than once, Reed caught him running to Cassie, whispering something in her ear. And he had a huge grin on his face. After practice, the two of them grabbed their stuff and headed off together. What was going on?

Reed kicked the ground. Had Jason had been lying to him about Cassie not being "his type" or whatever? Jason had zipped out of practice without even bothering to shower and change.

Reed decided to stop by Jason's room and ask him right out. Not that it was any of his business if Jason had changed his mind about Cassie, but seriously, they needed to stay focused. Reed could feel his blood boiling at the thought that Jason might have double-crossed him on Cassie. Would he lie to his face? He was probably laughing at Reed the whole time. It took a little while to register that Sam and Max were talking to him.

"What?" Reed had a hard time keeping his voice normal.

"Did you see Cassie and Jason? They were practically making out in the middle of the field. What's next?"

"Jealous?" Max snickered at Sam.

"Are you kidding me? She is so not my type. Too long and skinny. I like 'em curvy," Sam looked over at Reed.

"Uh, right. Me too," said Reed.

"What's up with you?" Sam asked.

"Me? Nothing." Reed decided to change the subject to the one thing he knew would get their attention. "I just want to get out of here and get some real food. I am sick of that 'nutritionally balanced' crap they give us in the caf. Do you want to come over and see if Rosa can fix us something big and greasy?"

Reed decided that bringing some leftover food to Jason's room later might be a good excuse for a one-on-one conversation.

"Yeah, now you're talking! I thought you'd never ask." Max's eyes lit up.

"Oh, sweet, sweet Rosa!" Max and Sam were chanting in unison. It certainly didn't take much to make those two happy. Reed rolled his eyes and grabbed their shoulders. "Let's go, or I'll change my mind about bringing you guys with me," he said, pulling them behind him.

Later, after a perfectly nutritionally balanced meal of steak and some more steak, they sank into the deep cushions of the chairs in Reed's den and sighed in contentment.

Reed had to admit that everything looked a little brighter with red meat in his bloodstream. Maybe he was just overacting. He was reading too much into things, that's all.

236

Reed's backpack was bulging with leftover food when he knocked on Jason's door. There were sounds of a scuffle from inside and then Jason opened the door just a crack.

"Hey, what's up?" Jason asked Reed, while standing in the doorway, blocking his view of the room.

"I just came from my house and our housekeeper gave me some leftovers that could feed a small army. Want some?" Reed was trying to sound friendly even though he was very close to kicking the door in.

"Just a sec." Jason closed the door all but a crack, and turned back to his room, talking to someone inside. Reed was sure it was Cassie. He felt his face flush with anger.

"I have to let him in," Jason said to whoever was inside. Reed had had enough. He shoved Jason into the room, slamming the door behind them.

"Do you want to explain what's going on?" Reed stopped suddenly as he got a good look at the guy sitting on the bed.

"Wow, there's something I never thought I'd see," Cassie remarked, "Reed, speechless. I think it was all worth it, just for this moment."

Jason chuckled, put his hands on Reed's shoulders, and pushed him to the chair.

"Yeah, it's Nate, you're not hallucinating. And clearly he's not dead." Jason sounded elated.

"Nate, how did you escape? What about Nikko? How did you get here? Does anybody else know you're here?" Well, at least the mystery of Jason's weird mood was explained. And it had nothing to do with Cassie.

"I don't think I can tell it all again," Nate said. He looked like he had been through hell, with scratches all over his arms and legs, and dark circles under his eyes. "Let me at the food first. I haven't eaten anything since this morning."

Reed handed him his backpack.

"Wow, your housekeeper is a genius. Are those brownies?" Reed watched as Nate piled a plate with food from various containers and could not keep himself from glancing back and forth between Jason and Nate. It was bizarre.

While Nate was rifling through the backpack of food, Jason told Reed about Nate and Nikko's escape from the training camp. Nate let Jason do the talking, happily inhaling Rosa's cooking, but occasionally chipping in some details. Reed could not believe that the guy sitting in front of him attacking a chicken leg, and making a complete mess of it, had been disabling delicate nuclear weapons less than a week ago. Jason explained about Nikko disappearing down the river, shot and probably dead. Nate paused in his chewing, but then doggedly continued.

"So, what's the plan?" Reed asked Nate.

"Good question. I think I'll stay with Jason till the end of the Tournament. Then, we'll see," Nate said, wiping his face and greasy hands. "Reed, thanks for the food."

"You can't stay here, Nate. You're supposed to be dead! If anyone found you, you're not the only one who'd get into trouble." Reed looked at them, and they all just stared back. Reed sighed.

"Okay, then. How are you going to keep Nate hidden?" he asked.

"Nate will stay in my room. He'll only go out if I'm in," started Jason.

"Right, and we'll never be anywhere besides this room together," said Nate. "No matter what, only one of us can leave at a time."

"So we'll have to switch at mealtimes, since we can't take any food out of the caf. I'm not sure it will be enough, though. Nate has some catching up to do," said Jason.

Reed now noticed that Jason was a little bigger, maybe by an inch and a couple of pounds. The pills, he thought.

"Not that much," said Reed taking a closer look at them. "What were they feeding you at that training camp?"

"We got those supplements, if that's what you mean. But I stopped taking them right after Jason told me about Luke." said Nate.

"We need a plan to keep Nate here. Reed, do you think you can bring more food?" Jason sounded like a kid planning a birthday party.

"No problem. It's a good thing that Rosa knows what pigs Sam and Max can be, so she won't be surprised if I ask for more food. This is pretty crazy, but we might be able to pull this off, at least until the Tournament ends." Reed was thinking aloud. "I think when Nate goes out, either me or Cassie should be with him, just to make sure he knows who is who. You probably don't know everyone on the team," he said, turning to Nate.

"Well, most of the country knows every single Alaska player. All those interviews you did at the beginning have been replayed a million times. I could probably fake it. But it probably wouldn't hurt," said Nate, glancing at Cassie.

"I can do that everywhere, except, obviously in the locker room." Was Cassie actually blushing?

"You two are always together anyway. I mean you and Jason. The whole team thinks you guys are a couple, now, by the way. So that should work." Reed was trying hard not to sound pissed off.

"We are not a couple!" Cassie and Jason both said at the same time.

"Okay, okay, sorry. Just saying, that's what everybody thinks," said Reed. There was an awkward silence.

"So it's agreed that Cassie will accompany Nate whenever he's out of the room, unless it's in the locker room, and then Reed takes over, right?" asked Jason.

"Sounds good to me," said Nate.

"Agreed. It's great knowing that you're alive Nate, but it's complicating things, and we really need to stay focused," said Reed.

"Yeah, we all need get to bed. Big game tomorrow," said Cassie.

Reed got up from the chair to head for the door.

"Hey Nate, I just want to say that what you and Nikko did was pretty sick. I overheard part of it from some guy with a Russian accent," said Reed.

"Colonel Gladov," supplied Nate.

"You really got those guys. I'm sorry about your friend, though." Reed waited at the door. "You coming, Cassie?"

"Yeah, I'm coming." Cassie got up from the bed reluctantly and quickly glanced at Nate.

"See you tomorrow?" she asked.

"I'm not going anywhere." Nate smiled at Cassie. Reed felt his stomach twist. He had to get this thing about Cassie under control. She was just his teammate. He needed to focus. He visualized himself blasting a goal past the Canadian keeper as he walked back to his room.

Chapter Twenty-Nine

JASON

"How'd it go?" Jason asked, as Nate entered the room after his first venture out with Cassie. They had gone to eat breakfast in the cafeteria, and Jason had been unable to relax the entire time they were out. He had been trying his old stress-reliever of throwing a soccer ball against the wall, until he realized he was supposed to be in the cafeteria and the thudding could give him away. He resorted to pacing around the room.

"You look like death. Pre-game nerves?" Nate was in good spirits. "The food wasn't as good as what Reed brings from home, but the company was a million times better. And after being cooped in here with nothing to do except sleep and think, I was so ready for a break."

"Glad you had your break, but I was in here thinking about the game against Canada and what would happen if, oh, I don't know, someone caught you! We have got to be crazy. If they find you here, we're both dead," said Jason.

"Hey, Jason, it was okay. Nobody could tell I wasn't you. I wore your hat the whole time. I even ran into Josh and Evan and they totally believed I was you. Just ask Cassie."

"Hmph," Jason grunted, and then turned his attention to more pressing matters. "I guess I'll eat the rest of the food Reed brought. I hope Reed will be able to get his hands on some more of that apple pie." With Nate back safely, Jason's appetite returned, and he dug into the rest of the delicious cinnamon coffee cake Reed had smuggled in. After a few bites, he noticed that Nate looked happy, *too* happy.

"You look pretty cheerful," Jason remarked.

"It's a good day. No one's shooting at me, for starters," said Nate. "Breakfast wasn't bad and Cassie's really great. And, since everyone thinks you guys are dating, I did a good job of staying in character." Nate ducked his head, and then looked up at Jason. Jason knew that look.

"What did you do? And more importantly, did Cassie kick your butt for doing it?" Jason erupted at the thought of his brother hitting on Cassie.

"Take it easy, I was joking. We were just hanging out together, no physical contact. I swear. You might as well tell me what's going on with you two."

"Nothing is going on. Look, I like her. She and Luke were my best friends here after you left, but to answer your real question—I don't *like* like her. But I worry about her. That business with Luke tore her up, and I don't want her getting hurt again. Especially right now. I know you don't have anything better to do, but I have a team to captain and a game to win tonight, so I can't have any of my team distracted." Jason sighed. "But I've seen the way she looks at you, and it's not how she looks at me," he admitted. Nate smiled.

"Wipe that stupid grin off your face," said Jason.

Over the years, Jason's easygoing nature was the one that had attracted more crushes, more girlfriends–though with their training programs, they couldn't go on real dates. But still, he had some experience in the kissing department. More than Nate. Nate had been more reserved, more likely to give Jason advice from afar. Jason wasn't used to girls being attracted to his twin, and not to him.

Nate reddened.

"Look, just be nice to her. If something more happens, at least don't go dying or anything. I don't think she could take it." Jason started pulling out his warm-up clothes, and dug under his bed for his favorite good-luck water bottle.

"Good point. And since there's a high likelihood of that happening, I won't do anything. I promise." Nate said.

"I have a warm-up in a few minutes, so I better head down to the locker room to get dressed," said Jason, pulling a flip-flop out from under his bed, and searching for the other.

"Nothing like the threat of a little nuclear holocaust to bring out the best in a team," said Nate, tossing Jason the other flip-flop that had gotten wedged behind the chair. "What's your strategy?"

There was a knock at the door. Nate slid into the bathroom and shut the door.

"Hi, Cass," Jason let her in.

"Hi Jase, hi Nate," Cassie spoke to the bathroom door. Cassie was already dressed for practice. Nate opened the door, and flashed Cassie a smile.

"We were just talking about strategy for today's game," said Nate. "How's your knee feeling?"

"Perfect. Seems to have recovered," said Cassie, twisting her leg to stretch her knee. Nate knelt down next to her and put his hand across her knee, pushing in on either side.

"Does that hurt?" he asked.

"Nope," she said. "Feels fine."

Nate's hand lingered for a few seconds on her leg, and then he pulled his hand away and stood up. Cassie's face seemed to flush a little. Jason rolled his eyes to no one in particular. This was Nate doing nothing?

"So what was the strategy you were talking about?" Cassie asked, turning to Jason.

"We'll just kick their butts. The old butt-kicking strategy. It's worked so far. Mostly." Jason was really looking forward to the game. He had a good feeling about it.

"Well, go kick some butt, you two," said Nate, wistfully. "I wish I could watch the game somehow."

"No way!" Jason turned to Nate. "The President is front and center at every single game. No way you can sneak out there. If someone sees you, we're all toast. Don't even *think* about it," Jason was adamant.

"We promise to give you a full report. And you can watch the highlights in the cafeteria with me afterwards." Cassie tried to soften the blow.

"Okay, okay. Just wishful thinking, that's all. I guess I'll just take another nap while you guys are out keeping the world safe from war. Just watch out for that Perry kid."

Perry was the star striker on Canadian team, and Jason knew he wasn't to be underestimated.

* * *

"Evan! Watch the left!" Jason was yelling from the goal, watching as the play moved predictably toward him. The cross was coming and Perry was perfectly positioned to take a left-footed shot, if Evan didn't block him. In the first 20 minutes of the game, Canada had come at them relentlessly, but Jason had been able to block all of the shots. Most of them had been weak, though, and Evan and Josh working together had put enough pressure on the Canadian front line that they hadn't really gotten a good shot. Alaska had been putting on the pressure, too, but the game was scoreless so far.

Then, there was a cross right in front of him. Jason swore. A Canadian slammed into Evan, preventing him from intercepting the cross, and bam, there was the shot. Dirty pool. There was no way Jason could stop it. The stands erupted in cheers and moans. Coach Andrews came out onto the field, yelling at the ref.

"That was a foul! A foul! This isn't American football! They can't tackle the defense!" Coach's face was turning red. Jason agreed with Coach, but he doubted the ref would do anything. It was rare to see Coach lose his temper, though.

The ref yelled back at Coach to get off the field, or he'd be ejected from the game. That's all we need, thought Jason to himself. Coach left the field, looking murderous.

"You okay?" Jason checked in on Evan, who was looking miserable.

"Yeah, I'm okay. Sorry about that, Jason. I thought I could get him. That moron!" Evan's legs were streaked with cleat marks from where the other player had practically run him over.

"It's early in the game. We'll get it back."

Being one down seemed to light a fire under Reed, Max, and Sam, who spent the rest of the half bombarding the Canadian goalie with shot after shot. Their defense was surprisingly strong, and Reed overshot the goal half a dozen times, to a chorus of moans both on and off the field.

"Another field goal," said Evan bitterly to Jason, after Reed lobbed what looked like a really promising shot into the bleachers behind the goal.

At the half, Coach laid into them, talking about sloppy shots, embarrassment to their country, and how they couldn't afford to lose this game with such vehemence that Cassie, Reed, and Jason all glanced nervously at each other. When he was done, Reed, Cassie, and Jason huddled together.

"What the hell, Reed? What's going on up there?" Jason asked.

"They're just really strong, today, dude. I don't know. Maybe they're on something." Reed was as frustrated as anyone with his performance. "And my dad's over there in the box with the President. See them?" Reed pointed.

Jason and Cassie squinted in the sun.

"Oh yeah," Jason could barely make them out.

"Look, we're only one down. We can get this back. Cassie, play up more, and I'll talk to Evan and Josh about guarding the left more. Okay, let's go." Jason jogged back onto the field, determined not to let the wave of hopelessness he felt building wash over him.

The second half started off well. Reed passed to Cassie, something Jason had noticed Reed doing more often lately, and Cassie dribbled up the field, passing player after player with her nimble moves. When she got near the goal, she passed to Max who passed to Sam, who passed a long ball to Reed, which was intercepted. The play headed toward Jason's end of the field, but Josh and Evan were on Perry and the other forward, easily stealing the ball. Perry seemed to be dragging. He stopped when Evan stole the ball from him, and didn't even try to get it back. Perry leaned over, put his hands on his knees, and stooped, breathing hard.

Then Cassie managed another breakaway, passed to Sam, and Sam slammed the ball in. Goal! The stadium was on its feet, cheering. Sam, Reed, and Max high-fived each other, and Reed high-fived Cassie, too. Jason punched his fist in the air. Yes! He knew they could do it. Okay, one more, one more, he thought. That's all we need.

Jason turned back to Perry, who was now on all fours on the ground. What was wrong with him? Then, Perry hurled. Ugh. That looked awful. The whistle blew.

Reed came and stood next to Jason.

"Holy crap," said Reed.

"What?" Cassie joined them in the goal.

"They did it. They poisoned Perry," whispered Reed.

"Whoa. I've never seen anyone throw up so much," whispered Cassie. "You think he's going to be okay?"

"This blows." Jason kicked the ground in disgust. "Now even if we pull off this win, it won't feel like we won."

"Yeah, and if we lose, we can just add Perry to the body count," said Cassie.

They watched as Perry was loaded onto a stretcher, barely conscious. A clean-up team came out and efficiently vacuumed the turf clean.

"Dude, that guy was seriously ill," said Evan, as he joined Jason, Cassie, and Reed, along with Josh, Sam, Max, and most of the rest of the team.

"Wonder what he ate?" asked Max. Was his mind just always on food, wondered Jason, or had Reed let him in on the secret. Jason looked over at Reed, and Reed shrugged his shoulders. A lucky guess on Max's part. Given what they were trying to pass off as food in the cafeteria these days, food poisoning wasn't a stretch. It was pretty clear that a month-long Tournament was taxing the country's supplies.

But how could only one guy get sick? The crucial one guy in the middle of a game they were losing? As Jason took a swig from his water bottle, he suddenly knew. All the players had their own sports-drink bottles with their names on them, to minimize germ transmission, of course.

The ref blew the whistle, calling the players back to the game.

"We've got a game to win," said Jason. "Let's get a goal!"

With Perry off the field, Canada's offense fell apart, and they were only able to get a few feeble shots on Jason, who blocked them easily. At the other end of the field, Cassie and Reed were on fire, taking shot after shot. By the end of the game, a disheartened Canadian team had let in three more goals, for a final score of 4-1.

Instead of feeling elated about advancing to the finals, Jason just felt kind of empty. Winning was better than losing, but winning this way kind of sucked. He wondered if Perry was going to be okay.

Chapter Thirty

NATE

Nate was pacing back and forth, just as Jason had earlier. Where was everybody? The game must be over by now, and Nate was going nuts. Did they win? Lose? Tie? What? He wished he could sneak to the cafeteria where there was a TV with a live feed, but it would be very hard to explain his presence at the field and in the cafeteria at the same time.

There was a knock on the door and then it swung open. It was Cassie.

"What happened?"

"We won," she panted, smiling. Nate let out a whoop, and then pulled her quickly into the room. She was freshly showered, and her long hair was hanging in wet strands around her flushed face. She looked so pretty, he felt an urge to kiss her right then and there, but he couldn't. He had promised Jason.

"What'd you do, sprint all the way from the locker room?" Nate asked. She nodded, and when she got her breath back, she explained.

"Jason's surrounded by reporters. It might be awhile before he can get back here, but I knew you must be going crazy," she said.

"I was. I was totally freaking out. I could hear the cheers from the stadium, but I couldn't tell which side it was for. I thought about sneaking down to the caf to check out the score, but I knew Jason would kill me," he said.

"I ran down here as soon as I could get away," she said, dropping onto Jason's bed. "It was a crazy game."

"I want every detail. I want the minute-by-minute recap you promised," he said as he sat next to her.

Cassie told him about the game, Perry, the mess on the field, and their suspicions about the President's interference. Even as he was listening and asking for more details, he was also thinking that in a couple of days there might be another war or he might be on the run or even dead. He might not have another chance. He looked at her, and took her hand.

Cassie stopped mid-sentence.

Before she could say anything, Nate leaned over and kissed her. For a few seconds, the rest of the world entirely vanished from Nate's mind. Cassie pulled away first, looking at him wide-eyed. Nate felt embarrassed.

"I... I had to do that," Nate stammered, waiting for a reaction. "At least once."

"I'm glad you did," Cassie whispered, smiling at him. She paused, and then said, "You know, I haven't ever kissed a boy before."

It shouldn't matter, but Nate felt like he might explode with happiness.

"In that case," he said, grinning, "I think we need to practice some more."

* * *

After Jason returned from an energy-draining press conference, Nate convinced him to take a nap and let him out to go the cafeteria.

"It really sucks that I couldn't see the whole game," Nate grumbled when he got back, even though he had watched all the highlights in the cafeteria with Cassie and Reed.

"The first half wasn't pretty," Jason replied, sleepily, as he rooted around the containers from Reed's house to see what food might be available.

Nate had heard all the details from Cassie and then Jason, but it wasn't the same as being there. Taking out the best player in the middle of the game by poisoning him was a desperate measure, and made it clear to the four of them that the President was willing to do anything necessary to close the deal.

Nate felt restless. The last 48 hours had been all about eating and sleeping and waiting. He felt fully recovered from his escape through the wilderness, and was starting to go a little stir crazy. He needed some exercise. He wondered if he could talk Jason into letting him go to soccer practice tomorrow. It would be great to play again. And to spend more time with Cassie, with ample opportunity to reinforce the rumors that they were a couple. Nate didn't even realize that he was smiling.

"What're you so happy about?" Jason asked. "Did I miss something?" Nate looked at his brother, remembering his speech about Cassie from before.

"Nothing," he said, his face wiped of all emotions.

The result of the other semifinal game was in. China had beaten Iceland, so Alaska and China would face off in the final championship game. Before the War, China had been the most populous country in Asia and had been rising in power, but it wasn't until after the War that it became the dominant world power, collecting what was left of the rest of the continent of Asia under its government. China had won the last five Tournaments, which meant they had had the top spot in the Global Government for the last 10 years.

Reed knocked on the door, bringing some food from Rosa. Jason dug in.

"So, it's China, again," Reed said to no one in particular. Nate just nodded.

"Yeah," Jason was talking while he attacked a chicken leg.

"Coach told me that they requested a four-hour slot in gym tomorrow—totally private, no observers, no media, no officials. Just the team and the coaches. What do you think they're up to?" Reed wondered.

"No idea. Guess we'll find out soon enough." Jason sounded unconcerned now that his stomach was nice and full.

* * *

"I need to get out of here, or I'll start my own nuclear war," Nate said to Jason the next morning. Jason reluctantly agreed to let him go to practice with Cassie and Reed. Jason was mentally and physically exhausted anyway, argued Nate, and he could use the extra rest.

It was like old times for Nate. He easily fit into the familiar drills. It felt so good to play soccer again. Nate was not a bad goalie, but lacked Jason's natural reflexes. No one seemed to notice, and Cassie and Reed lobbed him enough easy ones that he was able to keep his goal-blocking percentage near where Jason's usually was.

During a water break, a slew of secret service agents suddenly descended onto the field and with them came the President. Coach Andrews approached the President immediately and they spoke quietly for couple of minutes.

"Jason, could you join us for a moment?" Coach called, looking uncomfortable. Nate just stood, looking at the President. The sweat running down his back suddenly felt cold. What had he been thinking? Jase was right, it was stupid and reckless and asking for trouble. A look of terror must have passed over his face, because Cassie came over and gave his hand a little squeeze. She nudged him toward Coach, and Nate followed the entire parade down to the coaches' office.

Four agents positioned themselves in front of the door and two came in after Nate was waved in by the coach.

"I'll be outside if you need me Mr. President. Jason, everything is fine, don't worry," Coach said.

Oh sure, thought Nate. I'm sure everything is just peachy. The door closed and Nate was trapped with the President.

"Let's cut to the chase." The President looked at Nate. "I'm sure that an intelligent young man like you can guess what this is all about," he said. For a brief moment, Nate wondered if he could kill the President before the agents jumped on him. Probably not. He looked at the two guys with stony faces and hands on their weapons, ready. Definitely not. Considering the only weapon in his reach was a pencil on Coach's desk.

Nate looked at the President, trying to keep his face as bland as possible.

"Mr. President, I'm sorry, sir. I have no idea what you mean. What is this about?" Nate spoke respectfully, trying not to show his fear.

"Well, Jason, I'll lay it out for you. Your twin brother sabotaged a military operation that my government had been working on for the last two years. Thanks to him, it's ruined, and so are chances of Alaska's rise to power on the world stage. With this operation, life in Alaska could have become much better for all of our people. We'd have more and better food, more economic growth, and better lives for all of us, which Alaska deserves. But thanks to your brother, that option is out.

"We know that you communicated with your brother as recently as the day the sabotage was discovered. We also know that he told you about what he did, which of course is a treasonous offense, punishable by death." Nate couldn't believe what he was hearing. This guy was lecturing *him* about treason?

"I'm glad you aren't pretending you don't know what I'm talking about." The President waited for Nate to respond, which he did with another quick nod. He didn't trust himself to speak.

"Do you know what happened after they pulled their little stunt?" The President leaned forward, and stared at Nate, unblinking.

"No, sir," Nate responded automatically. Even as he said it, he felt his blood run cold. Could the President tell them apart?

"Well, I'm sorry to tell you that both your brother and his friend died as a result of their little prank." The President shook his head in an attempt at sorrow. "Such a waste, such a tragedy. I'm very sorry for your loss." His eyes searched

Nate's face again. Nate swallowed his anger, and tried to look appropriately devastated, but it took every ounce of his self-control not to attack this man for having Nikko shot in the river. The President waited a minute before speaking again.

"I hope you understand that winning this Tournament is our country's top strategic priority and we will do everything possible to guarantee that win. You are a smart young man. I have no desire to punish you for your brother's offenses, but I'm sure you'll understand me when I say that if you do not win this final game, there will be consequences. And not just for you." The President paused.

"I bring you greetings from you parents and sisters, by the way. They were most distressed to learn about your brother's untimely death in a training accident. I'd hate for them to lose another son. Or worse." Nate just nodded again.

The President seemed to take Nate's silence for assent, thankfully. Nate's heart was beating fast, and he wasn't sure he could hold it together much longer.

"We're done here," the President finally said, gesturing to his agents. "Looking forward to your final game, Jason. Make Alaska proud!"

The President left and Nate collapsed on the chair. His hands were shaking. He felt cold sweat trickling down his back. The President's words were echoing in his mind, "treason," "accident," "parents," "sisters."

Nate decided practice was over for the day. He headed back to his room.

"You want the good news or the bad news?" He asked Jason, after he shut the door firmly.

"Good," said Jason, observing the green tinge to Nate's skin.

"Okay," Nate took a breath. "The good news is that the President thought I was you." Jason's face started to lose color.

"What do you mean, the President thought you were me?"

"I mean, that just now, I had a little one-on-one with our fearless leader, and while he threatened my life—well, your life, really, because he thinks I'm already dead—he didn't catch on that I was you." Nate fell onto his bed, and lay there.

"So, the President came into practice to talk to me?" Jason asked. "Why? Oh. My. God. What if he had figured it out, Nate? We'd both be dead!" Jason's voice was rising.

"Calm down," Nate said. "That was the good news. He didn't know. He couldn't tell. We're still safe. For now."

"Great, so with that kind of good news, I'm not sure I can handle the bad news," said Jason.

"He knows that we talked. He knows that you know what I did. He suspects that you might be trying to sabotage the game. He has promised to kill you and whoever else he thinks is in on this, as well as our parents and Sarah and Christina, if we don't win the finals.

Nate looked for signs of panic in Jason, but he just stared at the floor. Finally, he looked up at Nate.

"Well, that's just super," Jason said. "Nothing like a little murder threat to really bring out your best game."

Chapter Thirty-One

REED

"Okay, so let me get this straight: The President has threatened to maybe kill you, and threatened your parents and sisters, if we don't win tomorrow? Wow, the guy isn't holding anything back, is he?" Reed got up and started walking around the room, too agitated to sit.

"Yup," said Nate shortly, still looking shaken even though it had been a few hours since the conversation. "I think he was serious."

Jason looked pasty, too.

"I guess the good news is that he believed that Nate was me," said Jason, quietly. Cassie was sitting on the edge of Nate's bed, with her knees drawn up to her chest and her arms clasped around them. Reed wanted to go put his arms around her. He stifled the urge, and sighed.

"So what do we do?" Reed stopped his pacing, and looked at Nate.

"I guess you guys better win," said Nate, grimly.

"Great plan," Reed replied. "I'll just go over to the Chinese team during the pre-game festivities and say, hey, our President is threatening to kill us if we don't win, so could you guys let us? I'm sure they'd understand." Reed threw himself down on Jason's bed, and looked across at Nate and Cassie. They both still looked shell-shocked.

"But if we win, you know what will happen," said Jason.

"And Nikko and Luke will have died for nothing. But if we lose…" Nate's voice trailed off.

"The President will have no way to take over. But, on the other hand, he's threatened our family," finished Jason.

Everyone was quiet.

Then Nate let out a string of swear words, some of which were even new to Reed.

"So that's what they were teaching you in that training camp," said Reed, flashing an unexpected grin. The mood in the room was too grim for anyone to smile back.

"Well, what do we do?" Reed asked. He really wanted to play and win this thing.

Jason and Nate looked at each other.

"It's not like it's just up to us," said Jason. "We could throw the game. We're the underdogs, so it wouldn't be a big surprise. But if the President has any plans to 'help' us, it might be out of our hands anyway."

"Reed, has your dad said anything to you about all this?" Cassie asked.

"I think he's starting to worry about what the President has up his sleeve, but there's nothing he can do about it." Reed had talked to his dad briefly after they beat Canada. His dad had been unhappy about Perry's poisoning, but laid some of the blame on Reed for not scoring in the first half. If the score had at least been tied at the half, he said, he felt like he could have talked the President out of taking any action. Everyone had been off in that first half, though. It was just one of those games, Reed had tried to explain.

"Did your dad say that the President would take action again if we were losing?" Cassie asked, again.

"He didn't, but I'd say it was a safe bet." Reed doubted the President was leaving anything to chance at this point.

"My dad also told me that this was probably the last year that the leadership of the Global Government would be decided this way, whether we win or lose. Too many other countries are unhappy with the system since China wins so often. If they win again, he thinks that they'll propose some other options for selection of the Global Government."

Jason snorted. "Yeah, well with the drugs and secret armies and stuff, it doesn't seem like it's working very well."

"At least they tried to come up with another way of doing things!" Cassie defended the system. "They had to have some way to choose the leadership. And I guess they thought this would be fair and was better than having armies bombing each other. Before the War, it was a rare thing for a country to win two World Cups in a row. Brazil did once, but no other country had. Brazil won five, and Italy won four, but France, Spain, West Germany, Argentina, Uruguay and England also won, so I guess they thought it would continue to change pretty much with each competition."

"Thank you, Miss Encyclopedia," said Jason, jokingly.

"Some of us actually like to read things other than comic books," Cassie replied.

"All that radiation obviously got to their brains to come up with a scheme like that," said Jason.

"I have a feeling no one knew how well China had prepared for nuclear war," Nate reminded everyone. "They had more than 3,000 miles of underground tunnels, not to mention all those bunkers loaded with food. They even had schools and complete gyms set up down there! If they hadn't agreed on a power-sharing system, we'd all probably be speaking Chinese."

"So, Cassie, China didn't win even one World Cup before the War?" Jason asked.

"No, not one. In fact, I'm not even sure they made it into the World Cup," Cassie responded. Reed could not help but be fascinated with Cassie. Again.

"Wow. How about our old country, the U.S.?" asked Reed.

"The U.S. got third place in 1930, but that's about it. They were in the World Cup several times, but never won," answered Cassie.

"So this is our chance, to win the first world soccer competition for our country, going back 100 years." Reed really, really wanted to win, even though he knew what was at stake.

"Right, we win, and then..." Nate trailed off.

"We get to live," Jason finished. "Well, for a while."

"Yeah, 'a while' being the operative term. China and Brazil will never go along with this," said Nate. "Either way, I'm pretty sure I'm a dead man walking. I don't know how long Jason and I can keep up the being-one-person act, but at some point, I'm probably going to have to leave if I want to survive." Nate took Cassie's hand in his.

What? Reed had a sudden urge to punch Nate, but he took a breath and reminded himself that he never had any chance with Cassie. It was his own fault. But, after this Tournament was over, life would go back to normal and there would be plenty of girls who would be into him, being a big soccer star and all.

"We can't throw the game," said Reed, into the silence. "It's not fair to us. We've worked so hard for so long, and we could actually win this thing."

"I agree with Reed," said Cassie, dropping Nate's hand, and looking at Reed. Whoa. Reed had not been expecting that. Cassie, on his side? "I don't think we could pull off not trying our hardest to win. I think we have to go out there and do our best to beat them. It's not our decision what happens next. It never should have been."

All three of them looked at Nate.

"Nate," said Jason, "I don't think we could do it. We're all used to going out and giving our all, and then some. We don't know how to cheat convincingly. And I have to agree with Cassie and Reed. We can't intentionally lose. We don't know what's going to happen for sure. Maybe the President will have a heart attack. It's different from your situation. You were dealing with nuclear weapons that were being prepared for launch. There are too many other things that could happen here."

Reed saw Cassie's relief, and he felt it, too. He wanted to play this game. He wanted to win. And maybe that's what Cassie wanted too, but he noticed it didn't take long for her hand to wind up in Nate's again.

"So, Reed, during tomorrow's game, I think we're really going to have come on strong at the beginning." Reed nodded, glancing away from Cassie and Nate. "If we don't score in the first 10 minutes, they're going to have momentum. We can't let that happen. Cassie, you too, if we're going to beat China, we have to do it early on." Jason spent a few more minutes talking strategy with Cassie and Reed, and Nate even chimed in with some suggestions.

"Okay, get out of here. Get some sleep. We've got a big game tomorrow." Jason got up, and started to usher Reed out the door.

"Right. Cassie, you coming?" asked Reed, waiting at the door. She disentangled her hand from Nate's and got up.

They walked down the hallway in awkward silence.

Finally, Reed broke it.

"So, you and Nate, huh?" He tried to sound friendly about it. They slowed down as they approached the corner where Cassie's hall split off.

"Yeah, me and Nate," said Cassie. "Why do you care?"

"I don't," he said. "Sorry I asked. But look, do you think we could put aside all the stuff in the past and be friends?"

"Friends?" she echoed uncertainly.

"Yeah, friends. I know I was kind of an idiot at the beginning, and I'm sorry. Can we just go out there and kick some Chinese butt as friends on the same team? If we're going to win this, we have to be able to trust each other on the field. I'm going to need you to really hammer those balls to me and Sam, or we'll never beat them." Reed waited for a response, watching as she considered him.

"I never let my personal issues interfere with what goes on in the game," said Cassie.

"I know," he said, "but, we're really going to have be connecting to make this happen, and I just want to be sure we're both all in."

"I'm all in," replied Cassie, then she paused. "You're asking because of Nate–because Nate said before that we shouldn't win."

"Yeah. I just want to be sure you really want this. We can do this, Cassie, I know we can win this." Reed searched her for any signs that she might be wavering.

"I said I agreed with you, and I do. I think we have to go give it everything we've got. I'm all in, Martinez." She sounded a little exasperated with him.

"Okay, then." Reed grinned at her, again.

"Good night," she said, rolling her eyes, and turnings towards her room. Reed watched her go, admiring the bounce in her ponytail. They could win this. Screw the consequences.

Chapter Thirty-Two

NATE

After Reed and Cassie left, Jason got into bed, and turned off the light.

Nate rubbed his tired eyes and sat down on the spare bed. For appearances sake, the mattress was still bare, but at night he pulled out the old sheets and blanket he had left behind, and converted Luke's bed into his own. After sleeping in the woods and in the wagons, a real mattress and pillow was heaven. He wondered how long he'd get to enjoy it.

If anybody had told him six months ago—when they were all agonizing about making the team—that he'd be better off just going home, he would have thought they were completely nuts.

"Jase?" Nate asked, "you asleep?"

"Almost," said Jason, drowsily.

"I can't stop thinking about tomorrow," Nate said.

"Well, I can. I'm going to sleep, and you should, too. Whatever happens, happens," said Jason, and turned over with his back to Nate.

"I know you're right," said Nate, "but I'm just wondering what we're going to do after the Tournament is over."

Jason sighed, and turned over to face Nate.

"Do we need talk about this right now? I'm wiped. And there's kind of a big game happening tomorrow," Jason said, yawning.

"I think I have to leave. I can't stay here. If you win, you guys will be famous, the champions of Tournament, but I'm supposed to be dead. I have to disappear…but, I hate to leave you again," Nate trailed off.

Jason sat up in the bed. "You're not leaving me. Are you nuts? We'll go together," Jason sounded wide awake now. "The only question is, where?"

"Our best chance is to catch up with Shaun and his group and go to Canada. They would help us and we could start a new life," Nate said. But then he thought about Cassie.

"Do you think Cassie would come?" he asked.

"Wow, you've really got it bad, don't you?" Jason asked.

Nate grinned at him.

"Guess it was finally my turn. But the timing's kind of awful," he said.

"I have no idea what Cassie would say. But you're not getting rid of me, that's for sure," Jason said, settling himself back in the bed.

"You'd leave all the glory and fame and come with me?" asked Nate.

"Yeah. Of course," said Jason, looking at him like he was the crazy one. "Now can we go to sleep? We can figure this out after the game tomorrow."

Nate lay on the bed and, despite everything, he was happy. Jason was coming with him. Whatever happened, they'd be fine. They'd figure out what to do.

He closed his eyes. After a while, he heard Jason's heavy breathing. You could always count on him to fall asleep within minutes. Not even a nuclear threat could give his brother insomnia. Nate chuckled quietly.

He tried to sleep, but it was useless.

He got up, careful not to make any noise, and crept down the deserted hallways until he got to Cassie's room. He wanted to see her. This might be his last night here. He might never have a chance to talk to her alone again. He knocked lightly. After a few seconds, he heard some shuffling inside. The door opened slowly and Cassie's face poked out from behind it.

"Hi," Nate said.

"Nate," Cassie whispered. "What are you doing here? Come in before someone sees you."

She pulled him in, and shut the door behind them. She flipped on her bedside lamp, and sat down on her bed, looking at him intently. Nate sat down next to her.

"Is everything okay?" she asked.

"Depends on what you mean by okay. But there's nothing new. I just couldn't sleep." He hesitated, suddenly feeling stupid for coming. Cassie needed her rest. Tomorrow was a big day.

"I shouldn't be bothering you with this right now. I'm sorry."

"No, that's okay. I was having trouble sleeping, too. Just too much in my head," Cassie replied.

"I know what you mean. I can't stop thinking about what's going to happen after the game," said Nate.

"I can't stop thinking about the actual game. What if we don't win? I put everything I got into this, we all did. How do we go on if we lose?" Cassie's voice shook.

"Cassie, I know you love the game and believe me I love it too, but…it won't be the end of the world if you lose. It might be just the opposite, in fact."

Cassie sighed. Nate reached out and took her hand and pulled her closer to him. His heart raced as she leaned into his shoulder. Screw the game tomorrow. Screw the President and Global Government. What Nate wanted was right here. He didn't want the moment to end. But he had come here with purpose. He had to tell Cassie his plans.

"Cassie, I came here tonight because I wanted to tell you that I have to leave soon."

Cassie sat up in surprise.

"How soon?"

"I'm not sure, maybe tomorrow. Jason is coming with me and I was hoping you would you come with us too," Nate said.

Cassie was silent for a while. She squeezed his hand and he knew she couldn't leave the team behind, no matter how desperately he wanted her to come.

"Where will you go?" she asked.

"I won't tell you any details. I don't want to put you in any more danger. But I have to get out of Fairbanks."

Cassie nodded in understanding.

"I've put you all in more danger than I realized. I never would have come if I had known…but then we would never have met," Nate trailed off.

"I'm glad you came," Cassie whispered. Nate pulled her into a hug, and let himself enjoy the moment.

"Cassie? Can I stay tonight? Here? With you?" he whispered softly, very aware that his voice was a little shaky.

Cassie leaned back slowly onto the bed, shifting and making space for him.

Nate moved in next to her, wrapping his arms around her. He pulled her in so close that there wasn't a speck of space between them. They held each other tightly, waiting for whatever came next.

* * *

Nate left Cassie's room early, and made it back to Jason's room without being spotted.

"So where were you?" Jason asked, arms crossed in front of his body.

"I, uh, well," Nate stumbled awkwardly. "I guess you wouldn't believe me if I said I went down to the gym for some early morning exercise?"

"Yeah, sure. I haven't checked out the window lately for flying pigs, but I'm sure they're up there."

Nate's face turned red. Then Jason punched him on the shoulder, and Nate couldn't help the goofy grin that covered his face.

"So?" asked Jason.

"So what?" said Nate, stalling. He started removing the sheet sheets just to be doing something that didn't involve looking at his brother.

"So, how is Cassie?" prodded Jason.

"She's really great," said Nate, blushing red and sitting on the bed. "I mean, she is so amazing."

He sat on the bed, thinking about how nice it had been to lie there with her, absorbing her warmth, even if she had fallen sound asleep within minutes. She never told him if she would come with him, but it didn't matter. While he was holding her close, watching her sleep, he had finally been able to think things through.

"Nate!" Jason's loud voice penetrated his thoughts.

"What?"

"I was just asking about...oh, never mind. I can tell you're off in la-la land. Let me know when you hit the ground." Jason started rooting through his pile of laundry.

Nate knew what he had to do. Now he just had to convince his brother.

Jason just stared at Nate when he was done talking. After a minute, he nodded. He would go along with the plan.

"It's the only way," said Nate.

Jason nodded.

"I have to go," Jason finally said. "Team breakfast."

"Yeah, I know. I'll eat one of those bagels from Reed's house."

"Okay, well, I'll see you later." Jason started walking out the door, and then turned around and gave his brother a hug.

"See ya," said Nate, quietly, after Jason had left.

Chapter Thirty-Three

CASSIE

Cassie and Jason were walking back to their rooms after the morning practice and strategy-pep talk from Coach. His belief in their team was infectious. They left the gym revved up and ready to go, but Coach had instructed them to go to their rooms and relax for at least an hour before lunch. Lunch would be followed by a free afternoon. She couldn't remember the last time she had a free afternoon. At 5:30, they would head to the locker rooms for some snacks and drinks, get dressed for the game, and then some light warm-ups.

"I don't think I'm going to get much rest," said Cassie, as they walked past the empty cafeteria.

"At least you're alone," said Jason, keeping his voice low. "Somehow I doubt the next few hours are going to be relaxing for me. But you *need* to get some rest." He gave her a look that said he knew where Nate had been last night.

Cassie sighed.

"I know, but I don't feel tired at all," she said.

"Ah, young love," teased Jason. Cassie gave him a shove, pushing him off balance.

"Shut up," she said, but she was grinning widely.

"Hey, Cassie!" Cassie turned to see Karen running down the hall.

"Oh my God, Karen! What are you doing here?" Cassie's voice hit full squeal, and she returned the hug. "Oh, this is Jason," she said.

"We met out on the field a few weeks ago," said Karen, holding out her hand.

"Oh, right, you were at the game with a bunch of kids." Jason shook her hand in that easy, friendly way he had, and Cassie watched Karen's dark eyes light up. Uh oh.

"My budding soccer stars are off with their parents, so I have some free time, and I thought I'd come wish you luck," said Karen to Cassie. "I gave the security guard my best kitten face, and he let me in." She did her big-eyed, sad look for them. Jason burst out laughing.

"I know, who could refuse that face, right?" said Cassie, also laughing.

Karen looped her arm through Cassie's, and said, "Let's go have some girl time. I'm sure you've been missing that, surrounded by all these gross boys all the time."

"Well, I know when I'm not wanted," said Jason, with mock offense, as he headed down the hallway. "I'll catch you later, Cassie."

Cassie and Karen headed toward her room.

"So, spill!" said Karen, when Jason was out of earshot.

"What do you mean?" asked Cassie, innocently.

"C'mon, he's majorly cute," said Karen, "and there's something going on between you two. I can tell these things. You know I can."

Cassie opened the door to her room, and Karen sat cross-legged on Cassie extra's bed. She patted the spot beside her, and said, "Come sit."

Cassie plopped down next to her. She was so happy to see Karen that she had momentarily forgotten about all the other stuff. Karen was rummaging around in her enormous pink bag that could hold her beauty supplies, her soccer uniform, and a ball, if necessary.

"What are you looking for?" she asked.

"Ah, here they are," said Karen, dredging out two paper bags from the depths.

"No!" said Cassie, reaching for the bag.

"Oh yes," said Karen, opening her own bag. Inside each bag was a mix of chocolate truffles, including Cassie's favorite, peanut butter, and Karen's favorite, white chocolate. Chocolate like this was almost impossible to find

"Where did you get these?" asked Cassie, her mouth watering as she unwrapped the first one.

"Oh, one of the kids on my team has a mother who plans fancy parties for visiting officials and big wigs, and when I told her how much *you* like them, she gave me some to give to you. She gave me some, too, just to be polite. Her daughter totally idolizes you. You should probably sign her daughter's soccer ball or something."

"Mmmmmmm," Cassie groaned with pleasure as the chocolate and peanut butter melted in her mouth. "I'm sure Coach would kill me for eating these before the game, but oh, they are so good. Especially after all this healthy stuff they give us."

"So," said Karen.

"So," replied Cassie.

"So what's up with that guy, Jason?" asked Karen, pretending to be very interested in her candy wrapper, spreading it out and folding it carefully into quarters.

"Nothing," said Cassie, "I mean, we're friends, and he's a really great guy. He's the Captain and he was nice to me when Reed was being so mean." Cassie explained about Reed and his sidekicks making her life miserable at first. And how Jason and Luke stood up for her. And then she stopped, not sure what to say about Luke. She saw Karen's eyes narrow and she got that cat-about-to-pounce look in her eye.

"Was there something going on between you and Luke?" she asked.

"How do you figure these things out?" Cassie was truly mystified.

"You forget, I've known you since you were eight, and you can't keep any secrets, Palmer. Everything's right on your face," said Karen.

"I think there might have been, something could have happened, but then, you know, he died." Her eyes welled up with tears, and Karen put down her bag of candy and leaned over and gave Cassie a hug. Cassie felt the tears dripping out of her onto her best friend's shoulders. She had missed Karen so much. She sat there, feeling like an idiot for crying, but letting the tears just fall.

"Hey, I'm really sorry about that, Cass. That was a terrible thing to happen, but such a fluke thing, huh? I mean, to die from a virus? That must have really scared you all." Cassie rubbed her eyes and sat up.

"It's worse than that," she said. "Much worse." She couldn't hold it in any longer. She wanted to tell Karen everything. She started with Jason, and then Reed and his father, and then about Luke and the pills.

"Oh my God! They doped you?" Karen was outraged.

"But that's not all," Cassie continued and then she told Karen all about Nate's training camp, their nuke tutor, Kraus, and the nuclear weapons.

"It sounds crazy, I know. I mean, nuclear weapons. War. Again," she said. It really did sound nuts. "Do you believe me?"

"I believe you," Karen said. "I do. I'm just having a hard time understanding how this could happen."

"Yeah, join the club," said Cassie, and she explained about Nate and Nikko disabling the nukes, and their escape, and him showing up at the stadium. Karen was sitting silently, for once not fidgeting, listening to Cassie.

"This is beyond crazy. Insane. How do you think about all this and still focus on the games? I'm such a chicken. I think I would just try to run away," Karen said looking at Cassie with wide eyes.

"Well, Jason's been great. He's really been the one holding us all together," Cassie said, then paused. "Karen, I'm in trouble." The words rushed out of her.

"How are *you* in trouble?" asked Karen, surprised.

"Because of…Nate," she said, not sure what to say.

"Oh. Oh." said Karen. "Nate. Not Jason, Nate." Karen looked at Cassie's face intently, all scary stuff forgotten. "I knew there was something going on! But why is that awful, Cass? That's good! If he looks like his brother, and of course he does because they're twins, then that is very, very good!"

"No, I mean, I never felt like this about anyone before. I just can't stop thinking about him. And I just met him! Am I going crazy?" Cassie looked at Karen.

Karen started to laugh.

"Finally! You desperately needed to do some catching up in the boy department. Seriously, Cassie. All it took was being surrounded by a bunch of hot guys 24/7 to do it!" Karen crowed.

Cassie immediately felt better.

"So tell me about Nate," said Karen, leaning back to the wall, like she was settling in for a long, romantic tale.

"There isn't much to tell. There's something about him that's different. The first time I saw him, my stomach flipped over–his eyes are so blue, and they just made me melt inside," admitted Cassie. "That never happened before. He's different from all the boys on the team. He's been in the real world, and he's so strong. Not just muscles, but, you know, character. But he also makes me feel like I can give him something, too. I just want to be with him all the time, even though I know that's impossible. Really impossible." Cassie sighed.

"I never thought I'd see the day," said Karen.

"He spent the night in here last night," said Cassie shyly.

"What?" Karen sat bolt upright. "Palmer, you've been holding out on me! You should have led with that!"

"No, no, nothing like that. He just slept here," said Cassie, feeling her face turn red.

"Hmph, cute and honorable?" said Karen, looking skeptically at Cassie. "He didn't try anything?"

"Well, I mean, of course kissing," Cassie said, looking down. Then she looked up and saw Karen's leer, and threw her soccer ball throw pillow at her. "Give me some credit."

"Good!" said Karen, throwing the pillow back.

"But after tonight, I don't know if I'll ever see him again," said Cassie, quietly.

"I guess dating a guy who is supposed to be dead does present some problems," said Karen, thoughtfully. "But the Tournament is almost over, and when it's over, win or lose, people will forget about it after a while and life will go back to normal, and things will be fine. There can't be another war. I'm sure someone will stop it before it happens. You'll see."

"I haven't told you the best part, I guess," said Cassie. "Remember when I told you about the President's plan? He came to our practice yesterday and took Nate aside—well, he thought he was Jason because Nate convinced Jason to let him out of the room to go to a practice or he'd go crazy—and told him basically, that if we don't win, he's going to kill Jason and his family."

"What?" Karen's eyes grew round. "That can't be true."

"That's what he told Nate." Cassie felt her good mood slipping away.

"He couldn't do that. That's just crazy. There are too many people watching all around the world." Karen shook her head, her face pale. "Maybe it was just some mental game he was playing to really motivate Jason to win. That would be pretty twisted, though." Cassie felt bad for laying all this on her friend. But she also felt better knowing that somebody outside the team knew what she knew, whether it was a mental game the President was playing or reality.

"Anyway, we're going to win," said Cassie, grimly. "We have to." Karen's normally playful demeanor had vanished, replaced with a hard edge.

"Yes," she said. "You have to win. This team is awesome, the best team Alaska ever put together. But when this is over, we're going to have to figure out a plan for you and Nate. And we will, don't worry." Cassie looked at the clock. There were still five minutes before lunch.

"So, how are things with your team?" asked Cassie. Karen rolled her eyes. And they both burst into hysterical laughter. When the giggles had subsided, Karen got up and gave Cassie a big hug.

"I'd better go," she said, "but I'll be there cheering you on and I'll come find you after the game so we can do some serious celebrating. Okay? And we'll think about all the rest of it tomorrow. Remember what Coach Jenny used to say, focus on one thing at a time."

"One thing at a time," nodded Cassie. "Okay, I'll see you after the game." Cassie watched as Karen disappeared down the hallway. She ran a hairbrush through her hair and headed toward the cafeteria, hoping that Nate had convinced Jason to let him come to lunch. One thing at a time.

Chapter Thirty-Four

FINALS

JASON

Jason was standing on the soccer field in the stadium filled with 50,000 people. This was it: The championship game of the Tournament. After today, his life would never be the same. He had always imagined this day as the most exciting day of his life. But reality bites.

He squinted against the lights, trying to see into the stands. He knew everybody was there: the President, all the ministers, and his parents and sisters. He wished he could tell his family Nate was alive. And about what he did. How he put himself at risk for the sake of others. What he planned to do. They would be proud of him. He was proud of Nate, too. Jason looked down the field at his teammates. Six months ago they were just a bunch of players from different teams, but now they felt more like a family. He could see their excitement and determination. He was grateful most of them didn't know what was at stake. Jason caught Cassie's and Reed's eyes. Reed gave him a thumbs-up, and Cassie smiled.

Jason took a deep breath and allowed himself to forget Nate and everything else for a moment. Despite everything, he loved this game. He was going to enjoy every minute he could.

* * *

CASSIE

Even though she hadn't gotten much sleep last night, Cassie felt great. Who needs sleep, she thought, as she pounded ball after ball at Jason. This was it. This was the day she had been training for. Nine years of wind sprints, stadium steps, endless drills, all came down to this. And it didn't hurt that she had spent the night in Nate's arms.

She looked around the stadium, and was amazed. So many people. So many excited people. She knew her family was in the stands somewhere. All of her brothers, her mother, her father, they were all there watching her. And Nate. Nate was somewhere on the field, she knew, but he wouldn't tell her where. He finally had told her he couldn't wait in Jason's room for this one. He had to be there. She figured that was the big secret they were keeping. And she could see why they didn't want to tell anyone.

Suddenly, she heard a huge gasp from the crowd. A buzz, even louder than the pre-game hum already going, grew. Cassie stopped the ball rolling toward her, picked it up and walked over to Jason.

"What's up?" she asked. Jason's eyes were focused on one of the large screens that were at both ends of the stadium.

"No way!" said Jason. Reed, Sam, Max, Evan, Josh, and the rest of them straggled over, staring up at the screen slack-jawed.

"Holy crap!" said Reed, throwing his ball down onto the ground with an angry throw.

The image finally made sense to her. It was Zhang Lie, a Chinese soccer star she remembered from the Tournament two years ago. He had been a powerful force, and had scored a record five goals against Argentina in the final match. About a foot taller than anyone else, he could outrun everyone. There had been rumors about what kind of drugs the Chinese team had given him, which had resulted in stricter anti-doping rules. Not strict enough, though, Cassie thought, thinking back to Luke and the drugs her team had gotten. It was probably where our dear President got the idea.

Cassie knew her team was larger than they had been. She was nearing 5'11", and many of the boys were hitting 6'2" or 6'3', but no one was near 7 feet tall, like Zhang Lie. But it couldn't be him. Players had to be 16 or 17 to compete in the Tournament. It must just look like him. The player's name scrolled under him.... "Wu Xi, Striker" read the ticker. He was the spitting image of Zhang Lie, minus the red birthmark on his left cheek.

Now she knew what the big deal about the "private training" session was. Here was their secret weapon. She turned to Jason.

"Do you think it's the same guy, or just someone who looks exactly like him?" Cassie asked bitterly.

"Probably his evil twin," said Jason. "This time his eyes spit venom at the keeper or something like that."

"It's Zhang, for sure." Reed joined in. "It's not like the Chinese have ever really cared about age limits when it comes to international competitions," he said, barely containing his anger. "This is BULLSHIT!" he yelled into the air.

"Shut up!" yelled Jason. "Do you want to be kicked out of the game before we even begin?" Cassie put her hand on his shoulder. Jason took a deep breath.

"Okay team," he called to the group, "I think we better run a lap or we're all going to explode." They took off running down the field, like something was chasing them. As she ran, Cassie tried to keep her mind off what would happen after the game if they lost.

* * *

REED

Reed was so angry he couldn't see straight. What was the point of all these stupid rules if no one was going to enforce them? This Wu Xi kid was probably at least 20 and was going to kill them. Maybe literally.

Before the game had started, Reed's father had come down to wish him luck. When he saw how upset Reed was, his father tried to calm him down. They knew, he said. They knew, and they were lodging a complaint. All the paperwork was in order. These kinds of things sometimes took years to sort out. Like that would help. They had to win today.

The ref called them onto the field, and blew the whistle. Within seconds, Wu Xi had the ball and was pushing towards the goal. Evan and Jack were scrambling to keep up with him, but he was too fast. Wu Xi immediately got a good shot on goal. Jason blocked it, and sent the ball down the field, only to have the ball turned around and back in the box within seconds. Another shot. Jason blocked it, but Wu Xi was there, and pounded it into the goal on the rebound. 0-1. Reed groaned. This was bad. Jason grabbed the ball, his face red from exertion, and threw it down the field to Max and Sam for the kickoff. At the whistle Sam passed the ball back to Cassie and she dribbled around a few Chinese players before sending the ball off to Max, who passed to Reed. Reed got a great shot into the corner of the goal, and the game was tied 1-1. Yes! The whole stadium was up on its feet. People were screaming Reed's name. Wow! Here you go. Show me some love. Reed was grinning from ear to ear as Sam and Max ran to him and patted him on the back. Okay, we can do this, he thought.

The next 20 minutes passed in a blur, with China dominating the field, and Alaska just holding on. After Reed made another unsuccessful shot on goal, the Chinese keeper kicked the ball out to Wu Xi, who flew past most of Alaska's defense. He knocked Evan down, and then Jack. He was like a bulldozer. Reed yelled an obscenity at the ref, but thankfully the ref didn't hear him. Reed saw Wu Xi take a shot. It rebounded off Jason's upper arm and the other Chinese forward finished the job. 1-2. Crap! They had to get it back. Reed was running on pure adrenalin now. After the kick-off, Wu Xi grabbed the ball again and barreled toward Jason. Jack stole it, and kicked the ball in an enormous arc that spanned almost two-thirds of the field, landing right in front of Reed. Yes! Reed dribbled around two Chinese defenders, but was tackled by a third. He lost the ball, but pivoted quickly, and stole it back. This was his chance. It was now or never. He slammed the ball towards the goal, and got it in over the keeper's head. 2-2! The fans went crazy. Reed pumped his fist in the air, screaming. The huge screens around the stadium showed his jubilant face close up. People were flashing "We Love Reed" and "Marry Me, Reed!" signs, cheering wildly.

The whistle blew for half-time, and Reed jogged gratefully off the field. He was exhausted. He grabbed his water bottle, slurping down as much as he could, and then listened to Coach lay out plans and plays that would win them the game. He seemed frantic. But then, they all probably did. As they headed back to the field, he looked at Cassie. She looked pretty wiped. Jason was last coming out of the locker room. He looked tense, possibly terrified, but he didn't look worn out the way Reed felt. Well, Jason hadn't been running sprints for the last 45 minutes. He just got to stay in the goal while the rest of them tried to keep up with Goliath. He couldn't believe that China pulled this. And that there was nothing they could do about it.

The whistle blew. The fans were cheering loudly. Reed tried to smile for the cameras he knew were focusing on his face. Just one more goal, he thought. One more goal.

Once he started playing, Reed's world was reduced to colors: the bright green AstroTurf field, blue jerseys, red jerseys, and a black-and-white soccer ball. He was giving it his all, dribbling, passing, running, blocking, stealing. This half wasn't going any better than the last, but Alaska was keeping Goliath from scoring, thanks mostly to Evan and Jack, who were double-teaming him whenever they could. Reed and Sam went back to help them, and they were able to keep the game tied. The Chinese defense was strong, too, and Reed couldn't stay open long enough to get a good pass or take a good shot. He was getting really frustrated.

"Time ref?" he asked as he ran by the one yellow shirt on the field.

"Two minutes." Oh crap, thought Reed. This was it. Not much time left. They had to score. They would never last in overtime. For a second he thought about all the agony he, Jason, and Cassie had gone through trying to decide what to do in this final game. It was almost funny now. The choice was never really theirs. Reed was just surprised that Wu Xi was not on the ground puking his guts out or something. The President was either losing his touch or the Chinese delegation really knew how to protect their players.

Before he had time to think, Reed saw Wu Xi grab the ball away from Sam, a move that left Sam on the ground, but no foul was called. Reed tried to catch up to Wu Xi, but his legs couldn't move that fast.

Wu Xi shot from far out. With so much power behind it, Reed knew it would be a good solid shot, but Jason could do it. He had seen him stop much worse. C'mon keeper! C'mon keeper! Jason leaped into the air, and tried to grab the ball.

The shot tipped off Jason's gloves, and slid into the goal. Reed could hear nothing but roaring in his ears. Time seemed to slow down.

The Chinese players were jumping up and down, and running over to high-five their enormous teammate. The crowd was roaring. Reed looked at Sam and Max, who both looked close to tears. Reed felt like crying himself. What just happened? He couldn't believe it. The exertion of the last 90 minutes hit him, and he felt exhausted. There was no time left in the game. No freaking time. This was it. The final whistle blew. They had lost. Lost. Reed was almost sick on the field. He couldn't believe it was over. He slumped to the ground.

The large screens around the stadium were showing the winning goal in slow motion, and Reed looked up to watch.

There was the shot, going long, there was Jason's gloved hand just tipping the ball, not quite getting it, and then it went into the goal.

The screen focused on Jason, who was still sitting in the goal, his face in his hands. He pulled his hands away, and looked up. The camera zoomed in on his dirt-streaked face. Reed looked at Jason's face and gasped. There, on the huge screen, magnified a million times, he saw it. The scar above Nate's left eyebrow.

Epilogue

JASON

Jason was slouched in the back seat of the car, with his eyes closed. He was so tired. The crazy adrenalin of the last few hours had finally dissipated, and he was drained. His dad was driving. His mom was sitting in the front seat, quietly staring ahead. His two sisters were next to him, also unusually quiet. It had taken a lot of convincing, and he had answered a barrage of questions, but he had finally talked them into leaving.

He was still hoping this was only a dream and he would wake up soon.

Who was he kidding? This wasn't a dream. It was a nightmare that he might never wake from.

Nate and the rest of team had been immediately escorted from the field by President's security force right after they lost the game. He had a funny feeling that it wasn't to bring them to the Banquet Hall to celebrate.

Jason felt powerless. He had waited at the stadium for as long as he could even though he promised Nate when they switched the places at half time that he would get his parents and sisters out immediately. He couldn't do it. He had to stay and watch till very end. Watched and hoped that Nate would change his mind. Yeah, good luck with that. Nate was even more pigheaded than Jason when it came to something that mattered to him. And this really mattered.

Jason replayed the speech Nate had prepared for him while he spent the night in Cassie's room. Did Cassie know about it? Did she help him to make that decision?

Nate had convinced Jason to switch places with him because Nate wanted to be the one to do it. The one to lose the game. Nate knew that Jason loved the game too much to lose on purpose. And honestly, Jason didn't think he could have done it. It was different for Nate. He had always been able to keep his emotions out of his decisions. That's why he was so good at strategy games. But in this case, Jason thought he was letting his emotions rule, too. Nate was in too deep after Nikko's death. It was for Nikko, Nate had said. He had to see this through for Nikko. But it was also for Jason, his "little" brother, and his family and Cassie.

Nate had said his life was forfeit anyway. He could never live openly. He would always be on the run and hiding. Well, he didn't want that life. There were things that were actually worth risking everything for, said Nate, and this was one of those things. When it came right down it, Jason wasn't so sure. He trusted Nate, and in the end, he decided to follow Nate's lead. Like always.

Jason looked out the window at the passing trees, the occasional pasture with cows. He was thinking about his promise to Nate. He would keep it, but not all of it. He would get his family safely to Canada. But then he would leave them with Shaun's group, and go back. Go back to get his brother, if he was still alive.

ACKNOWLEDGEMENTS

First, a big thank you to our sons Ben, Kubi, Luki, and Matthew, for being our first readers and providing invaluable feedback and soccer expertise. If nothing else, we finally understand–or think we understand–the offsides rule. A special thanks to Matthew, who read the book three times bouncing in the third seat of the car on the bumpiest roads in Africa, and to Luki, who caught our soccer mistakes and gave us many good ideas for the book. Sorry, Luki, that we had to take out most of the swears.

Thanks also to Ben, Kubi, Luki and Clara for posing for the cover in shorts on a very windy, cold day. We know it's embarrassing, and you'll probably want to move out of the state, but we love you for it.

Thanks to our husbands, Jamie and Marek, for supporting us through this process, encouraging us, and giving us time to "Escape to the Cape" for writing weekends.

An extra special thank you to Marek for designing our beautiful cover, posters, and website. It really came alive. We couldn't have done it without you. You're the best!

Thanks to Betsy Lawson, who edited the book for us and gave us great feedback. Her suggestions, ideas, and enthusiasm for the project lifted us up at a time when we really needed it.

And finally, thanks to all our friends and family, especially Jennifer's grandfather, Martin Levin, who read the early drafts or parts of them and gave us suggestions, encouragement, and legal advice.

ABOUT THE AUTHORS

Jennifer Goebel has always wished that "reader of books" was a paid profession. Born in the Philippines, she moved around a lot as a child and books were her constant companions. This near-pathological love for being immersed in an imaginary world has continued into adulthood, as the two-foot high stacks of books on her bedside table and her husband Jamie will attest. As a parent, she has tried to instill a love of reading into her two boys, Ben and Matthew, with some success. In return, both boys have led her into the unfamiliar world of sports. After many years of watching the boys battle it out on the field, she has actually started enjoying Premier League soccer.

Dagmar Jacisinova was born in a country that does not exist anymore and moved to the USA as wide-eyed, barely English-speaking "youth" at age of 25. She perfected her English by watching soap operas (yeah, no kidding) and talking to two-year-olds while babysitting. Dagmar never spent a day without reading and she started to read kids' and YA literature while trying to force the love of books on her twin sons. That twisted path also led her to writing this book, as she felt that most of the middle grade books out there were for "chicks." Dagmar still spends her "free" time watching her teenage kids dishing out and receiving punishments on various soccer fields and carpooling six sweaty Neanderthals to and from soccer games, while listening to them with her ears wide open.

Printed in Great Britain
by Amazon

42342441R00172